SURFACING

SURFACING

BOOK THREE
OF THE
NAUTILUS LEGENDS

EMMA SHELFORD

SURFACING

Kinglet Books
Victoria BC, Canada

ISBN: 978-1989677018

www.emmashelford.com

First edition: December 2019

DEDICATION

To my husband's fond memories of his old cherry tree

ALISTAIR

Alistair Brown shifted his weight from one foot to another then ruffled his graying hair with fidgeting fingers. Ryan Stokes passed a bulky briefcase to his other hand to check his watch.

"Here's hoping she's punctual," Ryan murmured. His eyes narrowed slightly, exacerbating the surrounding crow's feet. "I have places to be."

"Can you tell me about the project now, to save time?" Alistair said. He had been dying to know what he would be working on next, ever since he'd wrapped up his research project yesterday and Ryan had emailed him with instructions to meet him in this disused office space downtown. It was being renovated, but the workers had gone home for the day.

Alistair's hair prickled at the thought of meeting in secret. What sort of project would he be working on this time? He'd only been at Tellman Inc. for a year, but he'd never yet been bored. Not like that cosmetic testing facility he'd worked at a few years ago. His talents had been wasted there.

"Not yet," Ryan said. He patted the briefcase. "Let's get the relevant info from our mole, first. Once she's on her merry way, you and I can get down to business."

The door clicked open. It sent echoes through the cavernous office space, the sound hardly dampened by drop cloths piled nearby. A young woman with long auburn hair strode confidently toward them, her stiletto heels clacking on the polished cement floor. When she drew closer, she held out her hand.

"Mr. Stokes, it's a pleasure to see you again," she said. Her voice was even and pleasant, and Alistair could picture her comfortably hobnobbing with donors or calmly answering the phone. According to Ryan, she was skilled at both.

"Ms. Rossi, thank you for coming." Ryan shook her hand

and gestured to Alistair. "May I introduce Alistair Brown, one of my chief scientists. Alistair, meet Paula Rossi, personal assistant for Miles Callahan."

Paula turned to Alistair and smiled warmly at him. Alistair shook her petite hand and was surprised by the firmness of her grip.

"Nice to meet you." She opened her slim purse, which even to Alistair's untrained eye looked understatedly expensive, and drew out a folded piece of paper. She turned to Ryan.

"I have the correct frequency here," she said. "Does our agreement still hold?"

"Of course," Ryan said. He pulled out his phone and tapped it a few times. "There, the money has been transferred. Please, check and satisfy yourself."

Paula slid her hand into her purse once more and extracted a sleek new phone. She opened an application and scrolled down. Her mouth curved upward in a pleased smile, and she dropped the phone back into her purse.

"Just as agreed." She passed Ryan the piece of paper. "Goodbye and good luck, gentlemen. It was a pleasure doing business with you."

After the door had swung shut on Paula's clacking heels, Alistair gave his employer an inquisitive glance. Ryan grinned and laid the briefcase on a nearby sawhorse.

"Ready to hear about your next assignment? I think you'll like it." Ryan popped the clasps of the briefcase with a click and jerked open the lid. Alistair peered inside and frowned in confusion.

A strange machine was wedged into a surround of foam to keep it from shifting. There were various buttons and a screen, and the whole thing looked waterproof. Otherwise, there was nothing to indicate what the machine was for. Alistair glanced at Ryan, who looked satisfied with himself.

"It took my guys in the manufacturing department a full two days to slap this baby together, but they did it. It's ready for use."

"And what will it be used for?" Alistair tried to keep his voice simply curious. He wanted to know his next project, and Ryan was stringing him along. Ryan tapped the machine with one short finger.

"This, my friend, emits sound in whatever frequency you want. It's programable and has a few fancy options, which is what took my guys so many hours to tweak. Now that Paula gave me the correct frequency, we're ready to roll."

At Alistair's barely contained frustration, Ryan laughed.

"All right, I'll stop being mysterious, although you haven't heard the strange part yet. There have been reports of unusual sea life in local waters. Callahan found out how to attract the creatures using a certain sound. His assistant Paula was kind enough to ferret out the exact frequency in exchange for a decent sum of money." Ryan laughed again with a tinge of admiration. "She drives a tough bargain, but I think it'll be worth it."

Alistair frowned. Unusual sea creatures? How did Ryan think Tellman Inc. would benefit from them?

"What's my role in this?"

"I want you to collect and study these creatures. Apparently, some of these fish produce chemicals that enhance human abilities. It could be gold, but we don't know. I want you to find out everything you can about them." Ryan patted Alistair on the shoulder in a paternal way, despite their similarity in age. "Obviously, pursue the paths with the greatest chance of commercial success. You'll have complete control over the team, but I want frequent progress reports. You'll be working closely with Britta Lawson—I expect you'll put her dissection skills to good use—but keep the rest of the team segregated and in the dark. I trust you to keep the true nature of these creatures between you and Britta."

Alistair nodded his understanding. He was pleased to be working with Britta. She was level-headed and competent, and they made a good team. Keeping others in the dark would be challenging, but Alistair always craved a challenge.

"I understand," he said.

"Good." Ryan tucked Paula's paper into a file folder slotted against the top of the briefcase. "All the information I have is in that folder. You'll have access to boats, a lab, anything you need. Details are in the folder. There's a prototype trap in the lab already, to catch these creatures. Give it a once-over and call the shop guys for adjustments." He shot Alistair a steely glance. "I want a creature in your lab by the end of the week. We need to work as fast as possible. I don't trust Callahan not to tell others about this, despite what Paula says. Money is no object. Make it happen, and quickly."

"Understood," Alistair said. He could already foresee the corners he would have to cut and the ethics he would have to throw out the window. It didn't bother him too much. Some things were regrettable, but necessary. Despite the clenching in his gut over the pressure Ryan was already exerting on him, his heart raced at the new project. He wanted to dive in immediately.

"I'll assemble the team tomorrow," he promised. Ryan slammed the briefcase closed and passed it to Alistair.

"First thing tomorrow. I want results out of this, and soon."

CORRIE

Corrie's leg jiggled under the desk. Her supervisor, Dr. Jonathan Chan, stared intently at the figures she'd printed off for their meeting. Corrie looked at the mess of papers and office supplies on his desk and tried not to visualize how she would organize it all.

Her mind drifted instead to her analyses of the unicorn fish. *No, a strolia*, she corrected herself. That's what Zeballos Artino had called it, when he had showed her the logbook of creatures he had seen from his boat, the *Clicker*. She wasn't much further along with her analyses, mainly because Jonathan had been breathing down her neck. She thought wistfully of the kroll, a small shark unknown to science that they had rescued from Miles Callahan's private aquarium. What wouldn't she give for a sample from that creature?

Jonathan cleared his throat and Corrie dragged her attention to their meeting.

"This looks promising," he said. "The link between metabolic output and salinity is interesting. It's statistically significant. I agree, you should follow up with that angle." He frowned and looked at her. "Why haven't you run the nutrient autoanalyzer?"

If she had wanted to be truthful, Corrie would have said that she'd been too busy testing unicorn fish slime to get to that analysis yet.

"I had some problems with my reagent," she said instead. A twinge of guilt lanced through her stomach at the lie. "I'll do it next, though."

"Try to get on it shortly." Jonathan shuffled the figures around to look at the bottommost one. "When do you leave for your next cruise?"

"Thursday," Corrie said. Her stomach cramped again, but this time from excitement. She was heading out on the *Clicker* with Zeb and the others for another week of sampling. Would they see more strange creatures like the unicorn fish? She could only hope. A cold dose of uncertainty washed over her at the memory of Zeb diving into the ocean at night when he thought she had left the boat. What was he not telling her?

"If you haven't finalized your itinerary yet, I recommend traveling north. Samples from the Queen Charlotte Sound will give you high salinities and low temperatures, and some of the northern inlets that are freshwater fed will give you the opposite. It will be what you need to test this hypothesis." He pushed the figures toward Corrie. "If you can get those samples, I'm confident they're your best bet."

"Perfect," Corrie said. "I'll do that."

"Send me what you have with the autoanalyzer before you leave," Jonathan said.

Corrie left the office too excited to be grumpy at Jonathan's demands. She was going on the *Clicker* again, with all the excitement and mystery that entailed. She had big plans for her project. And she might see more creatures.

Thursday couldn't come fast enough.

TRIP

Sophie Trip loved summer and squeezed every drop out of the season. She lived outside, every minute she could spare away from her studies. Summer fruit emerging in the grocery store lined her kitchen windowsill and filled the refrigerator drawers. She spent weekends at the beach and the lake, as often as she could convince others to join her. She went alone if no one was free, just to soak up the heat and get her toes wet.

The evening shadows crept toward Trip's deck lounger, persistent and subversive, but Trip ignored them. She tucked a bowl of cherries closer to her side and popped one in her mouth with a defiant motion. Her teeth burst the soft fruit, and the potent flavor of fresh cherry juice coated her tongue. She gave a quick glance of gratitude at the massive cherry tree that leaned over the balcony, dripping with ripe fruit, despite the role it played in the encroaching dark.

She focused once more on the scientific paper that leaned against her bent knee and colored a sentence with a flourish of blue highlighter. See, she could work and enjoy summer at the same time. It was possible. Neither task was being done well, but they were being done.

There were footsteps on the deck boards behind Trip. She dropped her highlighter in her lap with relief and bent her head backward to see who had mercifully disturbed her studies.

Corrie smiled at her. She held a mixing bowl under her arm.

"You had the right idea," she said, pointing to Trip's almost empty cherry bowl. "I need some."

"I don't know," Trip said, considering the tree with mock concern. "There might not be enough to share."

Corrie giggled.

"I think the whole neighborhood could have their fill, and there would still be plenty for the birds."

"Well, I suppose you can have a few," Trip said. Corrie

made a silly face at her and started to pick.

"Still working?" Corrie said. "I have some data to work up tonight, too, but I need fuel first. Lots to do before my next cruise."

"Right." Trip had forgotten that Corrie was leaving for another week on the boat, helmed by the mysterious Zeb and his intriguing friend, Jules Elliot. "When are you leaving?"

"Thursday," Corrie said. "We'll spend the night somewhere in the strait then pick up Zeb's sister in Vancouver the next day and head north. I'm so excited to sample up there. After last cruise, I know exactly what conditions I need to test my hypotheses. This cruise is going to be great, I can feel it. I'll have so much data, I won't know what to do with it all."

Trip sat up straighter when a thought occurred to her.

"You're going to Vancouver first?"

"Yes." Corrie looked at her with a cherry in her mouth. She chewed and swallowed. "What are you thinking?"

"Can I hitch a ride? Your boat sounds way more fun than the ferry. I've been meaning to visit a friend over there, and Vancouver is great in the summer."

This was a chance for a summer getaway, the most she would manage this year, anyway. Nothing said summer more than strolling down Vancouver's beaches, drinking iced coffee, and watching windsurfers on the waves. She could afford a few days away. Her supervisor was on holiday, and no one was watching her.

An outing on the boat would also give her a chance to meet Jules again. She'd been intrigued by the easy-going deckhand. One evening of chat wasn't much to go on, but it was enough to try for more. Trip wasn't one to let an opportunity slip by without grasping it. It was unlikely they would ever meet again if she didn't orchestrate it.

Corrie looked bemused.

"I don't know. Maybe? I can ask Zeb. I don't see why not, but it's his boat."

"That would be amazing." Trip leaned back and gazed through the cherry branches with half-closed eyes. "So much better than the ferry."

Corrie was uncharacteristically silent. Trip looked over at her.

"What's up?" Trip said. "I thought you'd be excited to show me around. I'm not offended you're not, but it's weird. Will I be cramping your style?"

"No, no." Corrie twisted a cherry stem around her finger for a moment. Trip watched her with curiosity. Corrie was clearly burning up with something, and Trip could almost see words fighting to get out of her mouth. The words finally won.

"Trip, can you keep a secret?" Corrie said finally. Trip raised an eyebrow.

"Well, it sure looks like you can't. Come on, spill the beans."

"Seriously, you can't tell anyone. Oh, except Adrianna, she knows already."

Trip sat up.

"Wow, I'm the last to know? That stings." She patted the end of her deck lounger for Corrie to sit. "Come on, tell Aunty Trip your big secret."

Corrie hesitated then slowly sat.

"We found something out there," she said. "Last time on the boat. We saw animals that have never been documented before. New species, Trip. Do you know how crazy that is?"

"Do *you* know?" Trip frowned at Corrie. What was she trying to say? "Where are these animals? Why aren't you in the news with your big discovery?"

Corrie swallowed and gazed into her cherry bowl at the maroon globes piled high within.

"There's something weird going on with these animals. Something bigger that I need to find out first before I go to anyone else with this. They're all connected, somehow."

"Where's your proof?" Trip said, trying to inject reason

into this conversation that was quickly derailing. "Why do you think they are new species? What are they?"

"One is a salmonid with a horn like a unicorn," Corrie said. When Trip scoffed, she held up her hand. "I know, it sounds ridiculous. We had it on board, though, and I got samples. I sequenced them, and it's definitely not anything known."

Trip shook her head in disbelief.

"I don't know. I mean, a new species? That's a big pill to swallow."

"I didn't even tell you about the giant octopus yet." Corrie's eyes were wide with her earnestness, but Trip laughed.

"Okay, I get it. You're pulling my leg. Very funny. You got me."

"No, no, no." Corrie shook her head violently, then she leaped up. "Wait, I have pictures. Hold on."

She raced into the house. Trip frowned after her. What game was Corrie playing? This wasn't like her, not at all. Trip barely had time to wonder at Corrie's antics before she was back, her camera swinging from one hand. She flopped onto the lounger, which creaked alarmingly.

"Look." Corrie thrust the camera under Trip's nose. "Here's the unicorn fish."

The screen showed a fish in a tank. It was a glorious rainbow hue and appeared like a salmon with large fins.

"There's the horn," Corrie whispered. She pointed at a translucent tip that jutted out of the tank. "It's hard to see here."

"Yes, it is hard to see." Trip couldn't tell if the tip was attached to the fish or was simply a piece of plastic stuck to the tank. Corrie huffed and snatched the camera back. She flipped through photos until she found another one.

"Here's the giant octopus. What do you say to that?"

Trip frowned, then her eyes widened. Between two forested islands, in the froth behind a boat, two huge tentacles waved in the air. They approached the height of trees on the shore.

"What the hell is that?" Trip breathed. She glanced sharply

at Corrie. "Did you doctor this photo?"

"No!" Corrie said with angry earnestness. "I promise. This is all real, all wildly, ridiculously real."

Trip looked at the picture again and let out her breath in a whistle.

"Where has it been hiding?" she said. Corrie spread her hands.

"I know, right? That's part of the problem. There are others, as well, more than the unicorn fish and the octopus. The creatures seem to be connected, and only recently arrived on these shores. Where did they come from? Why are they here? What are they related to? These are things I want to find out before I tell anyone else. There's something big going on here, and I need to find out what it is." Corrie twisted her hands together. "I thought of going to my supervisor, but I'm not ready to give up control of this discovery."

She looked at Trip with pleading eyes, as if asking for permission to feel this way. Trip looked at the picture of the tentacles again.

"What if these things are dangerous? Shouldn't somebody be told?" Trip wasn't particularly worried, but it was important to play devil's advocate for others. It made them think more deeply about their answers. Corrie looked concerned.

"Nobody's even seen one yet, let alone been attacked. It probably doesn't go after humans and boats. Surely, if it did, it would have already."

"A weak argument, but probably true."

"I know I have to say something one day, but I wanted a little more time."

Trip handed Corrie the camera and leaned back on one hand.

"Hey, it's your secret to divulge. You don't need my approval. What's the plan?"

"I don't know." Corrie looked overwhelmed, then she brightened. "The *Clicker* has this sonar device that gives off a sound to attract these crazy creatures. Zeb doesn't know why—his dad knew something, apparently—but they flock to the boat when the device is on. I'd love to measure the frequency of the sound, but it's underwater. Do you know of anything that could do that?"

Trip nodded slowly.

"Yes, I think so. There's a team in my building that works on underwater equipment. I bet they have something I can borrow. Let me look into it."

Corrie nodded, and her shoulders relaxed.

"Thanks for listening, Trip. I hate keeping secrets."

Trip smiled wryly. These new species of Corrie's were a lot to take in, and Trip still wasn't sure what she felt about the whole thing, but she was glad to be in the loop.

"It was burning you up inside, wasn't it?"

Corrie stood and plucked a few more cherries off the tree.

"Like I'd swallowed coals."

ZEBALLOS

Zeb unlocked his apartment and pushed the door open. It was a depressing sight. Teetering stacks of boxes filled his tiny living room until there was only a narrow path from the kitchen to the couch, and a small viewing portal to the television. His father's rubbish, boxed up and delivered here after his death, cluttered Zeb's house, his life, and his mind. He wanted to throw it all away without looking at it.

But if he did that, he might miss something crucial. He'd found the storage locker key in one of these boxes, after all. It had held cryptic devices that might reveal George Artino's secrets. Zeb hoped so. And there was the chance that something of his mother's had survived. He owed it to himself to search the boxes before their destiny in the trash.

It was an easy task to put off, though. There was always something more important to do. Eating was necessary. Swimming took priority. Even wiping the kitchen counter was vastly more appealing than sorting the contents of his father's house.

"Today," Zeb said aloud. The door swung shut behind him. "It's happening today. Right now."

He'd just come back from a swim along the shore, where he'd played with a friendly seal, and was feeling energetic and ready to tackle the world, or at least the boxes. Determination filled him. He tossed his wet towel on the floor, shook his hand through his short, damp hair, and grabbed the nearest box. He settled at the kitchen table to examine it.

Most of it was junk that he recognized. Some of it, like the tea towel that his grandmother had sent her son from Greece, brought him some slight nostalgia, but the rest he passed over without regret. It was vestiges of a life he was finished with. He'd written off his father months ago, when the old man had steadfastly refused to divulge anything more about Zeb's heritage. Zeb had known that George knew something, but his old man had been adamant that the past was in the past and that no good would come of Zeb knowing anything. It had driven an irremovable wedge between the two. Even after George's death, Zeb's feelings toward his father were overwhelmingly of anger, not sadness.

He had glanced through ten boxes and was feeling proud of himself for his initiative, when his eye caught a flash of textured gray. His heart hitched. His fingers carefully pushed aside a pile of old facecloths and extracted a large abalone shell.

It was huge, the size of his outstretched hand, and ringed with holes from the shellfish's body. The outside was a mottled-gray, but the inside was a swirling iridescence of rainbow colors that gleamed like secret treasure.

He remembered his mother coming home with the abalone shell, enchanted with the find.

"I've never seen one so big," she had said. "And the beauty inside." She had twirled around his father, who had laughed in a way that he never had after her death. "It's like you, George, pretending to be a big gray rock, but with wonderful colors deep within."

If his father had had "wonderful colors" inside, he'd hidden them well. Zeb hadn't seen much after his mother's death except George's gray, hard exterior.

Zeb placed the shell in his "keep" pile. His mother had chosen the shell, and that was good enough reason to keep it. It would take pride of place on his dresser of treasures.

Nothing else of interest filled the rest of the box, nor the next five. Zeb's enthusiasm waned, and he considered wandering to the kitchen to see what his refrigerator had for dinner. Too bad Jules wasn't here—Zeb could use a good meal. He grew lazy after time on the ship with his best friend as cook. Nothing he could prepare would ever compare to a meal made by Jules, so why bother to compete?

One more box, he decided. He had made good progress. Already, he could see the hallway from his couch. A few more sessions like that, and he would be free and clear.

He peeled the tape off the final box from a pile by the couch. Nestled among holey socks and moth-eaten fishing sweaters was a small wooden chest. Zeb's heart squeezed. He recognized the carved whorls on the lid and the warm chestnut of the wood. His mother had called it her treasure box and had only let Zeb look inside while she watched.

Zeb lifted the box gingerly out of the rumpled nest of clothes and onto his lap. With reverent hands, he opened the lid. It creaked with age, caught, then opened. The scent of the treasure box wafted past Zeb's nose, salt and dried seaweed and cedar, and he closed his eyes to inhale the familiar smell. How could a scent take him so vividly into the past?

He allowed himself a few moments to enjoy forgotten memories, then he opened his eyes and examined the contents. It was just as he remembered. There was a folded strip of strange material, stiff and fragile, with creases staining the greenish brown with strips of white, a small drawstring pouch of the same material, a pile of tiny snail shells, and a necklace.

An amulet dangled when Zeb lifted the necklace into the air. The necklace's greenish brown cord was the thickness of a slender vine and stiff, although it turned pliant with the warmth of Zeb's fingers. The amulet was a translucent bone-white in the shape of a nautilus shell. Scratched on the back was a series of crossing lines.

Zeb didn't know what the shell carving signified, but it was his mother's, and that was enough. From his frequent encounters with legendary creatures of late, he'd felt both closer to his mother and as untethered as ever. He slipped the necklace over his head and tucked it into his shirt, where the cord relaxed and lay flat against his skin. It felt natural there.

The memory of the pale woman in the water crossed his mind, the one who had looked like his own mother, but he thrust it deep down. There had been no sign of her since then, despite his searches. He'd started to think that he'd imagined her, born of hopes and memories dredged up of his mother.

Zeb carefully carried the box to his bedroom, where he placed it on the top shelf of his closet. He was profoundly thankful that he had made the effort to look through the boxes. What if he'd tossed them all and had missed this treasure? He shivered at the thought.

He wandered back into the living room. Already, it felt more open, cleaner, clearer. He breathed deeply and straightened his shoulders. This was good. He could finally get rid of his father's influence in his life and move on. Tomorrow morning, he would finish the rest of the boxes before he picked Jules up for the drive to Victoria and the *Clicker*. Tomorrow, his apartment and his life would be his again. His father could finally be laid to rest.

JULES

Jules lay on his narrow bed. The ceiling made a dull thumping sound every time he hit it with the old tennis ball. He couldn't remember where he'd got the ball from—he certainly didn't play tennis—but it had hung around his trailer for months. Maybe it was an old dog ball, lost from his neighbor's German shepherd. There might be teeth marks. He didn't stop to check.

Throw, thump. Throw, thump.

He was supposed to be packing for his next trip with Zeb. Corrie and Krista would be back this time. He didn't feel equal enthusiasm for both women. Corrie would liven up the boat, which sorely needed enlivening. He could put up with Krista's snide remarks for a week. Probably.

Throw, thump. Throw, thump.

He hadn't packed anything yet, and Zeb was due soon. He hadn't even made it to the laundromat. It had seemed like far too much effort. There were clean boxers, somewhere. They might have a few holes, but it wasn't like anyone ever saw him in them. Jules threw the ball more savagely against the ceiling. It ricocheted back faster than he anticipated, and he swatted at it blindly. It bounced off his hand and dribbled to a halt against a bench on the far end of the trailer.

Jules didn't have the energy to be bothered by the loss. Instead, he resumed gazing at the ceiling with hands at his sides. He would pack soon. When he felt up to it. The trip was only for a week. He could scrounge up enough clean clothes, surely.

Jules had paid work for the next week, maybe a little longer if Zeb wanted it. But what would he do after the week? Would Zeb still want to drive around, searching for the mysterious creatures he felt such kinship with?

Jules closed his eyes to ward off the sight of the water stain above his bed. Maybe his dad had heard of someone needing odd jobs. The township was still working on the new library and was behind schedule. They probably needed extra bodies. The thought gave Jules no pleasure whatsoever.

He didn't know what was wrong with him. This was his life, and he'd always been happy with it. Maybe happy was too strong a word, but content. Or, if not content, then resigned. He wasn't good for much else than what he did, so why bother looking elsewhere? He scraped by. Rent was paid on time, usually.

People like Krista were in a different sphere of existence. She had so much ambition it practically oozed off her. That, and her confidence. Jules didn't understand her drive, how Krista could be so passionate about something that seemed so dull.

Maybe that was why he got on with Zeb. Zeb had never shown the same driving ambition as his sister, not until the recent obsession with weird fish. But Jules got that. Zeb wanted to know more about his dead mother. That was understandable.

Sophie Trip was interesting, though. Despite only spending one evening with her at Corrie's pizza party, Jules could tell she was as driven as Krista—surely, she would have to be to do that much schooling—but in a less claw-to-the-top way. She was truly fascinated by her subject matter, the wires and connections and whatever else an electrical engineer dealt with. That was worth pondering.

But Jules didn't have ambition, not like that. And no talents worth exploring. Odd jobs would have to do.

With that gloomy thought, Jules drifted into a wakeful sleep, with dreams where he tried to swim to the *Clicker* but could never quite reach it.

A sharp rapping on the door startled him awake.

"Who is it?" he mumbled. The unlocked door opened, and Zeb's head popped around the corner.

"Ready to go?" he said, then he frowned. "Where's your bag? Were you sleeping?"

"So, what if I was?" Jules said. His head was wooly with the nap and dream. He groaned and pushed himself to a sitting position. "It's my time, I'll do what I want with it."

Zeb put his hands up in a surrendering position.

"Fine, sleep away. But we're due to leave. I thought you wanted to do some grocery shopping on the way down. And I need to take the sheets to the laundromat. I hope we have those spare ones tucked away somewhere. We're having an extra guest on the first night, before we pick up Krista."

"Guest?" Jules rubbed his face. "What are you talking about?"

"We're taking Corrie's roommate Trip to Vancouver. She'll stay the night. I thought we'd anchor at Spirit Island."

Jules stared at Zeb, his sleepy brain trying to process Zeb's words. Then he cursed.

"I didn't make it to the laundromat. I need a load done when you do the sheets." He jumped up, filled with new energy. Why hadn't he packed a damn thing yet? He pulled a worn duffel bag from the floor and shoved the contents of a half-open drawer inside. One of his nicer shirts caught his eye from a pile on the floor, and he stuffed it in the bag. Zeb watched his antics with raised eyebrows.

"Shut up," Jules growled. Zeb put up his hands again.

"I didn't say anything. Man, you're in a bad mood today. What's up?"

"Nothing." Jules zipped up the bag and slung it over his shoulder. "I'm fine. Let's go. Do you have a pen in your car? I need to plan meals on the way down."

CORRIE

Corrie stifled a yawn as she followed her boyfriend David and the realtor into the condo's living room. David spread his hands and looked around.

"It's so roomy. And the view's not bad, either." He strode to the window, and Corrie trailed after him. She thought longingly of her lab bench with its samples waiting to be processed. Work sounded far more appealing than feigning interest in condo-shopping. She'd visited too many open houses in her childhood, tucked in a corner doing homework while her realtor mother talked up double-paned windows and the benefits of stucco.

The windows opened to a bank of balconies in the high-rise next door. Where was the view David spoke of?

"Can you see it?" David pointed to the far left, where a tiny sliver of ocean twinkled in the distance. "Ocean views."

"Right," Corrie said with mustered enthusiasm. "That's great." A sliver was better than nothing, she supposed, but her rental house had no views, and she didn't feel terribly hard done by.

"Open floor plan," said the realtor with a wave around. "Granite countertops, new appliances. Full-size balcony, too." She walked to the hallway. "The bedroom is right through here."

"Let's see it." David rushed to follow the realtor. Corrie lagged, trying to imagine herself visiting David here after a movie. It was comfortable, quiet, and private. She didn't have a problem with his current place, but this condo would be nice enough.

"This is great," David was saying when she squeezed behind him in the narrow room. "I only have a queen, so it will be roomier. I can put that big landscape painting I have up on this wall. And look, Corrie." He pointed at the window, through which evening sunlight was streaming. "You can see the ocean from your side of the bed."

Her side of the bed? Corrie hadn't realized she had a side of the bed, yet. The realtor nodded and smiled warmly at her and David. Corrie stiffened. What was David doing, talking about sides of beds to random strangers, like he and she had been together for years, like they were a done deal? Corrie felt manipulated into a corner by David's assumptions, and her breath grew sharp. She chose not to answer David's comment.

The realtor breezed to the hallway. Her voice floated back.

"And here is the den, a perfect little nook for a home office."

Corrie followed David and poked her head in the small space lit by one narrow window.

"Technically," the realtor continued with a conspiratorial lean toward David. "It can't be called a bedroom. No closet. But for a couple thinking of starting a family at some point it would be a stellar nursery."

She winked at them, and David chuckled.

"Multi-purpose. Good to know."

The realtor led the way to the bathroom, but Corrie was rooted to the spot. Her heart pounded and her face grew hot with confusion. From having a particular side of the bed to planning kids? Corrie could think only one thing.

Hell, no.

Did she want a family? Sure, someday. But talking about it now, with David? She was not ready for that discussion. She didn't know if she would ever be ready, with David. It was too soon to tell.

Anger took over. Where did David get off, planning their future without consulting her wishes? Did he have some master plan that he would gradually lay before her, expecting her compliance on her predetermined path? She felt like she was being led blindly by a puppeteer pulling her strings. She loathed the thought.

The rest of the viewing passed Corrie by, caught up as she was in a fog of seething resentment. Back on the street, David made a move to take her hand, but Corrie crossed her arms.

"I'm not ready to move in with you," she said. Better to be blunt and get her point across than to dance around the issue. She knew her voice had an edge to it, sharpened by her anger, but she couldn't soften it. She didn't really want to. David needed to understand.

He frowned with bemusement.

"Sure, I get that. No need to rush things, right? But we can talk about it sometime soon. I feel like we're moving in that direction, so whenever you're ready."

Corrie wanted to shake David's shoulders until the smug, satisfied expression slid off his face like greasy butter on a hot pancake. Why was he so certain that moving in together was inevitable? How was he so certain about them?

"Please, don't push me," she said. "I really don't like you pushing me."

"Pushing you?" David looked bewildered with his face colored by growing frustration. "What are you talking about? I'm only saying out loud what anyone in a solid relationship is thinking. What's so wrong with planning for the future?"

It was the assumption of a single future that angered Corrie. In some part of her mind, she knew that David was coming from a good place and truly cared for her. She was even a tiny bit flattered that he felt she was a long-term prospect.

The larger part of her, however, rebelled at the invisible constraints David was tightening around her. It was too much, too soon. She didn't want to go there, yet.

She didn't know how to put it into words that David would understand, so she didn't try.

"I guess I'm just not ready for that. Look, I should head home. I'm leaving on the boat tomorrow and I still have to pack my clothes." She stood on her tiptoes and kissed him quickly on the cheek. "We'll talk when I get back."

She left a quiet David looking hurt on the curb and walked swiftly to her bike without looking back. As kind as David was, she couldn't fall into the trap of being forced along someone else's path. She didn't want to repeat the mistakes of her past.

JULES

Jules tapped his pen against his knee while he thought.

"Do you think Trip likes salmon? Ugh, scratch that, you're not going to be able to get one this time of year. Lingcod just isn't the same for the recipe I'm thinking of, though. Maybe herbed lingcod cakes with caper sauce, those are good."

"Here's hoping she's not a vegetarian," Zeb said. He checked over his shoulder as he changed lanes on the highway to pass a motorhome on the hill. Jules gaped at him.

"Damn it, what if she is? I have some good meat-free ideas, but seriously…"

"Relax, Jules. She was eating pepperoni on her pizza when we visited."

Jules sank into his seat in relief.

"Good. Maybe I should text Corrie, see if Trip has any dislikes."

"Just do your thing. Everybody always raves about your food. Besides, maybe you can cook a disliked food so well that you convert her. Don't text Corrie—that's too far." Zeb glanced at Jules. "You really like her, don't you?"

Jules shrugged, his pen scratching out ingredients on his paper.

"I'd like to know her more."

"You'll get your chance tomorrow."

They lapsed into silence. Zeb focused on the road while Jules scribbled ideas for meals for their week on the *Clicker*. This was the one thing he was good at, after all, and he wanted to impress Trip. She was gorgeous, super-smart, and confident. He didn't have much, so he had to use what he did have, which was cooking.

Zeb hummed tunelessly, his thoughts clearly elsewhere. The notes were as random as one of his whistle songs that he played on the boat sometimes. Jules didn't pay much attention at first, immersed as he was with calculating amounts of carrots needed and the correct curry paste to buy, but when Zeb started to rub his forearm, Jules looked at him.

"You're itchy already? Didn't you go for a swim before we left?"

Zeb's hair had been wet when he'd picked up Jules, and the dried salt now clinging to the short strands didn't speak of a shower. Zeb grimaced.

"Yeah, I did. I'm fine. I'll be fine."

"What are you going to do this week, with Corrie on board?" Zeb had swum on their last trip with Corrie, but he seemed to need it even more now, two weeks later. Zeb hesitated.

"I don't know. Figure it out, I guess."

"There's that forward thinking that always endears you to Krista," Jules said. Zeb chuckled.

"Yeah, well, things usually work out okay, even so."

ZEBALLOS

Zeb heaved the pillowcases full of laundry over his shoulder, trying to reposition them for comfort, but they bit painfully into his muscles. He gritted his teeth and walked faster down the dock. When the *Clicker* appeared between a sailboat and an expensive-looking motorboat, he picked up his pace.

A line of scuba tanks rested on the dock beside the boat when he approached. Jules hauled one in his hands over the boat's edge.

"Good, you're here," he panted when he saw Zeb. "Give me a hand with these suckers."

Zeb dropped the laundry on the wooden slats of the dock and picked up a tank in each hand to take them to the hold, which already had three tanks strapped against the side wall. Jules passed his tank down to Zeb.

"Looking forward to squeezing into that wetsuit?" Jules said with a smirk. Zeb shivered with disgust.

"Not in the slightest. I honestly don't know how I'm going to do it." Zeb had avoided thinking about it, but Jules' words brought his formless fears to the surface. The way he'd been the past two weeks, needing to swim multiple times a day—would he be able to jump in the ocean with a layer of neoprene between him and the salty water? The thought made him physically sick. What would happen? Would he keep it together, or would be start ripping off his gear at depth as Corrie watched with horrified eyes? And how would he swim so frequently without Corrie seeing? He anticipated a lot less sleep this week, if he had to swim at night when Corrie was in her cabin.

"You'll figure it out," Jules said. He stood up from his crouch by the edge of the hold. "Repeat a mantra or something. 'I will not show Corrie I am part-whale. I will not show Corrie

"

I am part-whale.'"

Zeb threw an orange fender at him. Jules dodged it with a grin.

"Come on." Zeb climbed out of the hold. "The boat is a mess. Help get it ready."

"Aye aye, captain. Swab the decks."

Zeb grabbed the pillowcases of laundry and heaved them over the bulwark then swung them inside. The pillowcase of clothes he left in his cabin—Jules would be back in the top berth now that the women were joining them—and the second he kicked into the other cabin. Inside, clean sheets were roughly folded. He plucked a bottom sheet from the pile and shook it. His hands couldn't spread the wrinkles out, no matter how much he smoothed the sheet onto the bunk. He had a sudden vision of Corrie's body lying on the sheet.

He shook his head violently to get rid of the image. Why was his mind going there? Corrie had never shown any interest in him in that way, and she was already dating that David guy. His lip curled at the thought of David's smarmy face. Zeb wouldn't let an obstacle like David get in his way, except that he didn't want to get involved with Corrie. It was too messy. Her involvement with the creatures was already too close for comfort. He couldn't risk her getting closer. If she was interested in a passing fling, he wouldn't say no, but she didn't seem the type.

Maybe it had simply been too long since he'd been intimate with anyone, as Jules had suggested. Zeb rummaged in the bag for another sheet for the top bunk. He was having problems with control lately, with his cravings for swimming and jellyfish, so why should he be surprised that his mind was unruly in other ways?

Zeb stepped back and surveyed the room. It was as plain and sparse as his own, which had sufficed on Corrie's last visit but now felt spartan. He had a stroke of inspiration and darted to his cabin. When he returned, he placed a moon snail shell on a patch of non-stick mat on the dresser. It wasn't much, but it was something. He had a drawer full of shells and other treasures that he couldn't help picking up on his swims. There was so much beauty down there. He liked to be reminded of it when he was stuck on dry land.

A dull ache in his stomach diverted his attention from the shell. It had been a few hours since he'd had a jellyfish snack, and his body was forcibly protesting. Zeb picked up the now-empty pillowcase and wandered to the galley.

"Don't step on my pile," Jules yelled and brandished a broom at the end of the hallway. Zeb tiptoed with exaggerated motions around a mound of dirt and hopped into the galley. The counters were wiped clean and even the worn cupboard doors were as sparkling as Jules could make them. Maps in the eating space were straightened and tucked into their pouches in orderly rows.

Zeb smiled. Jules had been peppy ever since he'd heard about Trip's planned overnight stay. She and Jules had hit it off at Corrie's party last week, and Zeb was glad to see it. Jules had been lingering over his feelings for Carole, his old girlfriend. Zeb had worried that he'd never get over her leaving him—she'd even lived with Jules for a brief time, and they'd been together for over a year by the time she'd left—so it was a relief to see him interested in Trip. He hoped she wouldn't treat him poorly. Jules looked flippant and easygoing, but Zeb knew he was more brittle than he let on.

Zeb grabbed three pieces of dried jellyfish from his bag in a top cupboard and munched them gratefully. They were salty and chewy, and although the effect didn't last long, they were the only thing that even mildly curbed the terrible hunger that nothing seemed to cure.

Swimming helped, too. Did he have time for a quick dip before Corrie arrived? Zeb shoved the rest of the jellyfish in his mouth and walked outside. He grabbed his shirt back and started to pull it over his head when he heard voices.

"There's the *Clicker*! Make sure that box doesn't fall off. Most of my equipment doesn't float."

Zeb's heart jumped at the sound of Corrie's voice at the same time his skin crawled with the realization that he couldn't swim right now. He was too late. This week would be a test of his endurance, that was certain.

He hung over the bulwark to greet the two women, who pushed a cart teetering with boxes down the dock.

"Hi Corrie, Trip. Welcome aboard."

"Zeb!" Corrie looked at him for a moment with wide, uncertain eyes. Zeb barely had time to register the odd reaction before she hitched a dazzling smile on her face. "I'm so excited about this week. I have big plans. My dissertation will be so full of data points, they'll pass me from sheer data overload. And Trip gets to experience a night at sea! I love the rocking boat. I swear, I sleep much better here than at home. Do you think that's why people buy waterbeds? Do they come with wave action? That would be awesome."

"I think you have to make your own waves on a waterbed," said Trip with a grin. "Hi, Zeb. Thanks for giving me a ride."

"No worries," Zeb said.

He was both amused and slightly overwhelmed by Corrie's barrage of words. He had forgotten how much she talked. He liked it because he didn't have to contribute much, but it was a lot to get used to. He looked forward to getting used to it again.

"Is that all your equipment?" he said, then he leaned back and yelled, "Jules, give us a hand, will you?"

"That's everything." Corrie waved at the huge cart of plastic containers. "Everything I need to sample my anemones."

"Corrie Duval, dread conqueror of anemones everywhere," Trip said. Her eyes flicked sideways, and her mouth curved upward. "Hi, Jules."

"Hi, Trip." Jules hesitated, then his natural easiness took

over. "Hi, Corrie. Welcome to the *Clicker*, explorer of the seven seas. Here there be monsters."

"So I've been told," Trip said with a glance at Corrie. "I'm looking forward to hearing more."

Zeb wondered uneasily what she meant. Had Corrie told Trip about the creatures? He thought he'd made it clear that he didn't want anyone else to know, not just her professor.

Corrie avoided his gaze. She heaved a container in her arms and held it up to Jules.

"Let's get cracking. The anemones await."

They loaded Corrie's gear swiftly. After the previous week of sampling, the three of them knew where everything went, and Trip aided Corrie where she could. Once the containers were all in the lab or the hold, Zeb started the engine, and Jules untied the lines and hopped on board the moving boat. They were off again, and Zeb's heart thrilled at the thought. Last time Corrie had been on board, the world of his mother's stories had opened to him. What might happen this time?

Once they'd cleared the marina and were out in the strait among sailboats and pleasure cruisers, Corrie poked her head into the wheelhouse.

"Got a minute?"

Zeb waved her in, and she jumped over the threshold. She was wearing an old tee shirt that only hinted at her figure underneath, although they were tantalizing hints. Zeb banished the thought.

"Lots of them. What's up?"

"I want to go over our sampling plans for today." Corrie pulled out a chart from a pouch on the wall and spread it over the back counter. Zeb hid a grin. Corrie moved around the wheelhouse like an old hand. She pointed at a spot on the chart.

"We're spending the night here, right?" Her finger was on Spirit Island, and Zeb nodded. "Then, can we sample there this afternoon? Just a water sample, no diving. I want some water for a test of my analyses, and we can sample properly on the way home at the end of the week." Her fingers traced the coastline up the chart. "There are some amazing inlets that I want to sample, way up here. How far do you think we can go in a week?"

Zeb followed her finger with his eyes. The inlet her finger pointed at had an excellent shipwreck that he liked to explore. As far as he knew, no one else had ever discovered it.

"We can go that far, if you like."

Zeb was relieved to avoid testing his scuba diving today. He would have to face the challenge soon—diving with a restrictive suit felt more unbearable than ever—but procrastinating one more day almost made him sigh with relief. He rubbed his arm at the thought, his skin crawling with his need to swim. Corrie caught the motion.

"Are you okay?"

"Fine. Just some dry skin." As soon as he said it, Zeb silently cursed the words. What an unattractive thing to say. Not that he was trying to appear attractive to Corrie. Damn it, he needed a swim.

"Do you want some hand cream? I have some in my bag. Give me a sec, I can grab it."

"No, no, it's fine," he said quickly. "I'm fine."

Corrie looked at him with uncharacteristic silence, and Zeb started to sweat. After a moment, Corrie nodded slowly.

"Okay. I'm going to set up the lab. I'll see you later."

It was too quiet after she left. Only the waves and seagulls stayed with Zeb, and they weren't as good company as they usually were.

JULES

Jules pulled salt from the shelf and sprinkled it in the sauce bubbling on the stove. He tasted it—it still needed a pinch more. He reached into the box again.

"Hey, you."

He almost dropped the salt. Trip leaned against the door frame, looking at him like she knew exactly how her presence had made him react and was pleased about it. He flushed but hid it in a grin.

"Hey, yourself. Couldn't find anything to do in the lab?"

"Corrie's playing with her beakers, Zeb is doing whatever one does at the wheel, and I'm bored. What are you doing?"

"Working on dinner." Jules waved at the counter and stove. "Flank steak pinwheels."

"Mmm." Trip sniffed appreciatively. A series of rolling waves made Jules lunge for the handle of his saucepan. When they died down, he looked at Trip again, ready to resume their conversation, but her face had faded to a sickly shade of pale.

"Is this your first time at sea?" he said.

"I've been on the ferry before," Trip said weakly. Jules chuckled.

"Not quite the same. Sit at the table and look at the horizon. I'll fix you something to help with the nausea."

"Ugh, I feel awful." Trip sat heavily and rested her head on her hands. "And foolish. No one else is wanting to hurl."

"Sea sickness is really common," Jules assured her. "No sweat. I'll make you my secret remedy. Works like a charm every time. But just in case—" He slid a bowl onto the table in front of her. "I just cleaned the floor."

Trip gave a weak chuckle.

"Noted."

Jules flew around the kitchen. While water boiled, he grated fresh ginger and a licorice candy into a mug, along with peppermint, club soda, and a dash of honey. When he delivered the concoction to Trip with a flourish, she was paler than before. She wrinkled her nose at the fizzing, scented steam rising past her nose.

"Do I want to know what this is?" she asked.

"It will help," Jules said. "Promise."

He slid into the bench seat across from Trip and looked expectantly at her. His secret remedy for sea sickness had never failed yet, and he'd prepared it for many divers aboard the *Clicker* in the past. Trip looked in the mug, grimaced, then took a sip.

"Strong-flavored," she said and took another gulp, larger this time. "It doesn't make me want to revisit my lunch."

"Was that something you really wanted?"

Trip chuckled.

"Definitely not." She took another swallow. Color was already returning to her cheeks, and Jules nodded with satisfaction. Trip frowned. "I was looking forward to having your dinner. Corrie keeps gushing about the food on board. Stupid stomach."

"You'll eat," Jules assured her. "Drink up and look at the horizon if you feel a slip in your stomach. I'll make you more tea every hour. You'll be fine, I promise." He jumped up. "Speaking of dinner, I need to do a quick meal change."

"Do you want help?" Trip rose also. Now that they both stood in the cramped seating area, she was much closer to him. She didn't look the least bit uncomfortable about it, and Jules' heart beat faster. She clutched her tea tightly in one hand, but her color was back to normal. "I'm at loose ends."

Jules smiled.

"Absolutely. How well do you handle a knife?"

ZEBALLOS

Zeb drove for a while with his mind unable to settle on anything. Islands passed the boat, and a few harbor seals poked their heads out of the waves to watch the *Clicker's* progress. His skin itched, and he wished he had something to distract him from the sensation. He told himself sternly that he wouldn't be able to swim until tonight at the earliest. His body responded to the reprimand by itching even more strongly.

Zeb cast his thoughts around for some topic that would occupy his mind. With a start, he recalled the box of unknown devices from his father's storage locker. He hadn't even mentioned it to Corrie yet.

"Hey, Jules!" he yelled through the open doorway that led to the rest of the interior.

"Yeah?" Jules' voice floated back.

"Come drive for a minute, will you?"

Jules appeared a minute later, looking disgruntled and wiping his hands on a tea towel.

"I have stuff cooking," he said. "What do you want?"

"I want to show Corrie the devices from my dad's locker." Zeb gave Jules a pleading look. "Just for a minute."

"Fine, fine." Jules waved him away from the wheel. "But my timer goes off in ten minutes, and you'd better be back here by then, or you can eat all the burned bits. Got it?"

"Deal."

Zeb left the wheelhouse via the outer deck and strode to the aft deck. He'd tucked the container in the hold before Corrie had come on board. The door of the hold clanged against the deck, and he leaped in. When he climbed out with his load, Corrie peeked her head out of the lab.

"What are you doing?" she said with an inquisitive tilt to her head. Zeb cracked open the lid.

"Showing you some crazy stuff of my dad's that I found. I

think it has something to do with the creatures, in the same vein as the sonar device. I have no idea what the things are for, though. I thought you would want to have a look."

Corrie bounced out of the lab and over to the container.

"Yes, yes, yes," she said. "Amazing. Let's get it out. Ooo, that looks electrical." She pointed at the device with wires sticking out. "Trip might have a better idea. Trip!" Corrie yelled over her shoulder. "Come check it out."

Zeb frowned. He'd forgotten that Trip was around. What would they tell her? Corrie caught his expression.

"Don't worry, she knows about the creatures. It's fine."

Zeb's lips tightened. So, Corrie had told Trip. She wouldn't tell her professor, but everyone else was fair game?

"I thought we were going to keep all this between us."

Corrie had the grace to look chastened.

"She and Adrianna are sworn to secrecy, I promise. They won't go to my supervisor, or the press, or anything like that. They can help."

Zeb shrugged tightly. It was too late now. He only hoped that his disapproval stopped Corrie from telling any more of her nearest and dearest friends. Every extra person who knew was one more chance that the world of his mother's stories would come to mainstream attention. He hoped he could find his answers before that inevitable day.

Trip came out of the cabin and walked unhurriedly toward them. She clutched a mug of something steaming in her grasp. Zeb stood.

"I promised Jules I'd go back to drive," he said to Corrie's bent head as she examined the devices. "Good luck."

He walked toward the bow once more. His mind was now occupied, but it was with worry about leaked secrets. He wasn't sure if that was better than dwelling on swimming. On cue, his arm itched again.

JULES

Jules took his rice off the stove then wandered to the aft deck. Trip and Corrie were bent over the weird things from George's locker. Jules was surprised that Zeb's father had strange devices of unknown use, since he had always assumed that what he saw was what he got with George. It just went to show that even the most unlikely people had hidden depths.

Trip turned when she noticed Jules. She waved him over.

"Check it out, Jules. This stuff is bizarre."

Jules ambled over. He didn't have anything to contribute to an examination of the box's contents—Zeb had shown him already, and they were meaningless to him—but if Trip wanted him to see, he would come. He squatted next to Trip and peered at the things spread on the deck with an attempt at an interested expression.

"Find anything?" he said.

Trip shook her head, but not in negation.

"I have no idea why there's a dehydrator." Trip waved at the machine beside a bag of dried jellyfish that Corrie was prodding. "Or the creams and jars. But this thing is cool." She held up the device with wires extruding from it. "Let's have a look inside."

Before Jules could protest at her messing with Zeb's strange device, Trip had expertly pried the case open. It was the size of a large sandwich, with a tangle of wires and little connector things spilling out of the case, and weird blue tubes and what looked like a plastic English muffin inside. Although Jules didn't understand what anything was in the slightest, it was clear even to him that the wires belonged inside the case when functioning. Trip followed a few wires with her fingers, nodding to herself.

"Check it out," she said to him finally. He leaned forward, pretending the wires held interest to him. Trip pointed at an orange one. "This leads to the resistors, which sends the signal through this wire, here. But what's happening here?" Trip poked at the electronics. "What a mess. Whoever made this didn't know what they were doing. Now, I can only guess what's going on, but this output wire probably connects to the speaker. If I twist these ends together for a makeshift connection, and we install a battery and play with these dials, I'm guessing we can make some noise." She leaned back and considered it. "To what end, I don't know. But it's definitely producing sound."

Jules was fascinated by Trip's absorption with the device. He cast about for something to say.

"What's this bit, here?" He pointed at a flat disk over what Trip had said was a speaker.

"Looks like the whole unit is waterproof. That membrane allows the sound to transmit through water, while keeping the electronics dry." Trip finally looked at him and smiled. "See? Everything is connected in here, and everything has a purpose."

The wires did look snug in their casing, each one with a job to do, secure in their position in the device.

"I'm still not sure what this is," Trip said. She waved a piece of metal covered in black squares and other important-looking parts that was by itself in the box. "Can I take it with me to Vancouver and have a closer look? The friend I'm staying with has some tools."

"I'll ask Zeb, but I don't see why not," said Corrie. She rummaged through the box. "I have no idea about these jars, but these look like transmitter tags. I think someone tried to make terrestrial wildlife tags waterproof. I wonder if it worked. You'd have to wait until the animal surfaces, I presume—the signal wouldn't travel through water, I bet. They look pretty homemade."

"Zeb's dad wasn't the most sophisticated man," Jules said. "And he didn't like to throw money around. If he made it, I'm not surprised."

Jules felt strange saying negative things about old George Artino. Was it bad form to demean a dead man? Jules comforted himself by remembering he hadn't said anything that George wouldn't have proudly said himself. He had known what he was, and what he wasn't. There was no shame in knowing yourself. Jules felt a twinge of envy for George, but only a twinge. George might have known his place in the world, but he wasn't in it anymore. There were better things to be than dead, after all.

KRISTA

Krista Artino approached the human resources department with trepidation. The door was ajar, and the tapping of a keyboard floated into the hallway along with subdued voices.

She needed to inform them that she would be taking a few days of unpaid leave to join Zeb on the boat. In theory, this was acceptable according to her contract of employment. She was allowed to take up to seven days of unpaid leave every year, and her trip with Zeb a few weeks ago had used her vacation time.

In practice, no one ever used the unpaid leave. It was frowned upon by upper management and mentioned in disparaging terms during review time. Krista didn't know any junior attorneys who had ever taken any.

But Zeb needed her, whether he knew it or not. Without her guidance, he would make stupid mistakes and dig himself into deeper holes than he should. He might be technically an adult, but sometimes she wondered.

She took a deep breath, squared her shoulders, and marched into the office. They couldn't fire her because she took what was stipulated in her contract. She was a lawyer, after all. She knew what her rights were.

There were three desks in the spacious office, which was brightened by wide, west-facing windows. One woman and a man concentrated on their computer monitors, but the last woman leaned back in her desk chair while she spoke with Fiona Sullivan, Krista's colleague.

Krista grimaced. She didn't want a witness to her leave-taking, no matter how allowable it was. She had hoped to slide under the radar for the three days she would be gone. She twisted the grimace back into a neutral expression when Fiona turned to look at her. Fiona smiled warmly.

"Hi, Krista."

Krista nodded, and Fiona went back to her chat with the desk-bound woman. Krista approached the other woman, who looked up with a polite expression.

"Can I help you?"

"Yes," Krista said in a firm but quiet voice. She didn't have a hope that Fiona wouldn't hear her words, but she couldn't help trying to hide. "I'd like to apply for unpaid leave for next week."

The woman's eyebrows twitched involuntarily, but she recovered and pulled a form from the bottom of a stack behind her desk. Krista found herself trying to justify her actions.

"It's a family emergency. Just for three days."

"That's fine." The woman handed her the paper. "Fill out your reasoning on the form."

Krista nodded and walked stiffly out. Why had she blurted out the family emergency line? The woman didn't need to know. Krista was under no obligation to explain her reasons for taking unpaid leave. She cursed herself for being so weak.

Fiona caught up to her in the hall. Krista steeled herself for Fiona's particular brand of sugary speech, but Fiona was strangely straightforward.

"Be careful, Krista," she said and put her hand on Krista's arm briefly. "It's a tough time to be disappearing."

"Isn't it always?" Krista couldn't remember a time when everyone in the firm wasn't working their butts off at all hours. Fiona chuckled.

"True enough. There's a reason no one takes leave, though. I'm only saying, make sure you really need to go on your 'family emergency.'" She put the words in air quotations. "You don't have to explain to me, just be careful. I'll do my best to cover for you, but there's only so much I can do."

Fiona gave her a pat on the shoulder and turned to walk back down the hall. Krista's stomach twisted. Was she doing the right thing? Then she thought of Zeb. Surely, she should choose family over work. Shouldn't she? Didn't Zeb need her?

CORRIE

They had been underway for hours, and Corrie had set up her lab as before. Trip tossed a plastic eyedropper end over end while Corrie finished taping tubes to the wall.

"Surely that's enough tape," Trip said with a look at Corrie's organized wall. "No getting lost in here. Did you print off an index before you left?"

Corrie stuck her tongue out at her friend.

"What's your point? I'm organized."

"That's another word for it."

"I'm done, I'm done." Corrie pushed a drawer closed and clapped her hands. "We're not doing a proper station today, just collecting water, so I was thinking we could jump in the ocean and see some fish." She wiggled her eyebrows to suggest exactly what kind of fish she meant, and Trip stood up straight.

"All right! I brought my swimsuit for Vancouver, so I'm set. We can test the frequency of your so-called sonar device while we're down there." Trip frowned. "Won't it be freezing? It's not exactly warmed up from shallow sand, like at the beach."

"Yeah, it'll probably be freezing," said Corrie with an airy wave. She didn't care. There were fish to see. She could handle a little cold. "Whatever. We're tough, right?"

"Right." Trip grinned back.

They traipsed to the wheelhouse, where Zeb had one hand on the wheel and another holding an English-Greek dictionary. He snapped it shut when they entered.

"Studying for something?" Corrie pointed at the dictionary.

"My dad wrote a notebook that I found in the storage locker, but it's all in Greek."

"And you're learning Greek to decipher it? That could take a long time." Corrie picked the book up and rifled through it.

The letters were only familiar to her from math classes.

"I know Greek." Zeb shrugged. "To speak, I mean. My grandmother visited one summer from Greece, and that's all she spoke. She taught me. I can't read it, though. I need to figure out the alphabet, I figure."

"You learned how to speak Greek in one summer?" Trip looked impressed. "Enough to get around, or fluently?"

"Fluently, I guess." Zeb looked out the window to check for obstacles. "It wasn't too hard."

"That's insane. I had thirteen years of French class, and I can barely order bread in a bakery. I tried in Paris, once. It was terribly embarrassing. I finally had to mime a baguette, which everyone found highly amusing."

Corrie giggled and even Zeb's mouth twitched.

"If you don't have much luck, we can get it translated," Corrie said. "It can't cost that much, can it?"

"Yeah, that's true." Zeb drummed his fingers on the polished surface of the old wooden wheel. "I'd rather keep the contents private, though. Krista might help. She can read a bit. Maybe if she reads the words aloud, I can translate."

"Team reading. I like it." Corrie changed the subject to the one foremost on her mind. "Trip and I want to see the unicorn fish."

Zeb looked confused.

"We don't have one."

"You said the sonar device calls them to the boat." Corrie jiggled her leg. "We brought our swimsuits."

Zeb looked at her fully this time. His lips tightened in amusement.

"You know how cold it is in there, right?"

Corrie waved the objection away.

"I've done a polar bear swim before. It'll be fine."

Zeb looked to Trip for confirmation. She nodded.

"We're tough."

"Okay," Zeb said. "We'll be at Spirit Island in half an hour.

Meet me on the aft deck then."

Trip disappeared to get changed. Corrie jumped in place, unable to contain her excitement. Zeb let out a startled laugh and she grinned.

"We're really doing this. I'm going to swim with the unicorn fish."

"If one shows up, yes."

Corrie's eye fell on the Greek dictionary. She'd known for a while now that Zeb was wrapped up with the creatures, but she'd been too busy to fully explore how she had become involved. Something clicked into place in her mind.

"The award you offered," she said slowly. "For our first cruise. How did you select me?"

Zeb's smile turned into a look of discomfort. He opened his mouth a few times, but nothing came out. Corrie raised an eyebrow and leaned against the dash.

"You knew you were going to choose me," she said in astonishment. "Jules found out about the blog, and you wanted someone to hunt creatures with you. All along, you've been trying to find out more about the world of your mother's stories." She let out a huff of disbelief. "To be honest, I feel a little strung-along."

Zeb turned pained eyes on her.

"I'm sorry," he said. "That's not how I meant it. It was just a chance. You were the only person who might have been able to help me. You did get samples for your project, didn't you?"

Corrie shook her head in amazement at the preposterous scheme Zeb had created, then she nodded to answer Zeb's question.

"You're right, I did. And I wouldn't have missed finding out about all this craziness for the world." She beamed at him. "And now, I want to see a strolia in action. See you soon."

Corrie raced to her cabin. Her mind still reeled from the revelation that Zeb had concocted this elaborate plan to get her expertise on board. Should she feel manipulated? She wanted to—she hated being controlled behind her back—but her overwhelming feelings were of pride and gratitude that she had been chosen to discover the creatures. Imagine if she hadn't come on board and was still searching for answers with her blog posts? She shivered at the thought.

In her cabin, she slipped into her one-piece swimsuit. Maybe the extra fabric would give her a little more insulation, although she doubted it. Trip stepped through the door, and Corrie raised her eyebrows.

"Itsy bitsy bikini, really?"

"It's the only kind I own." Trip twirled in place. "Why would I have any other?"

Corrie shook her head with a laugh.

"Why, indeed."

They waited on the aft deck for Zeb to put the anchor down. Corrie jiggled impatiently. Where was he? She wanted to get in the water now. The fish were waiting.

Zeb finally strode onto the deck. He stopped in surprise.

"You're changed already."

"Of course," said Corrie. "We're ready to swim."

"I thought we'd do a few breathing exercises first," he said. "You'll get a lot more out of this if you can stay underwater for longer."

"Right, you free dive," said Corrie. "I guess that makes sense. Just don't make me wait too long."

"Corrie might burst if she doesn't get in the water soon," Trip added. Zeb smiled, but it didn't reach his eyes.

"I understand. This will help, I promise."

"How did you start free diving, anyway?" Corrie asked, curious despite herself. It seemed like an odd sport to get into, although she could understand the appeal. Being able to swim in the ocean without cumbersome tanks sounded wonderful. She would have preferred tropical water, but to each their own.

"I learned it from my mother," Zeb said. "And a lot of it was intuitive—she taught me when I was a kid. But I have read up on some helpful techniques. We can practice breath-holding on the deck before we get in the water.”

Trip raised an eyebrow, and Corrie agreed with her skepticism.

“How does that even compare to being in the water?” Corrie said. “We’ll be swimming and using up energy, and it’ll be cold, which won’t help.”

“You’re right. It’s totally different.” Zeb shrugged. “But if you can increase your breath-holding above water, it will translate. And when you descend, your body changes. Your heartrate slows and your blood vessels constrict to help you conserve oxygen. You’ll see.”

“All right.” Trip spread her hands. “You’re the boss. What do we do?”

Zeb looked around. When his eyes touched on two towels drying on the winch, he grabbed them and spread them on the deck.

“We’ll stretch first,” he said. “Open up the rib cage. I can expand my lungs much further because I have more mobility in the chest.”

“Go on, then.” Trip nodded at Zeb with a serious mouth and laughing eyes. “Show us your incredible expanding ribs.”

Zeb looked bemused. Corrie glanced at Trip with a quelling look. Trip looked back, entirely unrepentant.

“Shirt off. Chop, chop,” Trip said. “For our education.”

Zeb frowned in confusion, but he reached behind him and pulled his shirt over his head in one smooth motion. Corrie’s stomach clenched, but she maintained a calm expression. It was apparent that he truly swam frequently, and the motion of his arms above his head showed off his physique beautifully. Corrie moistened her suddenly dry lips.

“Okay, watch while I take a breath,” Zeb said, thankfully unaware of her reaction to his shirtless state. She didn’t know why it had sent her into such a lather. It wasn’t the first time she’d seen him shirtless—he had been in a swimsuit for much of their previous voyage when he had changed into his wetsuit on the deck.

"I'll watch carefully," Trip said with a straight face. Corrie shot her a look of consternation. Trip studiously ignored her, although the corners of her mouth twitched. Zeb placed his hands behind his head.

"Here's a normal breath," he said and breathed in. It sounded deep to Corrie, and Zeb's chest visibly expanded. A strange necklace on his chest rose with the motion. Zeb shook his head at her disbelieving expression. "Here's a breath for diving."

He inhaled again, but this time the breath seemed to go on for ages. His chest grew round and ribs hinted underneath his tanned skin. Corrie's eyebrows rose when he finally stopped his inhale.

"Okay, I get it," she said. "We need to stretch. You can put your shirt back on now."

Trip elbowed her when Zeb's head was in the shirt, but she mercifully kept her disapproval at Corrie's reserve non-verbal.

Zeb led them in a series of stretches designed to work the muscles between ribs and along the back. By the end of the sequence, Corrie had to admit that she felt much more open than before. Her breath flowed easily into her lungs, and she felt energized. Zeb pointed at the towels on the deck.

"Lie down on your back and close your eyes," he said. Trip twitched one eyebrow at Corrie. She ignored it. "I'll lead you through your breath-holding."

Trip and Corrie lay on their towels. Zeb kneeled between them. Corrie closed her eyes and let the rocking of the boat soothe her. Her mind wandered to her lab—she shouldn't spend too long fish-watching—but there would be time later to prepare for her anemones. Once they were in the water, she would get a chance to see a unicorn fish in its own habitat. That was worth a late night of sample processing.

Corrie tensed when the gentle pressure of a hand rested on

her stomach.

"Fill up your stomach first," Zeb said quietly. "I want to feel my hand rise."

Corrie inhaled deeply and pushed against Zeb's palm. She squashed the thought of her stomach looking distended and concentrated on the breath. Zeb moved his hand to press his fingers on her sternum, where the ribs joined together.

"Now, inhale to fill the ribs," he said. "Use the space that you made when we stretched. Then, hold."

Corrie wrenched her mind away from Zeb's fingers on her chest and inhaled still more deeply. She held the breath.

It wasn't so bad, at first. The deck rocked gently below her back, and a crying seagull flew past the boat. The pressure of the huge breath in her lungs pushed against her tongue that held the breath in her body, but it wasn't unpleasant.

After a while—it couldn't have been long—a strange cramping sensation crawled through her chest. Her tongue twitched in its need to release the breath, but she held firm. Some indication of her discomfort must have crossed her face, for Zeb spoke in a low, soothing voice.

"Don't think of the breath. Think instead of the waves, of cool water rushing through your fingers as you swim, of your hair floating in the silky green of the ocean. Think of the silvery, sleek bodies of fish as they dart past you. Watch the smooth body of a dolphin as it rushes by you in the dimness, the currents from its passing pushing streams of water against your skin. Hear the call of the deep blackness of the chasm, the darkness that descends forever, waiting to be discovered. See the beams of sunlight lighting up millions of tiny creatures in the water, some glittering with arcs of rainbow light, each one a little spark of life. Think of how you belong here." His voice changed, from the hypnotic lilt of his descriptions to a harsher command. "Breathe."

Corrie's body spasmed. Her throat felt stuck closed, but with concentration she released it. She exhaled forcefully and brought in a new breath with a gasp. Her eyes fluttered open to the too-bright blue of the summer's sky. Trip coughed beside her.

"Congrats." Zeb gave Corrie a half-smile, but his eyes were troubled. "You held your breath for two and a half minutes."

"What?" Corrie sat up. Despite the wrenching end to their experiment, she felt fine now that breath flowed into her lungs. "That's insane. I'm sure I topped out at thirty seconds before, max."

"Me too." Trip looked dazed.

"Technique," Zeb said without elaboration. He stood and held his hands out to help her and Trip up. "Ready to try it in the water?"

JULES

The voices of the others floated through an open door, and Jules wandered to the deck to see what was happening. His eyes glossed over Zeb's bare chest and swim-suited form and glanced appreciatively at Corrie's curves encased in her sleek one-piece. They stopped at a rounded bottom partially covered by a white bikini. The rest of Trip's figure was as exquisite, and when she turned, he tore his eyes away from the tiny triangles of her bikini top to look at her face. Her mouth twisted in amusement.

"Did I die and go to Mexico?" Jules said, covering his reaction with banter. "Did the weatherman say it was bikini weather in BC?"

"It's always bikini weather," said Trip with a cheeky smile. "We're going down to see these famous fish."

"In just a swimsuit?" Jules eyed the cold water with horror, but found his gaze returning to Trip's curvy body and smooth stomach like a fish to a lure. He forced his eyes back to her face. "You'll freeze your tits off in there." As soon as the words were out, he regretted the vulgarity, but Trip only grinned widely.

"We wouldn't want that, would we?" She winked at Jules. "Don't worry, I'll bring the girls safely back."

"Do you want to come, Jules?" Corrie asked.

Jules shook his head reflexively. Zeb jumped in.

"He probably has stuff on the stove, since it's almost dinner. We won't be long, anyway—too cold."

Jules shot his friend an appreciative glance and Zeb nodded. There was no way he was getting in the water again. The last time he did, a ligan—a ridiculously long sea serpent with fangs the length of Jules' arm—had swum right at him. He didn't want to say that in front of the women, though. Corrie would look at him with sympathy, and Trip—who knew? He didn't want her to know he was so spineless.

He suppressed a shudder at the memory of the ligan and wished the others didn't feel the need to see the fish for themselves. He would rather none of them risked their lives in the ocean. Zeb had assured him that the ligan was a friend, but what if there was another one that wasn't so friendly? And what if it took a dislike to Trip? Wild animals were unpredictable.

"I'll hold the fort up here. Someone will have to get the hot chocolate ready after your polar bear swim."

"We'll definitely need warming up,'" said Trip with a sideways glance at Jules. Jules' mouth twitched in a smile. He liked the way Trip thought.

Corrie rubbed her hands together and strapped on her mask and snorkel.

"Let's do this before I lose my nerve. This is definitely not Mexico." She stepped forward to the opening in the bulwark where Zeb had installed the ladder and jumped in, holding her mask to her face. After a tremendous splash, she bobbed to the surface. Her shrieks were piercing.

"Damn it, it is so cold in here! Hurry up, Trip. This is going to be a very quick swim."

She huffed explosive breaths out of her mouth while she swam out of Trip's way. Trip adjusted Jules' borrowed mask, clutched a handheld frequency monitor in her hand, and leaped into the water with a cannonball and a yell of glee. When she surfaced, she cursed far more eloquently than Corrie had.

"I'm putting the girls' chances at fifty-fifty," she yelled up to Jules. "Wish me luck."

Jules gave her an exaggerated look of dismay, and she laughed before cursing again. She and Corrie treaded water.

"Hurry up, Zeb!" Corrie yelled.

Zeb dangled his mask from one hand, looking at it with loathing.

"Do I really have to wear this?" he said to Jules in a low

voice. "I hate it so much."

"I thought you didn't really use your eyes much down there, anyway," Jules said reasonably. "Just ignore it."

Zeb sighed.

"Fine. I'll be good. They get in the way, though."

Without another word, Zeb took two quick steps and launched himself in a perfect dive. He flew in a wide arc from the deck and slid into the water with barely a ripple. Corrie's and Trip's mouths gaped open, and Jules winced. It was hard, sometimes, being Zeb's friend. His athletic skill didn't reflect well on Jules, and Jules worked hard on his engaging personality to make up for it. He glowered at Zeb's wake and tried to ignore Trip's impressed look. More difficult to ignore were two proofs of Trip's coldness poking through her bikini top.

"Good luck," he called out. "Say hello to Spiky for me."

He turned back to the wheelhouse for somewhere to sit. The boat was anchored, but the chair behind the wheel was the most comfortable one on board, with the added benefit of being out of sight of the swimmers. He didn't particularly want to watch Zeb cavorting with the women.

Jules flopped onto the main chair and put his feet on the dash with a discontented sigh. He disliked being grumpy, but the mood had come to him more often than usual this past week. He picked up an old fishing magazine for the fifth time, then threw it aside in disgust.

Jules pulled his phone out of his pocket instead. They were close enough to shore that he had connectivity, so he started to browse. It was aimless at first, but he eventually found himself perusing recipe sites and dreaming of ways to improve each recipe. Thai red curry was fine, but what if he replaced the bamboo shoots with sliced turnip and substituted sockeye salmon for chicken for a West Coast fusion feel? Would a dash of birch syrup in the coconut rice be too much?

His stomach clenched with eagerness at the sudden thought

of culinary school. What did they learn there? He searched online. "Chef school" was not the right term, but it led him to "school of culinary arts," which opened a few links.

He looked at their class listings. "Knife skills" made him scoff—he could handle his knife just fine—but "sensory and palate training" made him pause, and "molecular gastronomy" sent him back to the search bar, where he read with growing interest. Maybe there was something here, after all.

Not that he would do something like this. Most of the places were in Vancouver, to start, and where would he get the money? Not to mention, they probably wouldn't even take someone like him, with no qualifications. It was too snobbish for him. He liked to cook, and that was it—even if the "charcuterie" topic awoke in him more fascinating questions than he could answer.

ZEBALLOS

Zeb's eyes itched and watered in their disapproval at being trapped behind a mask. He longed to rip it off and allow them to adjust to the cool water. It seemed unfair that the rest of his body got to enjoy the water while his eyes suffered.

At least he wasn't wearing a wetsuit. He shuddered to think of squeezing into the tight black neoprene. He didn't know if he could do it again when Corrie needed to sample. What would he do? He had another vision of himself tearing off his equipment at sixty feet below while Corrie watched, dumbfounded.

He would have to keep it together, that was all. He was strong. He could handle it. Too bad about the eyes, though.

Zeb looked up at Corrie and Trip's legs treading water above him. They peered down at him with owl eyes behind their masks. He waved and propelled his body to the surface.

"Ready?" he said when above water. Corrie and Trip glanced at each other with nervous, expectant looks. Corrie nodded with resolution.

"Let's try it."

"Don't forget to equalize your nose," he said. When Trip looked puzzled, he mimed holding his nose. "You know, like in an airplane."

"Right." Corrie frowned. "You didn't."

"I have a lot of practice. I don't need to hold my nose. Now, deep breath—stomach and chest—then dive."

Zeb flipped upside down to wait for the two underwater. His eyes itched again, and he had a brilliant thought. He took off the mask, pretending there was a leak, to allow cool water to flow over his eyes. They instantly soothed. Regretfully, he put the mask back on and blew air through his nose to empty the mask of water. His eyes adjusted to see in air once more.

Corrie paddled with her arms to stay in position. Trip

fiddled with the frequency monitor in her hands and watched the screen carefully. Corrie's eyes showed her nerves and exhilaration, and Zeb smiled widely. He held up a finger for them to wait and closed his eyes. The sonar device thrummed. He reached out with his senses to feel for movement in the water.

Below them, to the left, rising…

A squeak from Corrie traveled through the water and Zeb grinned again. Corrie pointed to a small school of strolias that emerged through the dimness. She and Trip clutched each other's arms in their excitement.

Zeb swam cautiously toward the strolias and held out a hand, in which he'd carefully held onto a piece of dried jellyfish. It was one of his last ones—he hoped Krista remembered to bring more onto the boat tomorrow—but if it helped Corrie see the strolias more clearly, than it was worth it.

The bravest strolia came forward and snatched the jellyfish out of his hand. It swallowed with a jerk of its head, its shimmering rainbow scales glinting even in this dim light. Zeb turned back to the women and gestured them forward.

Trip shook her head and aimed her body for the surface, but Corrie swam forward. She clutched her chest, clearly feeling the lack of air, but her curiosity won. Zeb made a soothing noise, deep in his throat. His mother had used to make it when he was learning to swim, when he was only a tiny child.

Corrie's hand left her chest and Zeb pressed a piece of jellyfish into it. She smiled at him with excited eyes and held it out to the fish.

A different strolia darted around the first brave one and grabbed the jellyfish with a quick snap. Corrie snatched back her hand, but the fish merely swallowed and swam back to its kin.

Corrie put a hand to her chest again, her eyes now fearful. She looked to the surface with growing horror and kicked her legs.

Zeb watched her feeble attempts to swim with consternation. If she were that air-starved, she was rising far too slowly. Without thinking, he wrapped an arm around her waist and kicked with powerful strokes to the surface. She clung to him with frightened fingers that dug into his side. Her body was warm and soft against his chest. She spasmed, and he kicked faster.

They burst from the water in a fountain of splashing. Zeb held Corrie up so she could take her first gasping breaths without needing to tread water. Trip watched with worry in her face.

"Are you okay, Corrie?" she said when Corrie was finally quiet. "You were down for way too long."

"I know that now." Corrie disengaged from Zeb's arms and treaded water on her own. Cool water flowed into the empty space where Corrie's warm body had once rested. She smiled apologetically. "Sorry about that. Now I know my limits. It's just, there were unicorn fish down there. How could I resist?" She turned to Zeb. "Thanks for getting me out of there."

"Of course." Zeb pondered. How could he make this safer for Corrie? "What if you wait on the surface while I scout around for fish? If I see one, I'll send up bubbles."

Corrie's eyes lit up.

"Yes! I'll be watching."

Zeb flipped over once more and dived down. He glanced at the two before low visibility stole them from view. Both had their heads in the water and watched his descent.

Once he was deep enough to comfortably stay neutrally buoyant, he sent out a sonar call, deep in his chest. The device was already calling the creatures here, but another call couldn't hurt. Within a minute, the small shark that he called a kroll came to investigate. Grinning broadly, Zeb released a series of bubbles from his mouth and continued to hum.

Seconds later, Corrie arrived. She pointed at the kroll with frantic gestures, and Zeb did a somersault to show his own excitement. He held out a hand for Corrie to wait, and he increased the hum in his chest. He approached the kroll and held out his hands.

The kroll swam through them like an affectionate cat. Corrie pulled something out of her swimsuit and flapped it at Zeb. It was a piece of gauze in a sample bag. Zeb grinned widely—of course Corrie wanted a sample—and waved her forward. She swam to him with nervous glances at the circling shark. She must have remembered the poisonous teeth of the kroll they had rescued from Miles Callahan's aquarium.

Zeb hummed again and the kroll swam toward him. He touched its sandpapery skin then wrapped an arm around its middle to keep it still. It couldn't breathe without swimming, he knew, but Corrie wouldn't take long. Zeb hummed still louder to calm the kroll while he had it contained.

Corrie swiped the gauze over its skin and bagged the sample. Zeb released the kroll with an affectionate pat and it swam away. Zeb pointed to the surface and started to rise, spinning the whole way to release his feelings. It was wonderful to swim with someone else again, even if Corrie's frequent need for air was limiting. He felt much more himself down here, and it was so liberating to share his world with someone. He caught Corrie's eye as they ascended, and they shared a grin.

TRIP

Trip was done. The weird fish had been cool, no doubt, but she was freezing and didn't have Corrie's fascination with the strange creatures. She swam with sure strokes to the ladder and hauled herself up. Even after five minutes in the freezing water, she was almost shuddering with cold. She grabbed her towel and wrapped it around herself, but it wasn't enough.

The clanging of the ladder as she climbed must have alerted Jules to her presence, for he appeared with a thick blanket and a mug of something steaming.

"My savior," she said through chattering teeth. "It's insanely cold down there."

"There's a reason I stayed aboard," Jules said. "An ice bath isn't my idea of fun." He draped the blanket over her shoulders and pressed the mug into her hands. Trip sighed in relief.

"Thanks."

Jules glanced at the cabin, then looked at her in apology.

"I need to get back to the galley. Wouldn't want to ruin dinner."

When Jules left, Trip sipped her drink—his special seasickness tea, which went down like a dream—and watched the water for the others. Within moments, Zeb and Corrie popped their heads out of the waves. Trip waved at them then regretted the movement that disturbed her blanket. Corrie had a wide smile and she waved a plastic bag at Trip.

"I got a sample," she screeched. "Of a weird shark. Amazing!"

"Great," Trip called back. "Now get on board before you freeze to death."

Zeb glanced at Corrie with worry, as if the cold wasn't something he had considered. Now that Trip thought of it, Corrie's lips were blue and her head shook from shivers, but Zeb looked as comfortable as he did on deck. Trip frowned.

That was strange.

Once the two were on deck and Zeb had found another blanket for Corrie, Trip had warmed up enough to think about their adventure.

"Let me get this straight," said Trip. She had a professional interest in the sonar device, and she longed to open it up and see what the mechanism of sound production was. "This sonar device produces a deep humming noise, once every ten seconds, and draws unusual creatures to the boat."

"Sort of a humming boop," Zeb said. He looked sheepish when Trip glanced at him. "That's how I would describe it."

"The boop. Got it. Highly technical jargon around here. And you're the only one who can hear it." Trip looked questioningly at Zeb, who nodded.

"So far."

"The sound is at fifteen hertz, by the way. Most people can hear no lower than twenty hertz. Here's a question: when you got the shark sample, how did you get the fish to come to you? Why didn't it ignore you and swim straight to the device on the hull?"

Corrie looked at Zeb with interest. Zeb shrugged.

"I tried to make the same noise. Sort of a deep hum in my chest. It seems to work."

"Do it now," Corrie said. Zeb gave a look of concentration then glanced at her expectantly. Corrie shook her head. "I didn't hear it."

She placed the flat of her hand on his bare chest. Zeb's face tightened, then he made a visible attempt to relax it. Trip hid her smile. There was clearly something going on between these two, even if Corrie couldn't see it. It was cute, like watching two bumbling teenagers. If nothing happened during this week on board, she and Adrianna would have to put their heads together to figure out how to force the issue.

"Okay, do it now," said Corrie. Zeb closed his eyes for a moment. They popped open when Corrie squealed. "I felt it!

There was a vibration. So cool. You're a walking sonar device. You can call the creatures on your own. Hey, could you teach me to do that?"

"It shouldn't be humanly possible," Trip said slowly. To make a noise that was lower than most humans' audio range? She'd never heard of such a thing. She tried to catch Corrie's eye, but she was too busy trying to hum. Trip resolved to talk with her later. Something wasn't adding up with Zeb. He seemed like a good guy, and he and Corrie clearly had a thing going on, no matter what Corrie said, but there was more to him than he appeared.

She left them to their noise-making endeavors and wandered to the kitchen—galley—to find Jules. He was stirring a pot on the stove. His eyes lit up when he saw Trip, and a warm glow stole over her. He was so transparent in his attraction to her. It was sweet. She liked his easy conversation, the way his mind was wired the same as hers, and his eagerness to get to know her. He held out a spoon.

"I'm glad you're here," he said. "Taste this and tell me what you think."

She didn't take the spoon from his hand. Instead, she opened her mouth and leaned forward. Color rose in his cheeks, but he grinned and slid the spoon into her mouth. She closed her eyes and let the flavors flow over her tongue.

"God, that's good, Jules. I want more. What are you making?"

"Thai ginger beef with cracked pepper." When Trip opened her eyes again, Jules beamed at her. "The more ginger, the merrier, I figured. We can't have you unable to eat. That would be a disaster."

"Apparently. I had no idea of the dire consequences. Missing dinner would be tragedy on an epic scale." Trip looked around with an exaggerated motion then nodded at the pot of sauce. "One more taste, come on."

Jules dipped the spoon in again and lingered when he took

it out of her mouth. This time, Trip maintained eye contact. She wasn't looking for a relationship currently—it wasn't her style, not now with her studies and too many interesting people to meet—but she might make an exception for Jules. For now, at least.

"Trip?" Corrie's voice broke the spell. Trip straightened and Jules dropped the spoon in the sink when Corrie appeared in the doorway. "Zeb and I are going to take a quick water sample before dinner. Are you good?"

"Go for it," Trip said. Corrie bounced out and Trip turned to Jules. "Can I help? I can't manage anything too tricky, but I can probably chop vegetables safely. Unless you're very particular about size and shape."

Jules colored again, even though Trip hadn't meant anything by her comment.

"No, chopped is chopped. Although, if they aren't the same size, some will cook faster than others…"

"You are particular." Trip swatted his arm playfully. Jules dodged with a grin.

"I'm sure you'll do great."

ZEBALLOS

Dinner was lively. Corrie was in fine form, talking and laughing more than the others, although Jules gave her a run for her money. He was transformed from sleepy and surly when Zeb had picked him up in Campbell River to engaging and animated with Trip on board. Zeb was happy to see it, even though it meant he was lost in the conversation. He was used to that. Even if he wished that Corrie would look his way more often, he didn't know how to break through the happy cacophony. He shouldn't wish it, anyway. No good would come of Corrie's attention. He had a hard time remembering that, though.

By the time dinner was long over and the beers had been drunk, Zeb's skin was itching. It had been hours—hours and hours—since he last swam. The women's arrival had distracted him, and their group dive had been a brief reprieve, but now his body asserted itself with a vengeance. When Trip started to yawn and Jules looked toward his cabin, Zeb encouraged them to go to bed. They wandered off, but Corrie moved in the opposite direction.

"I have a few samples to process in the lab. Are you heading to bed?"

Zeb tried not to let his grimace of disappointment show.

"I have a few things to tidy up first. Good luck with the samples."

Corrie disappeared, and Zeb put his head in his hands, which had started to tremble. He could hold out for a while longer, surely. His stomach cramped and he gasped. Corrie poked her head back into the eating area.

"Are you okay?" She looked at him with concern. "You don't look well."

"Fine," he forced out. The cramping subsided but left a residual ache. "Maybe dinner's not sitting well. You go on."

"If you're sure…" Corrie waited until Zeb waved her feebly off, then she disappeared again. Banging drawers and running water followed her departure.

Zeb stood up. The ache in his stomach was a familiar one, although the cramping was new. A few pieces of dried jellyfish would settle him. He took one step toward the galley.

Blackness swept in from all sides of his vision, until only a pinprick of light remained. He gripped the back of the bench with white-knuckled ferocity until the light slowly crept back.

He didn't know what was going on with him, not at all. Was his body so in need of a swim that it was rebelling in other ways beside itching? Or had it simply been a long day, and he needed to sleep? He'd never suffered from faintness in the past, not until that episode in Victoria the other week.

Jellyfish would help. He walked to the galley, his feet surer with every step. He reached into the top cupboard and pulled out a bag of jellyfish. Two pieces were work of a moment, and he reached for more. Four hardly scratched the surface of his need. By the time he had swallowed eight pieces, the bag was almost empty and his stomach, while not entirely satiated, complained far less. He hoped Krista would remember to bring more when she boarded tomorrow, otherwise he would have to take an emergency trip into town. How would he explain that to Corrie?

Zeb walked to the wheelhouse, where he tidied charts and magazines, trying to pass time. How long would Corrie be working for? He strode quickly to the lab and poked his head in. Corrie was pouring water into a tube with headphones on, and her head bounced to an unheard beat. At the cheery sight, Zeb's face relaxed from the worried frown he hadn't realized he'd been wearing. He knocked on the doorframe, and Corrie turned with surprise.

"Zeb! Hi." She pulled the headphones off her ears. "What's up?"

"Just seeing how you're doing. It's getting late." He looked at the rack of tubes she was filling. Most were empty. "Can I help?"

Corrie smiled.

"That's sweet, thanks, Zeb. It's a one-woman job now, but I appreciate the offer. I'll only be another twenty minutes, I think. Then off to bed. Big day tomorrow, right? Get Krista, sampling twice, cover some ground. I'm so excited to get samples from those northern inlets. I really think they're going to show us something spectacular. My data hinted at freshwater influx as being an important factor in production of the cancer-fighting metabolites. It's still only a hypothesis, but I would love more data to back it up. This could be really something."

Zeb smiled at her enthusiasm. Although he would have liked to talk more—or have her talk at him more—she had stopped filling her tubes while she spoke. Zeb's skin crawled with heat and discomfort.

"North it is," he said. "Tomorrow. Good luck with the rest of your samples."

He withdrew his head and Corrie put her headphones back on. Twenty minutes. He could survive twenty minutes. Probably.

Corrie finally drifted to bed while he was pretending to coil rope, over and over. The door to her cabin closed with a soft click.

With a gasp, Zeb tore off his shirt and pants. His swimsuit was underneath, as always. He barely managed to extract his flippers from the life ring in his haste, and he didn't bother putting them on until he dived into the water.

Immediately, his skin cooled. He imagined it soaking up water like a sponge. His face and shoulders relaxed, and his entire body loosened. He did a lazy roll in the water to work out the kinks of his difficult afternoon then twisted to fit his flippers on his feet. He closed his eyes against the glimmering phosphorescence of phytoplankton and opened his other senses.

The bay was shallow, and the seafloor only a few long kicks of his flippered feet away. Scuttling creatures moved on the bottom, likely crabs or squat lobsters, and he wondered if Jules wanted any for dinner. He didn't have a collecting bag, though, and it was probably more hassle than it was worth, trying to explain where the crabs had come from to Corrie and Trip. He swam an arm's length from the seafloor, occasionally soaring up in a burst of relieved energy. A patch of kelp attached to the rocky bottom with firm holdfasts was no obstacle to Zeb, who slid through the algae with a smile as the smooth stipes knocked gently against his body.

It took a minute of hearing the noise before it consciously registered with Zeb. Every few seconds, a deep, humming thrum passed through his body. He felt it more than heard it. It was the sonar device on the *Clicker*, it had to be. Except, he had turned it off after he and Corrie had come aboard from seeing the kroll. And the noise came too frequently from this source. And it was in the opposite direction from the *Clicker*. Zeb was never wrong about direction.

He had to know what was making the sound. His heart beat faster as he kicked swiftly forward. The noise got louder, and Zeb opened his eyes in a vain attempt to see in the blackness of the water. Higher and higher he rose, until his other senses picked up a disturbance in the water. It might have been a net, or a cage of wire. Something thrashed desperately inside, and Zeb sped up.

When he was close, Zeb stopped, wary. Nothing was nearby, only the cage with the thrashing thing and the sound, distressingly loud. It thrummed through Zeb's body, an undeniable call forward. Zeb resisted.

He held onto the bars of the cage and cautiously pressed his body against the wire. The thing inside moved too quickly to understand its shape. Zeb hummed and clicked in a soothing melody. The currents that buffeted Zeb's body subsided. Slowly, an image appeared in Zeb's mind, of an arm's length fish with a horn on its head.

Zeb jerked back in surprise. The cage had captured a strolia. Indignation swelled in his chest, and he felt around the cage for a release.

The strolia thrashed again when he stopped making his calming sound. Zeb could hardly hear himself over the incessant thrum of the sonar device, but he hummed and clicked again to soothe the strolia. Finally, his fingers stumbled on a clasp. With relief, Zeb flicked the door open and growled low in his throat with a noise that meant "this way."

The strolia didn't hesitate. It whooshed past Zeb, leaving currents in its wake that tousled Zeb's short hair.

Zeb didn't stop running his fingers over the cage until he found a smooth container where the sound was loudest. He tried to pry it open with his fingers, but it was immovable. He had to stop it, but how?

Inspiration struck, and he dived straight down. There were plenty of loose rocks on the seafloor, and he picked one that was large and without too many anemones encrusted on it. He shot up to the cage. When his fingers found the device once more, he raised his arm and brought the rock smashing down onto the plastic.

It took three hits, but finally, blissfully, the noise stopped. Zeb's lungs burned, and he remembered that it had been a long time since his last breath. He followed a rope that suspended the cage to a buoy on the surface and took a huge, gulping gasp when moonlit air hit his face. His breath came in pants, not from lack of air, but from rage. How could someone else be hunting strolias? Hadn't Zeb stopped enough people? Why did everyone seem to know more than he did about his mother's world?

CORRIE

Corrie finally finished filling her tubes and was ready for bed. She could have started earlier, but they were having such a nice dinner and conversation that she hadn't wanted to cut it short too soon. Trip had gone to bed a half-hour ago, and Jules had disappeared into his and Zeb's shared cabin shortly after. Zeb was floating around—he kept popping his head into the lab to see how she was doing—but she couldn't see him now.

She turned off the light in the lab with a sigh of relief. Day one of her second cruise was done. She was excited to get into it properly tomorrow. They had to pick up Krista first thing, but after that, it was on. Tanks were filled and ready in the hold for scuba diving to find anemones. It would be fun to collect them by free diving, but finding them would take way too long, and they were quite deep. She wondered how deep Zeb could go.

Corrie opened the door to her cabin carefully, but Trip was still awake, reading a book in her bunk. When Corrie closed the door behind her, Trip snapped her book closed and looked at Corrie with a serious expression.

"We need to talk," she said. Corrie's stomach gave a jolt. Those were never good words to hear. Although, coming from Trip, she couldn't think of anything serious that would warrant those words. She perched on the end of Trip's bunk and Trip scooted her feet to the side to make room.

"What's up?"

"It's Zeb." Trip gazed at her steadily. Corrie frowned.

"What about him?"

"What do you really know about him?"

Corrie narrowed her eyes, trying to figure out what Trip was getting at.

"About the same as you, I imagine. I've only known him for a few weeks. He owns a boat, got some money from his dad, likes science enough to spend it on me.”

Trip waved away her words.

“Not that stuff. I mean, have you noticed anything strange about him?”

Corrie stilled. Yes, she had. She was surprised that Trip had picked up on it, but her friend was very observant. She liked to figure out mysteries and find connections between things.

“What have you noticed?” Corrie said carefully. She wanted to hear her own ideas separately confirmed.

“He’s far too comfortable in freezing water for someone with hardly any body fat,” Trip said. “He can hold his breath for a very long time, although you can train for that, to a certain extent. And that noise he made, the hum that only he can hear? That shouldn’t be possible.”

Corrie nodded slowly.

“Yeah, I’ve noticed the same things. He kept sneaking off somewhere, last time on the boat. I don’t know where he went, but sometimes his hair was wet. And he fended off a bunch of sharks in Miles Callahan’s aquarium, I don’t know how. He was even bleeding, and they didn’t bother him.”

They were silent for a moment. Corrie’s mind was whirling. It all added up, but to what?

“But what does it mean?” she burst out. “I don’t get it. Do you think he’s using the enhancer from the unicorn fish slime? Or something else?”

Trip let out her breath in a long, reflective sigh.

“I don’t know. I just think there’s something he’s not telling you. Be careful, okay?” A smile crossed her lips. “Especially since he’s got eyes for you.”

“Not you, too,” Corrie said in exasperation. “Adrianna was trying to set me up with him. I’m dating David, remember?”

“And how’s that going?” Trip raised an expressive eyebrow. Corrie pursed her lips.

“There are bumps in every road.”

“Mm-hmm.”

"Besides, you just finished telling to be careful with Zeb and his secrets, and now you want me to date him?"

"I didn't say anything," said Trip. "Keep your eyes open, that's all. Do whatever you want to do but do it knowingly." She slid into her covers and nudged Corrie off the bed with her blanketed foot. "Go to sleep."

"Not likely, now." Corrie stood, indecision pulling her both to her bunk and away from it. The door won. "I'm going to make some tea. Good night."

The ship was quiet. Corrie didn't know where Zeb was. Maybe he'd gone to bed. She boiled water and made her tea. The warm mug felt good under her fingers, and she walked out to the deck and sat against the wall on the bow. Stars twinkled overhead but didn't provide any answers.

She sipped her tea and remembered Zeb in the water today, when they were swimming back from sampling the strange shark. Zeb had slid through the water as sleek and graceful as a seal. The beauty of his movements thrilled her even now, in remembrance. He had no sudden motions underwater. Every move was smooth and fluid.

And he was light-hearted, she realized with a start. On the boat, he was quiet, taciturn even, with only hints of amusement that she occasionally surprised out of him. There was a weight on his shoulders that stopped him from fully engaging.

But, underwater, she had glimpsed a different side of Zeb. His face was expressive and joyful. He was downright playful when they ascended after the shark sampling. He'd even done a somersault. Corrie wouldn't have believed it if she hadn't seen it with her own eyes.

Corrie wished she could see that side of him more. It was like she only knew half of him. She wanted to know both parts of Zeb, to discover what he was like whole.

ZEBALLOS

Zeb swam back with swift undulations of his legs and torso. He burned with fierce indignation. To think that someone was trying to catch the creatures of his mother's stories, again. They'd only just stopped Matt Nielsen and Miles Callahan. How could someone else know? He had to do something. This was getting out of hand. His affinity with these creatures ran deep. He needed to know what they were, and his true connection to them. If even half of his mother's stories were true…

He sensed the *Clicker* in the dark and directed his body straight to its metal hull. The ladder was out, as he'd left it, and he climbed aboard, still seething with fury.

"Zeb?"

Corrie's incredulous voice dampened his fire with a cold wave of fear. What was she doing up? She had gone to bed a half-hour ago. He had watched her door close.

He turned slowly to face her. She had an empty mug at her side and a bewildered expression on her face.

"Were you swimming? It's so late. And dark." Her eyes raked his body and he felt self-conscious. "And you're only wearing your swimsuit, again. And no mask. What the hell were you doing?"

Zeb's news about the cage dried up in the face of her confused accusations. How had he planned to tell the others about the cage, anyway? He hadn't thought that far ahead.

"You know I free dive," he began with no idea how to end. Corrie didn't let him finish.

"That won't fly this time." Corrie crossed her arms. "It's dark. There's nothing to see. You can't even tell which way is up or down without light, not if you're far enough under. It's too dangerous."

Zeb wondered how she knew that. It was true—at a certain

depth, human bodies no longer naturally floated to the surface—but it wasn't common knowledge. Had she been reading up on free diving?

"And no mask?" Corrie continued. "I guess if it's dark, you don't need to see, but seriously. And you're not even shivering. When are you going to tell me the truth?" Her face was set in determination. "I get it, we hardly know each other, not really. But whatever is going on with you is obviously tied up with the creatures. If you want me to help properly, I need the whole story."

Zeb gaped at her. How had it come to this? He thought he'd been careful. Corrie was too smart for him. She saw everything.

"I don't know what you mean," he said feebly. Corrie shook her head.

"Don't start." She held up one hand. With the other, still holding the mug, she checked off fingers. "One, you never get cold. Two, you swim without a mask. Who does that? Three, you can hold your breath forever. Four, that weird noise you made to attract the shark. Five, you're ridiculously graceful underwater."

Zeb took a moment to appreciate the compliment. Then his ire rose. It wasn't directed at Corrie, but at the fears and uncertainties that had plagued him for years. How was he supposed to explain something when he knew so little himself?

"What do you want me to say?" His voice came out louder than he'd meant, but he couldn't modulate it. "There's nothing. I don't have anything I can say." Zeb turned away, breathing heavily. He was already ashamed of his outburst, and knew it hadn't helped his standing with Corrie, only hurt it.

"The only explanation I can come up with is that you're secretly taking the unicorn fish enhancer," Corrie said coolly. "So, until you tell me otherwise, that's the assumption I'm running with. If whatever you're doing has something to do with the mystery creatures, I'd appreciate you telling me. I can't solve problems until I have all the information." She exhaled sharply. "I don't do well with secrets and lies. If you won't tell me what's going on—I'll finish this week, because you were kind enough to offer more scientific cruising, but when that's done, we're through. Understand?"

She turned to go.

"Wait," Zeb said hoarsely. He'd almost forgotten the cage. No matter what Corrie thought of him, she needed to know that. "I found a trap in the water. Tonight. There was a strolia in it, and a different sonar device. Someone replicated it and is trying to capture creatures."

Corrie turned back. Her eyes were wide.

"Not again," she whispered. "Who is it this time?"

"I don't know." He shook his head. "I released the strolia and bashed up the sonar device, but I don't know if that will stop whoever it is."

Corrie drummed her fingers on her crossed arms.

"I don't know what's going on," she said at last. "Let's talk about it in the morning. You should get dry, so you don't get cold." She looked pointedly at his wet chest then walked inside.

Zeb stood still for a minute. His stomach churned. What had he done? What could he have done differently? He wanted to run after her, explain everything—everything he knew, which wasn't a lot—but Krista's admonishing face floated in his mind's eye. He really didn't know Corrie well at all. Only last week, he was concerned that she would expose the world of the creatures to her university, and now he wanted to tell her his darkest secrets? It was a foolish notion, and he suspected that his growing attraction to Corrie was biasing him in her favor. That she thought ill of him rankled, and that she thought he was taking the enhancer on the sly rubbed at his ego the wrong way. If she knew that his abilities were all him, would she be impressed or frightened? He didn't know.

CORRIE

Corrie slept badly. It took forever to get to sleep—her anger at Zeb's secrets kept her tossing and turning for ages—and her eventual dreams featured friends and relations with their backs turned to her, murmuring unintelligible whispers.

A closing drawer alerted her to Trip's motions in the morning, but she resolutely kept her eyes closed until her friend had left the cabin. She was too bleary to talk about her argument with Zeb. Hot anger roiled in her stomach again at the thought of his lies to her face. He had said he had nothing he could say. What did that mean? That she wasn't worthy of telling the truth to?

Corrie punched her pillow in frustration. She hated lies, hated them with a passion. Her ex-boyfriend Dylan had done nothing but lie to her. When she had finally extricated herself from his toxic clutch on her life, she had sworn that she wouldn't put up with lies, never again.

It was too bad this had happened so early in the cruise. It would be a long, tense week on board the *Clicker* with this between them. And she'd been so looking forward to it.

It was fine. She could be professional. She had anemone samples to collect. She would simply do her science, do it well, and leave at the end of the week with a cooler of samples to analyze.

Zeb's words last night came back to her, and she sat up with a start. What would they do about the trapped strolia? This week wouldn't be as simple as she had hoped. She swung her legs out of bed and hurried to dress. They needed to discuss the strolia. They needed a plan.

Jules was cooking breakfast when she emerged, accompanied by an attentive Trip. Despite her sour mood, Corrie could help smiling. Trip wasn't subtle with her actions or words, and Jules responded eagerly. Zeb wasn't there, which made entering the galley easier. He must be driving the boat, because islands crawled past the galley window and the floor rocked gently.

"Good morning," Corrie said. She grabbed a prepared plate of pancakes and drizzled syrup over them. "Yum. Has either of you talked to Zeb this morning?"

Jules gave her a sharp glance. Trip didn't notice.

"Sorry, not yet," she said. "I need to grab a sweater. Brr, it's cold this morning." She disappeared into the hall. Jules waited until Trip had left before answering.

"Yeah, he had breakfast before we pulled anchor. He said—" Jules visibly searched for words. "He said he told you about the cage."

Corrie wondered what Zeb had told Jules. Everything, presumably. They were good friends, after all. She kept her face impassive, even as she wondered how much Jules knew about Zeb.

"Yeah, okay," she said. "I guess we need to figure out what to do about it."

"He wanted to wait until Krista was on board." Jules made a face and Corrie giggled despite herself.

"No love lost between you, is there?"

"Oh, she's fine," said Jules as he flipped pancakes in the frying pan. "If you like scorpions."

JULES

Too soon, they were motoring toward Vancouver and approaching the marina where Zeb had arranged to meet Krista. Jules found himself dreading it. Not only would they pick up Zeb's half-sister, who never had a kind word to say to him, but Trip would be leaving. Less than twenty-four hours, and Jules was smitten. He'd fallen hard and fast for this smart, beautiful, funny woman. She seemed to enjoy his company, but he didn't know if she felt even a quarter of what he did.

Where could it go? He didn't know. They didn't even live in the same town, so the slow unfolding of getting to know each other would be restricted to random visits. All he knew was that he was forced to stay on this boat, away from Trip, for a whole week. He would do it, for Zeb, but it wouldn't be easy.

Jules gazed at the marina with a frown from the aft deck. The subject of his musing materialized beside him.

"Where's your phone?" Trip asked. Her shoulder brushed his, and Jules shivered. He pulled his phone out of a back pocket and handed it to her. She hummed tunelessly while she typed in her contact information.

"There," she said. "Now it won't be an unknown caller sending you naughty texts."

"But those are the best kind," Jules said. His face warmed under his grin. Trip nudged his side.

"Thanks for saving my bacon with your special tea," she said. "This cruise would have been awful without it."

"Vomit is never attractive," said Jules. "I was saving everyone."

Trip laughed, and her full-throated chuckle tingled Jules' spine. She ran a hand down his arm, then reached up and turned his face toward hers with a hand on his jaw. They were so close that Jules could smell minty gum in Trip's mouth. She looked into his eyes.

"I think this is a first," she said.

"A first for what?" Jules breathed. He was proud of himself for emitting a coherent sentence. Her closeness was stopping all brain activity.

"Talking about vomit before a kiss." Trip smiled then leaned forward. Jules met her with ready lips of his own.

Her lips were so soft, yet so firm. Jules pressed harder, wanting to taste her, wanting more…

"Jules!" Zeb's voice yelled from the wheelhouse. "Get the fenders ready."

Trip pulled away. Jules' face squeezed in a grimace of frustration. He couldn't have had one uninterrupted minute?

"Jules?"

"I'm coming!" Jules shouted back, his voice louder and harsher than usual. He rubbed his face then looked at Trip. "Sorry."

She reached up and tweaked his nose with laughing eyes.

"Duty calls," she said with a smile in her low voice. When Jules turned to find the fenders, Trip gave him a smack on the bottom. Jules looked back at her. She winked. "To be continued."

The boat slid smoothly into dock. Krista was waiting for them with a small backpack. Jules leaped overboard to tie the stern line to a cleat and she grabbed the tossed headline for the bow.

"Hey, doofus," she said to Jules. "Another cruise, hey?"

After a night aboard with Trip, and her parting kiss that was so rudely cut short, Jules had no patience for Krista.

"Yep," he said without elaboration, and climbed on board again. This would be a long week, he could already feel it.

CORRIE

Corrie hugged Trip goodbye on the dock.

"Call me if you need to talk," Trip said with a glance at Zeb, who spoke to Krista near the bow. Corrie nodded.

"Thanks. I might."

She hadn't yet had a chance to tell Trip about her ultimatum with Zeb last night. The memory roiled unpleasantly in her stomach. She hitched on a parting smile and waved Trip off.

"Untie the stern line, will you?" Jules called to her. "We're leaving right away."

Corrie untwisted the heavy rope from the cleat and climbed aboard. Krista followed her after unhitching the bowline.

"Hi Corrie," she said. "Got your tubing all color-coded?"

"Of course," Corrie said with a smile, remembering Krista's previous reaction to her carefully organized lab space. "Doesn't everyone?"

The boat pulled away from the dock. Jules ambled over, his hands in his pockets and an uncharacteristic glum look on his face.

"What happened to you, sad sack?" Krista asked him. "I've never seen such a gloomy face on you."

Jules' face twitched, but he otherwise ignored Krista's comment.

"Zeb wants to talk about the cage." He nodded toward the wheelhouse. "Come on."

Krista raised her eyebrow at Corrie, who only shrugged. She didn't know why Jules was unhappy, although she had a shrewd guess it had something to do with Trip's absence. Krista kept her eyes on Corrie.

"You've hardly said five words. Normally, no one can get you to stop talking. What happened on this boat? And what is the cage?"

"Zeb will tell you about the cage," Corrie said. She didn't

answer Krista's other question. She didn't know what Krista knew about Zeb—presumably everything, but who knew—and Krista didn't inspire confidences. Zeb would likely fill her in. Until then, Corrie didn't feel the need to gab to Krista.

Jules was already in the wheelhouse and propped against the doorframe to the interior cabins when Corrie entered through the outside door. Zeb sat in the chair with one hand on the wheel. He glanced at Corrie when she stepped over the threshold, and his face tightened with emotion before he looked forward again. Corrie squeezed in beside Jules and Krista perched on the fold-out chair. She looked at the other three.

"Okay, we're all here," she said. "What's going on? You can't manage one night without supervision?"

"I found a cage with a new sonar device at Spirit Island," Zeb said without preamble. "Inside was a strolia. I released it and bashed up the device so it wouldn't attract any more creatures, but this means that someone is after them. Again."

Krista stared at Zeb, who kept his eyes on the sea ahead.

"And how did you find this cage?" she said quietly.

Zeb's eyes flicked toward Corrie with an involuntary motion. Corrie crossed her arms and looked away. Krista glanced between her and Zeb, and her eyes widened.

"Okay, whatever," she said in a new tone. "It doesn't matter. The point is, someone is messing with these weird animals again. Are we going to do something about it, and if so, what?"

"I want to know how they found out," Zeb said, his even tone not entirely hiding his anger. Not for the first time, Corrie pondered what these creatures meant to him. There had to be more than a few bedtime stories.

"Did Miles Callahan talk?" Corrie said aloud. Krista shook her head.

"It's possible, but I really doubt it. If those documents I have got out, he would be ruined. It would be a huge risk, and for what? A possible chance at a new drug that may or may not be effective?" Krista looked at Jules. "You didn't get loose-lipped at the bar, did you?"

Jules' face darkened with anger.

"No," he said shortly. "I didn't."

"Maybe it was Matt Nielsen," Corrie said. "Although I don't know why."

"I agree, Matt wouldn't make much sense," said Zeb. Corrie had the feeling he was trying to be agreeable to her. She scowled and held her arms more tightly across her chest.

"There isn't a lot we can do without knowing who's behind it," said Krista.

"I'd like to check the cage again, see if it's been fixed," said Zeb. He glanced at Corrie. "If that works for your sampling, of course."

'I can make it work," said Corrie. The northern inlets called to her, but she didn't want to see creatures being caught by unknown entities, for unknown, likely nefarious, purposes. "Let's sample around here today, then head north tomorrow." She pulled a chart toward her and checked it over. "I wanted to sample Horseshoe Bay on the way home. Spirit Island is right there, so we can head there today instead and be near the cage."

Zeb nodded, and Corrie turned to go. Krista gave her a look of surprise at her abrupt departure.

"I need to set up my equipment," Corrie said. "I'll be in the lab if anyone wants me."

ZEBALLOS

Jules followed Corrie out the door, mumbling something about lunch. Krista turned to Zeb with a bewildered expression.

"What the hell was that about?" she said. "I've never seen Corrie so quiet. And how did you explain finding the cage?"

Zeb's jaw tightened. He hated explaining himself to Krista, especially when mistakes were his fault and she had warned him. It grated his pride.

"I didn't," he said shortly. "Corrie saw me come back. I thought she'd gone to bed."

"What did she see?" Krista's eyes were wide with dread. Zeb kept his own on the horizon.

"What do you think? Me in a swimsuit, wet from the water, with no mask."

Krista cursed, low and long. She dropped her chin to her chest as if in contemplation, and Zeb waited for the inevitable outburst.

Surprisingly, it didn't come.

"So, it's happened," Krista said. She stared at the side of Zeb's face, but Zeb didn't look back. "Now, what? What did you tell her, what does she think?"

"I didn't tell her anything. She thinks I'm on the strolia enhancer. I didn't confirm or deny it. I don't know, maybe I should tell her everything."

"What do you mean by everything? Your abilities? Your mother? Your minimal facts or your wild suspicions?" Krista shook her head. "Better that she thinks you're on the enhancer than the truth. No good would come of it. You hardly know her. Who's to say she wouldn't run off to the press, or her scientist friends? Then what would become of you?"

Krista pressed a fist into her stomach. Zeb looked away from his sister's unusual display of fear. Her advice was practical, but it didn't account for other factors.

Zeb wanted to tell Corrie. He hated—loathed—the way she looked at him now, like he had let her down. He missed her laugh and her constant chatter. He wanted to recapture the joy and excitement of their previous cruise, with everyone pulling together to find Matt Nielsen and the lost strolias. It had all changed, and it was because of him.

Krista was probably right. His head agreed with her—barely—even though his heart did not. He wanted to trust Corrie and felt he could. But Krista's fears had proven true a few weeks ago, when he'd been captured for his strangeness and knowledge of the creatures. He shouldn't dismiss her advice too readily.

"I won't say anything," he said out loud. To himself he added, *yet*.

CORRIE

Corrie slammed a drawer open and pulled out tubes then grabbed a permanent pen and flopped onto her stool to write labels. There was nothing she urgently had to do, but she didn't want to stand in the wheelhouse any longer than necessary. Zeb was full of secrets, Krista was her usual abrasive self, and even Jules was out of sorts. She was starting to regret coming back for another week aboard the *Clicker*.

She squared her shoulders. It was only a week. She could handle anything for a week. And it was for her project.

"Somebody has to think of the anemones," she muttered under her breath.

Corrie wondered who was capturing unicorn fish, but she didn't have any brainwaves. She thought longingly of the northern inlets, where anemones waited for her, but then an image of a trapped unicorn fish crossed her mind. A day of figuring out what was going on wasn't a big deal. There was plenty of time for both.

With her tubes labeled, there wasn't much else to prepare that hadn't already been done. Corrie straightened a few pieces of errant tubing, but even she couldn't find something to tidy after a minute. She sighed and turned to the door. Maybe Jules was in the galley.

ZEBALLOS

Zeb was hungry for dried jellyfish, again, so he left Krista in charge of the wheel and ambled to the galley. Jules was banging pots around, but he'd lost his frown and was humming quietly to himself. Zeb grabbed a few pieces of jellyfish out of the top cupboard—thankfully replenished by Krista—and leaned against the wall to munch them.

"I need some crab," said Jules. "For tomorrow's dinner. Grab me some the next time you're down."

Zeb nodded and continued to chew.

"I'll get them tonight."

Corrie wandered in, looking bored. She spotted Jules and opened her mouth then snapped it shut again when she saw Zeb. Zeb straightened and swallowed hastily.

"Corrie, I've been meaning to ask." He tried to speak quickly so that she wouldn't leave right away. Her body was half-turned to the exit, but she stayed with a polite expression on her face. "I was hoping you could help us with the logbook while we're driving to the next station. Jules drew the creatures, and I put in a few notes from what I've seen, but we could use your input." She was silent, so Zeb cast about for more things to say. "Maybe you have some data to add?"

Corrie's eyes brightened at his suggestion, and he drew a relieved breath. Her shoulders turned to face the galley.

"Sure, I could have a look." Her voice was guarded, but her eyes followed Zeb's hands as he fished the logbook out of a pouch on the wall. They sat across from each other at the table, and Corrie leafed through the book. Jules came out of the galley and leaned against the wall, wiping his hands on a tea towel.

"We're getting quite the collection, aren't we?" Corrie said as she flipped a page. "Ugh, there's Sucker. You call it a brigar?" Corrie didn't look at Zeb, but the question was directed at him.

"My mother did," he said quickly. "Look, I tried to remember what she'd said about it. There's a story about it chasing some people, but I couldn't remember the details. It was a long time ago that she told me."

Corrie shot him a sympathetic look at the reminder of his early loss. Zeb was heartened by this. Maybe Corrie could still be reached. Deep down, he knew exactly what to do to get her to open up again—tell her what he knew—but he pushed that thought down. It was too soon.

"If we see that thing again, I'm moving to Alberta," Jules said with an exaggerated shudder.

"Unfortunately, I don't have any data on Sucker, beyond descriptive qualities," said Corrie. She turned the page. "For the unicorn fish—strolia—though, I have some. The specimen we captured, Spiky, was forty-eight centimeters long, and appeared pretty typical in size." She looked to Zeb for confirmation, and he nodded.

"They're all about that long."

"I have behavioral observations, and I can print off protein analysis readouts for the slime, if you like, but they won't mean much. Better to wait until I come up with something conclusive." She read the rest of Zeb's entry and frowned. "The horn is poisonous at the tip?"

"So my mother said."

Corrie looked at him with accusation.

"That would have been nice to know before I started doing my tests on it. Do you know an antidote to this poison?"

Zeb's shoulders sank, but he tried to rally.

"I was watching carefully."

"Except when you weren't." Corrie shook her head and turned the page. She jabbed her finger at the next image. "This is the shark in Miles' aquarium, the same one that I got a sample from yesterday. Nice drawing, Jules."

"I aim to please," Jules said.

"I will have data from this one, I hope. When I get back to the lab."

The next page showed an otter-like creature that Zeb had seen a few days ago. Corrie stared at the drawing.

"What is this?"

"It's a *dobar*," Zeb said. "It's like a river otter, but heavier and with a larger face and nose. I saw it near Nanaimo, under the boat. It tried to nibble my hair, thought it was seaweed."

"Did it rip off your mask?" Corrie said innocently.

"No, I wasn't wearing one." As soon as the words were out of his mouth, Zeb winced. Corrie's face had a resigned, disappointed expression which ate at Zeb.

"Figured," she said without further comment.

"Do you have any stories about that one?" Jules jumped in. Zeb was grateful to his friend for trying to diffuse the situation. Jules was good for that.

"Unfortunately, no. Only a mention in passing. I vaguely remember more, but so much is gone." Zeb felt a wave of regret and sadness wash over him, so familiar from the early years after his mother had died, but rarer now.

Corrie snapped the logbook shut.

"Let me get together my notes, then I'll write down my observations. And, Zeb." She looked him in the eyes. "Don't forget about your father's notebook. Krista's on board now. We can find out more about the stuff from the storage locker."

A spark of interest ignited in Zeb. Part of him didn't care what his father had written down in his cryptic notebook and didn't want anything to do with him. A larger part salivated at the thought of finally getting answers.

"Should we do it right now?" he asked. At Corrie's fervent nod, he turned to Jules. "Jules, could you—"

Jules waved him off.

"I'll go drive, since I don't read Greek. Honestly, the qualifications for deckhand on this vessel are too intense."

Corrie giggled, and Zeb relaxed into the sound. She said no

more after Jules left but opened the book again and perused the entries. Zeb let her be. He didn't want to force his company on her, since he didn't want to ruin whatever tiny bit of goodwill he might have won during their previous exchange.

Sitting in the quiet with Corrie was peaceful, broken too soon by his sister breezing in and swatting him around the bench so she could sit. Zeb scooted closer to Corrie, but not too close. She felt skittish, and he didn't want to scare her off.

"You think I remember any Greek?" Krista said. "It's been ages, and I wasn't any good at it then. You and Yaya chatted away like natives, and I could hardly say a word."

"But you learned how to write to Yaya, didn't you?"

"Pitiful three-sentence letters, yes."

"I only need you to read." Zeb opened the notebook, stashed in one of the many useful pouches by the table, and spread it in front of Krista. "You read the words aloud, I'll translate."

"I can write down what you say," Corrie offered. Zeb nodded gratefully and opened the logbook to a fresh page.

"Use this, there's lots of space."

Corrie looked uncertain about writing in their logbook, but Zeb didn't have anything better. Krista scanned the page.

"Oh, man, this takes me back." She began to stumble Greek words out, stopping at the end of every sentence for Zeb to translate. Her words were slow and halting at first, but gradually picked up speed. Zeb closed his eyes to concentrate. Corrie's pen scratched under the sound of his voice.

It has begun. She didn't think it ever would, that he was safe. I hoped but didn't believe. And I was right. Now she's gone, and he isn't safe. I must start from the beginning. All I have are stories. I'll start at the beginning, with the creation story of her people.

Ramu looked up at the dry and dusty people on the shores of her ocean, and she grieved that they would never know the wonder of her watery realm. They would gasp and choke on her smooth water, freeze in her cool waves, and flounder blindly in her green dimness.

Then Barlo, of the wind that whips the sea into a foamy froth when a storm approaches, saw Ramu's distress.

"You have the means to make any creature what you will, do you not?"

Then Ramu recalled the leftover grace entrusted to her from the making of the world, when she and the other goddesses had pooled their powers to create the creatures of the earth and ocean. Even now, she remembered that Gula, she of the rock and dirt, had contributed more to the dry folk than the others. Ramu, busy with her ocean-dwelling creatures, hadn't noticed until the dry folk had been fully formed.

"I do," she replied to Barlo. "Gula took the dry folk for her own, which grieves me. What joys they are missing, away from the waves! But I was entrusted with the leftover grace, to keep it safe and unused."

"I will distract her," said Barlo, and he flew to Gula's favored rocky cliff. A whirlwind blew dust in the air for three days and three nights, and Gula hid her face until the storm was over.

Meanwhile, Barlo flew to the ocean where Ramu waited, and blew her up into the sky. She held the urn full of grace, and as she rose high into the heavens she waited for the right moment. When the darkness of the night was overwhelming in its obscurity, she dropped the urn.

The first time the urn shattered, it broke into three pieces. Two of the glowing shards flew over the horizon and out of sight. The final piece hit the blackness again and shattered into a thousand glowing fragments. They fell into the shoreline glowing with the grace of a dozen goddesses.

Ramu smiled.

"The people on these shores will be blessed with further grace, the grace of the ocean waves that they were earlier denied. They will be the people of my heart, the wild children

of the currents."

Zeb's heart squeezed so tightly that he could barely force the final words of the story out. It was as if his mother were telling the story, with crisp detail that he had no chance of pulling from his memory. When Krista stopped reading, the three sat silent. Zeb turned his face to the ceiling to hide the tears threatening to fall.

"I remember that one," Krista said quietly. "It's been a while." She rested a hand on his forearm and squeezed. Zeb blinked furiously until it was safe to bring his face down without danger of tear tracks.

"That was one of your mother's stories?" Corrie said softly. At Zeb's nod, she frowned. "I don't understand. Where was she from? Her heritage?"

Zeb shrugged without looking at Corrie.

"I don't know. She never said."

"I've never heard a story like that before." Corrie traced the edge of the logbook with an absentminded finger, and Zeb's eyes followed the motion. "It sounds almost Polynesian, you know, an island people with the ocean theme." Her eyes raked Zeb's features, but he didn't look up. "Do you take after her much?"

"He looks a lot like Dad," Krista said. "Just the hair and eyes are different."

"And what was that beginning part, about somebody not being safe?" Corrie said.

Zeb finally looked at Corrie with a frown. He'd been so immersed in his memories, that he'd forgotten about the cryptic message from his father. When he looked at Krista, she refused to meet his gaze, instead fidgeting with her fingers and looking pensive.

"I don't know," said Zeb slowly. "I assume 'she' is my mother."

"Are you the 'he?'" Corrie said. "Now, who's after you? I swear, I led a quiet life before I met you."

An escaped breath of laughter forced itself out of Zeb's mouth and surprised him.

"I don't think your life was ever quiet." He chanced a look at Corrie and was gratified to see amusement cross her features.

"Yeah, I know I talk a lot. Somebody has to."

"I think I've done enough for today," Krista said abruptly. She pushed the notebook toward Zeb and stood. "I'll take over from Jules on the wheel."

Zeb frowned after his sister until she left the room.

"She knows something she's not telling us," he said slowly.

"That's strange," said Corrie. "I wonder what that's like."

Zeb grimaced. Despite a few moments of decent conversation, his secrets hung over him and Corrie like a dark cloud. He didn't know the best way to blow them away.

"I'll be in lab," Corrie said, standing. "Let me know when we're on station."

Zeb whiled away the next half-hour with his Greek dictionary and a pencil, trying to decipher the foreign alphabet of the notebook. It was slow going, but he persisted, partly because he wasn't welcome in the lab or in the wheelhouse, but mostly because he wanted—needed—to know what it said. It was his mother's words in his father's voice, speaking to him from beyond the grave. He supposed his father would talk about the devices at some point, but Zeb hardly cared. His mother's stories were a piece of his history, and he needed them fresh and real, especially given the creatures that flocked to the *Clicker*.

When the boat slowed near the east side of Spirit Island, Zeb tucked the books in a nearby pouch and rolled his neck with a relieved sigh. He rubbed his arm. Scuba diving with

Corrie was next, and he feared what would happen in the water. Would he manage to resist the siren call of cool water? Would he be able to stay cooped up in claustrophobic neoprene for a full half-hour while Corrie collected anemones? He didn't know, and his jaw tightened at the unpleasant prospect.

Corrie was on the aft deck when Zeb emerged from the cabin, blinking in the bright summer sun. She didn't acknowledge him and continued to check her sampling equipment. Zeb jumped into the hold and silently passed up two air tanks and their equipment. Corrie nodded to him and set up her gear.

Zeb sometimes grew overwhelmed by Corrie's chatter, but he hadn't realized how much he had enjoyed it until it was gone. This quiet, solemn Corrie was not an improvement. He wracked his brains to think of topics to break the silence, but the more he thought, the more his mind froze.

Corrie finally spoke. Her voice startled Zeb.

"Zip me up, please."

She turned around in her dry suit to expose the long zipper that ran from shoulder to shoulder across the back. Zeb stepped up and gripped the heavy zipper pull. A faint scent of something floral wafted past his nose. Was it her shampoo? He shook his head to clear it and tugged the zipper closed.

He reached down to pull his wetsuit from a pile of gear.

"Why are you bothering?" Corrie's voice held a hint of exasperation. "We both know you don't need it. Unless you have a time limit on feeling the cold." She raised an eyebrow in question.

Zeb shook his head mutely. He looked at the wetsuit in his hands then at the ocean. He tried to hide the naked longing he felt at the thought of swimming without the hated neoprene, but he knew he wasn't succeeding. He glanced at Corrie in appeal.

"I—I don't…"

Corrie held up a hand to stop him.

"Do whatever you want," she said. "I don't care. Let's collect my samples."

Zeb drew a deep breath. If he did this, dived without a wetsuit, he was confirming everything Corrie suspected but had no proof of. There was no going back after this.

A slosh of water against the hull of the *Clicker* decided him. He couldn't refuse the call of the sea.

Corrie bent down and wriggled into her diving vest. Zeb slipped on his own vest and followed her march to the ladder. Her hair was in a ponytail, and a few strands had caught in the seal around her neck. The breach would cause a slow, uncomfortable leak underwater.

"Wait," he said. When she turned, he stepped forward and reached to her throat. He slipped his fingers under the lock of hair and tugged it gently free.

Corrie shivered with such a small motion that he wouldn't have noticed if he hadn't been touching her slender neck. His breath hitched, and their gaze met. There was such confusion in her eyes, confusion and anger, mixed with something else that had caused her to shiver. He drew his fingers back along her neck as he brought his arm down, and her eyes fluttered involuntarily. Then, they snapped open with embarrassment.

"Come on," she said abruptly. "Let's go."

"Zeb?" Krista's voice shot out from behind them.

Zeb's jaw tightened. He knew what she was about to say. He turned and watched her stride down the side of the boat.

"What the hell are you doing?" she said sharply. "Where's your wetsuit?" Her eyes flicked to Corrie, who crossed her arms with a defiant tilt to her head.

"Are you playing the game, too?" Corrie said. "Go on, tell him he'll get cold without it. Spin a few more lies."

Krista's eyes widened. She looked to Zeb, speechless for once.

"Leave it, Krista," Zeb said. Everything was such a mess. He couldn't see how his sister's involvement would improve matters. The sea called to him, beckoning him with gentle waves. He stepped toward the ladder with resolution.

Krista shook her head in disbelief.

"I try, I really do," she said. "But I can't help someone who won't help himself."

She turned on her heel and marched back to the wheelhouse. Zeb threw the weighted dive flag overboard then glanced at Corrie, his face set. She looked at him appraisingly.

"Ready to sample?" he said. He needed to distract her, to remind her of their task. Corrie nodded and followed him down the ladder.

Although the mask was irritating, the flippers too large, and the vest awkward, scuba diving was a thousand times better without a wetsuit. Zeb descended the dive flag line with a smile on his face that wouldn't be suppressed. Corrie's eyes were questioning when she noticed, but he pointed in the direction of the shelf to divert her.

Corrie found a cluster of anemones right away. She snipped fronds from a few of them then continued along the edge of the shelf. At their depth, the visibility was much clearer than at the surface, and yet the seafloor descended to their right into the darkness of the void. Zeb longed to explore, but he dutifully followed in Corrie's wake.

Another cluster clung to the rockface, and Corrie stopped to collect samples. Zeb hovered nearby with his eyes closed to sense the surrounding currents more easily. A school of perch flitted above them, and a dogfish glided into the depths. The breathing apparatus made it almost impossible to listen to the sounds of the sea, but Zeb strained to hear familiar noises.

A faint groan made him frown. It was repeated, along with the clicks and squeaks of a distressed animal. Zeb slowed his breathing and focused his senses. It was far away, but gentle currents against his legs spoke of a tremendous thrashing.

Zeb's eyes flew open. The commotion was coming from the direction of the cage.

Corrie tucked her completed samples into a collection bag at her side but looked around when Zeb grabbed her arm roughly. He pointed back in the direction of the *Clicker*, then signed "follow me" and "up." She looked confused and held up three fingers next to her sample bag. She always took clippings from three clusters of anemones.

Zeb shook his head violently and pointed back. With a confused look, Corrie nodded and followed him.

At the surface, Corrie pulled her regulator out of her mouth.

"What the hell, Zeb? Why couldn't I get my samples?"

"The cage," he said. "Something's happening there, something's in trouble. I need to go look. Please, I'll help you get more samples after."

Enough of his worry must have got through to Corrie, for she didn't object further.

"Okay, we'll do it later. How do you want to check it out? Should we get the dinghy?"

"No time." Zeb kicked toward the ladder with the dive flag in tow. He held onto the side while Corrie climbed up. "I'll check it out in the water quickly. Let Krista know, okay?"

"What, you're going to dive there?" Corrie hung over the side to stare incredulously at him. "It's not safe to go again so soon after our first dive. And you don't have enough air. And you should always scuba dive with a buddy."

In reply, Zeb wriggled out of his vest and strapped it to the ladder. He ripped off his mask and threw it over Corrie's head, where it landed on the deck with a clatter.

"I'll be back as soon as I can."

Without waiting for an answer from a speechless Corrie, Zeb flipped backward off the ladder and dived under the surface.

The long diving flippers, while bulkier than he preferred, gave him an added boost of speed. He flew toward the cage. The thrashing was fainter now, although clearer in his ears without the bubbles of the scuba tank to distract him. The roar of a motorboat taking off thundered through the water. Was it related to the cage? It had to be. Zeb willed his body to swim faster.

The signature of the cage flowed past his body as a distinctive disturbance in the currents. It was empty, but below it, something wiggled feebly. Zeb focused his eyes. A dark form flopped in the dim green light.

Zeb slowed. He didn't want to scare the creature, whatever it was. It was clearly hurt, and likely frightened. If he startled it, it might dash away and cause greater injury to itself.

Zeb hummed quietly, deep in his chest, with a soothing rhythm. He paddled with unhurried kicks toward the creature. The flopping slowed as the creature heard his hum. Zeb hummed louder and poured every bit of reassurance he could into the sound. The creature stopped its movements and turned its head in his direction.

Zeb's hum caught for a moment before he hastily resumed. The creature was a *troba*, a gentle animal that appeared as a hairless horse at its front end, with streamlined hindquarters in which the legs were connected. The hooves on both foreleg and hindleg were elongated into hard paddles. The skin on its top half was a dark brown which faded into white on the underside. It was much smaller than a land horse, and the whole body was no longer than the length of Zeb's legs. Large, liquid eyes gazed at Zeb with fear and hope.

It was only after the initial shock of discovery had passed that Zeb noticed a deep gash on the troba's flank. Dark blood seeped out of the wound.

Zeb had to help, but how? He couldn't do anything here, that was certain. He continued to hum while he approached the troba. Its flank shivered, but it allowed Zeb to come alongside it and wrap his arms around its middle.

Carefully, gently, Zeb kicked his legs, dragging the troba beside him. He hoped Corrie knew how to help, because he was fresh out of ideas.

CORRIE

Corrie was beyond fuming. Not only had Zeb called their dive short, leaving her a sample shy of a full set—she shuddered to think of how she would deal with the statistical analysis of the resulting data—but he had zoomed off with hardly an explanation after coming to the surface. Without any gear but his flippers, no less, and for what? Because he somehow knew that the cage was being tampered with? Was he clairvoyant, now?

Corrie ripped her vest from its tank with a savage yank at the Velcro. It was going to be a long week if Zeb was going to flaunt his abnormalities without any explanation. She could take whatever he dished out. Anything was better than this ridiculous charade that everyone knew about except her. She climbed out of her dry suit, wanting to rip it off as well, but mindful of the expensive seal around her neck. In her current mood, she wanted to throw it across the deck.

Corrie busied herself with putting away her equipment until Jules wandered outside.

"Ready to get your water sample?" He looked around. "Where's Zeb?"

"Oh, just off for a swim," Corrie said. "You know, as one does. He brought us up early—before I'd collected all my samples—said something was at the cage, and tore off." She slammed the hold shut with a satisfying clang. "His gear is strapped to the bottom of the ladder, if you care."

She stormed to the lab and shoved her samples in her little fridge. Now, what? Was she supposed to wait until Zeb was back before she and Jules sent down the sample bottle to collect water? The thought of waiting for Zeb grated at her, especially since he had given her no explanation. Did he think her science was not worthy?

She squared her shoulders. Forget Zeb. Her project was

important, and she was going to sample right now. He could just swim around the line if it bothered him.

She marched out the door and opened her mouth to call for Jules. He was still on the aft deck, dismantling Zeb's gear that he must have fetched from the ladder.

"Let's sample," she said. Jules looked up.

"Shouldn't we wait for—"

"Let's sample now," she said firmly.

Jules hesitated then nodded at the sight of her determined face.

"Yeah, okay. I'll start up the winch. Where's your bottle?"

Corrie bent to pick up her collection bottle from its case by her feet but looked up at the sound of a gasp. Jules ran to the side of the boat. Corrie followed despite herself and looked over the bulwark.

Zeb treaded water by the ladder. In his arms was a bizarre creature. The best Corrie could describe it was as a half-horse, half-fish, covered with hairless skin like a seal. A deep gash oozed clouds of blood into the water.

Corrie's mouth dropped. Was this what Zeb had somehow sensed in the cage? What was it?

"It's hurt," Zeb panted. "Get the tank, Jules. It's losing a lot of blood. We need to get it on board."

Jules ran to the hold with Corrie close at his heels. He threw the doors open and leaped down.

"Pass it up," Corrie said. "I'll get it filled with water."

Jules heaved the heavy glass tank to the edge with straining muscles. Corrie grabbed the edge and pulled it onto the deck then ran to the saltwater hose. She turned on the tap, threw the end in the tank, then raced for her phone.

"What are you doing?" Jules yelled as he ran to the ladder. "We need to get it up."

"I'm calling Adrianna," Corrie shouted back. "I don't know anything about medicine. How do you stick a bandage on a water animal?"

Corrie grabbed her phone from the lab and dialed Adrianna's number. Mercifully, her friend answered.

"Corrie, hi! How's life at sea?"

"Adrianna, I need your help," Corrie said. "I have a sea creature with a wound. I have no idea what kind of animal it is, and I don't know how to help it. It's not like I can stick a Band-Aid on the wet thing. It seems calm right now, but I don't know for how long. How do we help it?"

"Get me on video," Adrianna replied in a brisk, competent voice that Corrie imagined she must use at work. "I need to see it."

Zeb appeared at the ladder, his face red with effort at carrying the creature. Jules grabbed the back end and they maneuvered it into the tank. It lay limply, its flank fluttering with shallow breaths and its dark eyes following Zeb. He crouched at the side of the tank and put a hand on the creature's head.

"Wow," Adrianna's voice said from the phone. Her face took up the screen as she gazed at the creature. "Just, wow. Okay, where's the wound?"

Zeb reached in and turned the creature to the side with gentle hands. Blood seeped out of the gash.

"Get the wound out, expose it to air if the animal will let you," Adrianna instructed. "Grab your first aid kit."

Jules ran off. Zeb lifted the hind quarters over the edge of the tank until the wound was above the water. The creature twitched, but Zeb stroked its tail and it fell still. Jules returned with a red bag labeled with a white cross.

"Now what?" Corrie said, her voice high-pitched. Blood dribbled down the side of the creature. It continued to stare at Zeb with big, trusting eyes like a fawn.

"You're all doing great," Adrianna said firmly. "Get gauze out of the first aid kit, along with tape. Use half of the gauze to dry off the skin and dab around the wound, then lay fresh gauze over it and wrap the tape around as best as you can. That will do for now, until the blood clots. The wound looks superficial, so I think you can avoid stitches."

Jules took over the wound-dressing while Zeb kept the creature steady and Corrie held the phone so Adrianna could call out advice. Jules' hands were deft and sure, and he neatly taped up the creature's flank within minutes. He and Corrie sat on the deck in relief once he had finished, although Zeb continued to hold the tail and stroke it softly.

"Thanks, Adrianna," said Corrie. "That was intense. Now what?"

"Keep the tail out of the water for fifteen minutes, if it lets you. Then keep the creature in the tank so it can't move much for the next twenty-four hours. Give it something to eat and make sure the water in the tank stays fresh. Otherwise, there's not much else you can do. Keep me posted, and good luck."

Corrie said goodbye and hung up the phone. They stared at each other.

"What do we have this time?" Jules said finally.

"It's a troba," Zed said quietly. "A gentle creature. No poisons this time." He shot a guilty glance at Corrie.

"Good to know," she said. A thousand questions cluttered her mind, but she could only rake her eyes over the new creature. Jules whistled.

"Incredible. I'll get the logbook." He jumped up.

"Can you tell Krista what happened?" Zeb said without taking his eyes off the troba. Jules wrinkled his nose out of Zeb's sight. "She should know. And head to our next station, near the river."

"Yeah, sure."

He disappeared into the cabin. Corrie tore her gaze away from the troba and contemplated Zeb. He crouched over the creature with one hand supporting the connected hindlegs and the other resting on its topside. His face wore a look of concentration. Corrie's eyes wandered to the rest of him. Of course, he was wet and nearly naked, although he didn't shiver.

His muscles were taut from holding up the troba's hindquarters, and Corrie remembered his fingers tracing her neck before their dive. She pushed the thought away angrily. Her body was betraying her, not letting her be as incensed as she should be at Zeb.

"What are you doing?" she said to get her mind off Zeb's wet body.

"Trying to keep the troba calm," he said without looking at her.

Were his hands on the creature's body keeping it calm, or was there something more? Corrie shuffled over and sneaked her hand over Zeb's arm to place her palm on his chest, underneath the strange necklace with the shell pendant. It was a new addition since their last cruise, and Corrie wondered where it had come from. Before his secrets had come between them, she would have simply asked.

He stiffened and looked at her for the first time.

"What are you doing?" he said hoarsely.

"Testing a theory," she said. "Keep doing whatever you were doing."

He gave her a bewildered glance, but when the troba twitched under his hands, his face stilled into concentration again. As Corrie had predicted, his chest began to vibrate. She kept her hand there until she was sure that she wasn't imagining the vibration, but when her mind wandered to the warmth of his chest and the firmness of his pectorals, she withdrew it hastily.

"Satisfied?" Zeb said.

"Not quite the word I would use, but my theory was correct. You're humming to calm the troba, aren't you?"

Zeb didn't answer but only stared at the creature. Corrie rolled her eyes. What would it take for him to come clean?

"Whatever," she said. "I'm getting equipment from the lab. I might as well sample this creature, since we're lucky enough to have it on board."

ALISTAIR

Alistair tapped his fingers on the lab counter while he watched Britta work. With smooth, deft motions, Britta drew her scalpel through the belly of a hooked-fin shark.

"Skin without scales, impedes scalpel action," Britta said aloud for her recording device to pick up. "Two centimeters of subcutaneous fat."

"When is Terry going to finish?" Alistair burst out with an irritated glance at a nearby closed door. "He only had to hook up a few hoses, for pity's sake. Things would go so much faster without all this secrecy."

"Can you imagine the paperwork?" Britta said. She calmly peeled back the incision flaps. "And you know Terry would blab. Ventral organs intact. Removing liver next."

Britta slid a gloved hand under a thick slab of dark red organ, lifted it slightly, and sliced carefully at the membranes underneath to release it from the body cavity. Alistair peered inside, then he looked at the closed door again with a huff of disgust. He could have set the tank up faster himself, but he'd been in the middle of other preparations and had assumed delegating tasks was a good use of time. Relying on incompetent people would give him more gray hairs than he already had.

"What do you plan to do about the vandalism?" Britta asked without moving her eyes from her work. She prodded the cavity with inquisitive fingers. "Excessively large kidneys for the size of the animal. Will weigh them shortly."

"If it happens again, you mean?" Alistair drummed his fingers again in thought. If the destruction of their sonar were vandalism, it was done by a highly dedicated vandal who also owned scuba equipment and a boat. No, Alistair was sure this was a targeted attack. *Why* was a stickier question. "We have spare traps and devices, but every attack puts us back another day, and the boss was clear on the timeframe."

"He wants answers yesterday, of course." Britta smiled wryly. She dropped two glossy kidneys into a waiting container. "I wonder what Kelly will make of these. She's convinced herself we're studying porpoises."

"She's close, but she'll never guess," said Alistair. "I wouldn't have believed in these creatures without seeing them. But about the vandals, I'll have to think of something, and soon. It can't happen again."

There was a knock on the door, and Alistair leaped to answer it. Britta calmly pulled a sheet over her dissection.

"Terry," said Alistair at the sight of a short, bespectacled man in rough, grease-stained jeans. "All done?"

"Ready to go." Terry glanced at Britta and the lumpy sheet on the counter. Britta smiled blandly back at him. "I'll head back to the shop. Let me know if you need anything else."

"Will do. Thanks, Terry." Alistair steered him to the hall door with a friendly but persistent hand on his shoulder. The sooner Terry left, the sooner Alistair could get on with his work.

When the door clicked shut behind Terry, Alistair strode to a tarp-draped cube on a cart, as tall as his chest. He whipped the tarp off with a flourish.

"There you are, my pretty," he crooned to the water horse. It was a spectacularly ugly beast with a hairless, earless horse head, and awkward fused legs that ended in heavy keratinous fins. It was a face only a mother could love, but it had a sort of dignified elegance despite that. Alistair beamed at the water horse, their first after a slew of horned fish. "Time for your special tank."

"Need help getting Specimen B into the tank?" Britta asked while she carefully drew back the sheet to expose the hooked-fin shark once more. Alistair shook his head and positioned his hands to push the rolling tank.

"Thanks, but I've got this. You carry on with your

dissection, I've distracted you long enough. I'm off to run a few tests on this bad boy." He patted the tank fondly, and the creature swam to the other end of the tank with sluggish movements. "Definitely some of the sound modulation scenarios with the improved equipment to start. There are a few more invasive tests I'd like to run, as well."

"Will it survive?" Britta's voice was calm, measured, spoken while she continued her dissection. Alistair admired her professional detachment. It was one of the reasons he enjoyed working at her side.

"I'll leave the most invasive to the end," he said and wheeled the cart to the door. "If it doesn't survive, well, then your dissection skills will be needed again."

PAULA

Paula smiled blandly at no one in particular. She held a folder in the crook of one arm, her pen grasped loosely in her other hand. She shifted her feet in their skinny stilettos, and the fabric of her gown swished pleasantly against her legs.

The ostentatiously old-world room in this downtown boy's club was filled with the well-heeled and well-dressed. It was supposed to be a charity event, but most of the attendees were here to mingle with each other. It was the sort of event that Miles couldn't resist, and he'd been making the rounds since seven o'clock, despite his obvious unease earlier. Paula wondered what had disturbed him, but Miles wasn't talking, and Paula wouldn't ask. She was only here to support him and provide facts as needed. She didn't mind dressing up—especially since Miles had provided a generous stipend for buying evening wear—but after a few hours, even her ready smile was flagging.

Miles chatted to an older couple nearby. His rich laugh caused the man to smile and the woman to titter with a beringed hand on his arm. She was draped in gems and a ridiculously low-cut dress, revealing her wrinkled cleavage. Paula sniffed and promised herself she would never become so classless when she was lined and gray. Her own dress dipped low in the front, but she smiled as she glanced down. She was young enough and perky enough to support it.

"Paula," Miles said to her. "Do you have the numbers for last quarter? I want to convince Jim here that I'm not making this up."

"Of course," she said smoothly and opened the folder to read a few statistics for the couple. So, Jim and Susan Broadbeam were interested in this side venture. Paula filed that information away. She didn't know how it might be useful, but she didn't know it wouldn't be. Who knew when she might come across a tidbit that would be profitable? She'd learned from the best, after all. Miles was a master at gleaning information.

She stepped back to give Miles space to talk to the couple. Her eyes scanned the room and settled on a familiar figure. Ryan Stokes sipped a glass of red wine, but when he saw her looking, he toasted her and walked her way.

Paula glanced at Miles, but he was immersed in his conversation with his back to her. She sidled toward a tall table with a candle in a hurricane glass and tried to look at ease.

Ryan joined her a moment later but kept his attention away from her. She followed his lead and looked around the room with a disinterested glance. A thrill spiked through her stomach at this clandestine, cloak-and-dagger meeting.

"Good evening, Paula," he said quietly. "I thought you might be interested to hear that your information was good, and we've caught a number of strange creatures so far."

"Of course it was good." She smiled knowingly toward the room at large, but it was meant for him. "To think you doubted me. I wouldn't reward your generosity with bad intel."

"I'm sorry I ever let the notion cross my mind."

"What sort of creatures?" Paula asked, curious despite herself. She didn't really care what he did with the information she'd passed on, but strange animals that no one had ever seen before couldn't help but pique her interest.

"I shouldn't really say, but I wanted to thank you in person. And give you a chance to help more, since our previous business was so profitable."

Paula shifted the folder under her arm and looked at Miles. He was still engaged with the Broadbeams, clearly in the middle of an amusing anecdote. She was intrigued by the thought of another chance to earn the kind of funds that Ryan could provide. She was so close to a down payment on that condo in Yaletown she'd been eyeing. It was out of her price range on her salary, but she lusted after its granite countertops and exquisite views.

"I'm listening," she said.

"There's a hint, in the papers you gave me, of a man who knew more than he let on about the creatures. There's a reference to information stored in the Tangled Net database, in Callahan Security. Tell me more about this man and what he knows, and I'll make it worth your while."

Paula nodded slowly. Miles was wrapping up his story, and his body language spoke of moving on to the next group. She smoothed her dress over her hips and stepped away.

"I'll see what I can do," she said with a glance over her shoulder. Ryan smiled in satisfaction.

"I look forward to our next meeting."

Paula was on edge, but she smiled brightly as Miles passed through the antechamber where her desk sat. He smoothed his hair in a mirror on the wall, hung for that purpose.

"How do I look?" he asked when he turned around.

"Very dashing, Mr. Callahan."

"That's what I was going for." He winked at her.

"Don't forget your lunch with Jade Yeo at one o'clock."

Miles checked his watch and nodded.

"Got it."

Paula waited two minutes after Miles left the room before she rose and walked unhurriedly to his office. Just yesterday, she had discovered a scrap of paper taped to the inside of Miles' desk drawer. On it were five passwords. She'd taken a picture of all of them—she didn't know when the others might come in handy—but the one for the Tangled Net database was what had really caught her eye.

She slid through the door and closed it partway. Her heart beat faster, but she walked confidently to Miles' desk. She was pretty good at this spy business. No, she was damn good at it. Maybe she'd found her calling.

Paula sat in Miles' swivel chair and breathed in the scent of warm leather for a moment, before she poised her hands over the keyboard. She logged into Miles' account—that password she knew legitimately, as his assistant—and opened the application for the Tangled Net database. Without hesitation, she typed into the password prompt. Her breath whooshed out of her lungs when it was accepted.

"Need to tighten up your security, Callahan Security," she murmured with a satisfied lift to the corners of her mouth. "That was too easy."

Paula scrolled through the database until she found the correct files. She opened them and started to skim.

Her brow furrowed as she read about the kidnapping of a man named Zeballos Artino, and of Miles' suspicions about him. She didn't know what Ryan would make of this information, but it was what he was looking for, she was sure. She snapped a few screenshots with her phone.

The door banged open. Paula's heart leaped into her throat, but she quickly closed the Tangled Net application and opened Miles' calendar program. Miles looked at her and frowned.

"I wore the wrong tie," he said. "Came back to change. What are you doing?"

Before Paula could answer, Miles' face drained of blood.

"You're the mole," he whispered. "You've been snooping. Damn it, Paula, do you know what you've done? They'll expose everything if they know the leak came from my office."

Paula swallowed but kept her face politely confused. How had he guessed so easily? Her vision of herself in a skintight black leather spy outfit vanished in a puff of smoke, but she kept her cool. She could still salvage this. She was Paula Rossi, damn it, Miles' trusted assistant and spy extraordinaire.

"I was checking your calendar app," she said with a puzzled frown. "I was afraid it wasn't syncing properly. The tech department warned me that they'd been having issues lately. What are you accusing me of?"

Miles stared at her for a long moment. Then he sighed heavily and rubbed his face.

"I'm sorry, Paula. That was uncalled for. I've been so on edge lately over this, that now I'm seeing enemies where only friends are. Will you forgive me?"

He came around the desk and glanced at the screen. His calendar program filled the screen, and Paula thanked her quick flexes. She stood.

"Of course," she said warmly. "I understand you've been under a lot of strain. It's forgotten."

She touched his shoulder and sauntered out of the door. A minute later, when Miles had rushed out for his meeting once more—correct tie in place—Paula pulled out her phone.

"I have it," she said when Ryan was on the line. "Send me the money and I'll send you the pictures."

CORRIE

Corrie banged a drawer open to look for a swab. She stopped and took a deep breath. Being angry with Zeb was only causing her angst, no one else. This week would be far more pleasant if she accepted his silence, did her work, helped with the troba, and didn't expect anything else from Zeb. There was clearly something strange going on with him, but he wasn't going to tell her, and working herself into a tizzy over it was futile. She was tempted to search his cabin for the enhancer, but she quashed that thought. If that was his game, it didn't matter to her. She could be calm and professional and not take his secret-keeping seriously. He was a colleague, and she should keep him that way, and not expect anything else from Zeb. Even if he walked around in his swimsuit, dripping wet…

She grabbed the swab from the drawer and slid it shut. Her phone rang and she jumped to answer it. Maybe Adrianna had thought of something else for the troba.

The screen said David was calling. Corrie froze. Did she want to talk to David now? She had really hoped that he would leave her alone this week. Harsh words had been said when they had parted, and she'd wanted time to ruminate on them. Had she meant it? What did she really want? She still wasn't sure.

Putting off the call wouldn't help in the long run, so she sighed and answered.

"Hi, David."

"Hi, Corrie. Do you have a minute? We really need to talk."

"Not really, I need to take a sample shortly."

"We need to talk about what happened." David's tone was wheedling. Corrie's ire rose, but she tried to keep calm.

"I said we'd sort it out when I got back. I can't do this right now, okay? I have stuff to do. This isn't a phone conversation."

"We have to figure this out. I can't wait a week, hung up to dry. It's too long."

Corrie breathed through her nose, trying to keep her cool. It didn't work.

"Okay, you know what? Fine. You win. We'll do this now. You know what the problem is? You are going way too fast. You're a nice guy, David. We have good times. But you're talking about the condo like it's a given that I'll be moving in shortly, and I'm so not there. I mean, really? We've only been dating a few months. It's way too much, too fast."

"But we're great together. Why wait? It's not like I proposed to you."

"Moving in together is a big deal! How can you not see that? Or do you see it, but you're trying to back me into a corner so I can't escape? It's way too soon."

David huffed in amazement.

"'Back you into a corner?' Can you hear yourself? What kind of monster do you think I am? I want you there because I love you. And yeah, I think we might have a future together, is that a crime?"

Corrie's leg jiggled in her agitation. He sounded reasonable, her logical side told her, but her emotional side cringed from his persistence.

"What are you afraid of?" David said.

He said he loved her. She wasn't nearly there yet and was afraid she would never be. She was afraid of being trapped. She was afraid of being manipulated into doing things she didn't want to do.

"I'm not afraid," she snapped. "It's just too soon."

"Why wait?"

"Because I don't know that I love you."

There. She'd said it. The words hung in the ballooning silence, filling the growing space between them.

"Right," David said. "Right. Yeah. Well, then. There's not much point to this, is there?"

Corrie's anger flipped to self-loathing. How could she be

so cruel to David? Maybe it was better now, than when they had gone too far down that road.

"I'm sorry," she said. There wasn't much else to say. "I might, in time, but it's too soon for me to tell."

"Forget it," said David. "You obviously don't feel the same way I do. I'm not going to hang around, waiting for you to magically develop feelings for me. There are plenty of fish in the sea, and I'm a good catch."

"You are," Corrie agreed. It was a lame thing to say, but her words, usually so plentiful, had dried up.

"It's Zeb, isn't it?" David said sharply. "He got to you, on the boat. That's what's going on."

"What?" Corrie yelped. Her pity for David dried up in her indignation. "What the hell are you talking about?"

"Enjoy your cruise, Corrie." David's words dripped with sarcasm. "I'm sure you'll find plenty to amuse yourself with."

He hung up, and Corrie gaped at her phone. She cursed and slammed it on the counter then buried her head in her hands. Her body coursed with emotions: anger, regret, and—relief?

She lifted her head. Maybe this was the right thing to do, after all. What was the point in sticking with someone she wasn't sure about, even if he looked good on paper? Surely there was more to a relationship than pleasant conversation and mild compatibility. Was she naïve to hope for passion and real love with a decent man?

JULES

After a brief look at the creature on deck, Krista had returned to the wheelhouse.

"I don't have any more patience for Zeb and his animals," she growled to Jules. "I'll drive to the bay. Go make yourself useful elsewhere."

Jules didn't need a second invitation to escape Krista's hostile presence. By the time he had wandered back to the aft deck via the galley to pick up their logbook and a unopened bag of Zeb's jellyfish, Zeb had lowered the hindquarters of the creature into the tank and was watching it rest on the bottom, its big eyes closed in repose. Zeb looked up at Jules.

"Are you going to get dressed anytime soon?" Jules waved at Zeb. "At least pretend a swimsuit isn't like a second skin for you?"

"Why?" said Zeb, but he stood up and walked toward the cabin. "Corrie already knows I'm impervious to cold."

"For the rest of us, then. I'd rather not see you prance around in your speedo."

Zeb huffed but disappeared inside without further comment. Jules sat down and stared at the troba. His pencil hovered over the paper for a full minute before he committed to the first line. Once he'd started, the rest was easy. The creature poured onto the page, cartoonish but accurate. Corrie came out while he put the final touches on the ears. He signed his name with a flourish and held it up for her approval.

"Yes, that's it exactly," said Corrie. "Nicely done."

She sank down to the deck with a sigh and placed a large container beside her.

"What are you planning?" said Jules. "And why the long face?"

"Sampling this guy," Corrie said, then she looked at Jules. "And David just called. We broke up." She fidgeted with her fingers. "I'm not even sure what the issue was. It ballooned out of his going condo shopping. He expected me to move in with him soon, I think."

"I guess he knows what he wants," said Jules. It was a bold move on David's part, which Jules both admired and scorned. Jules wished he had someone he wanted to move in with him. His mind drifted to his ex-girlfriend Carole, who had lived with him for a time, but the thought didn't pain him the way it usually did. Another beautiful face entered his brain, which brought him momentary pleasure until he imagined Trip in his trailer. The vision popped like a burst bubble.

"Yeah," Corrie said with gloom in her voice. "The problem is, I don't know what I want. Or, truthfully, I don't know that I want him. Not the way he wants me, anyway. It's not really fair to have a lopsided relationship, is it?" Corrie twisted a swab between her hands. "It's better to leave him now and let him find someone who really cares for him. He deserves better."

It sounded to Jules like Corrie was convincing herself. He wondered whether Carole had bothered when she'd left him, or whether she'd had no regrets.

"What do you have in your container?" Jules said to distract her. Corrie's face didn't suit sad. She looked more natural in merriment. Luckily, her eyes brightened at the diversion.

"Baggies for collecting that bloody gauze. Perfect DNA sample right there. And Zeb's stuff from the locker. I've been wanting to play with them, and since we have a creature on board, what better time to test them?"

"Didn't we just save this one from certain death?" Jules looked at the sleeping troba. "Do we really want to be testing on it?"

"I thought I could test them on myself, first, to make sure nothing would hurt it." Corrie pulled out a jar of cream. "If I don't react, it will probably be fine. Besides, the sonar device isn't harmful, it only calls the creatures here. And we'll wait until the troba wakes up and we give it some food, make sure it's doing okay."

"I brought snacks," said Jules. He held up the bag of dried jellyfish. Corrie wrinkled her nose.

"Why does Zeb eat that stuff? I tried one last time I was on the boat, and it was nasty."

"To each their own. I agree with you, it's not pleasant. But the unicorn fish gobbled it up, so it's worth a try."

"Good thinking."

Corrie opened the jar and sniffed. Her nose wrinkled.

"It smells like seaweed. Weird."

"Here, try it on me." Jules offered his arm. Corrie looked at him askance.

"We don't know what it does, and you want to go first?"

"It's fine." Jules had tried worse than this old hand cream in his life. "For science, right?"

His comment elicited a smile.

"For science," Corrie said. She stuck her fingers in the green-tinged cream and spread it on his forearm. She and Jules stared at the spot for a minute. Nothing happened.

"I'd better check me, too," she said and spread more on her own arm.

"Maybe it's a delayed reaction," Jules said. "We'll grow three extra arms tonight."

Corrie snorted.

"More hands to hold pipettes, I guess."

"And imagine how many knives I could chop with at once."

"A one-man commercial kitchen."

Corrie put the lid on the cream and looked in the container for more. Jules glanced at the troba in its tank and jumped when he noticed its large eye gazing at him.

"Hey, look," Jules said. "I think the horse thing is waking up."

Corrie spun around.

"Hi," she said softly to the troba. "You're okay." She

looked at Jules with hesitation. "Do you think we should try the cream?"

The creature didn't appear in distress. It waved its front appendages lazily through the water but kept its tail-end with the bandage stiff. Jules shrugged.

"Sure, a bit. It seems fine now."

Corrie opened the cream again and dabbed her finger into the greenish substance. Carefully, she slid her other hand under the creature's tail and lifted it to the surface. The troba kept its eye on Jules, but it seemed to sense they were friends, for it made no move away from Corrie. She rubbed cream on a spot gently, waited a moment, then lowered the tail into the tank once more.

The troba's eyelids lowered halfway, and its fins waved slowly through the water. It leisurely rolled over, looking for all the world as relaxed as a sunning seal.

"I think it likes it." Corrie whispered with a complicit grin at Jules. He snorted.

"Too bad it didn't work that way on us." Jules stood up. "While the horse thing chills out, I'd better get on dinner. It will be here before we know it."

"Let me know if that arm starts budding," said Corrie. Jules grinned and walked inside.

So, Corrie was a free agent once more. He should tell Zeb. Zeb hadn't said anything to him, but Jules wasn't stupid, no matter what Krista said. He'd seen the way Zeb looked at Corrie. Jules knew Zeb would be interested in the news of Corrie's breakup.

Zeb was in the galley, rummaging in a top cupboard.

"Get out of my galley," Jules said. "You're messing everything up, as usual."

"I thought Krista brought me three bags of jellyfish," said Zeb, his eyes trained on the cupboard. "But there are only two here. I could have sworn…"

"I took it outside. Treat for the troba when it wakes up."

Zeb sagged against the wall with relief.

"Don't scare me like that. I was worried I'd run out."

"Three whole bags? I think you'll be fine." Jules looked at his friend more closely. He'd known Zeb a long time, and this obsession with swimming and dried jellyfish wasn't normal for him. Was he ill? Zeb did look more tired than usual, although that could be from the midnight swim he'd sneaked out for last night. Otherwise, he seemed okay.

"I don't know." Zeb ran a hand through his hair, then he tried for an encouraged smile. "Yeah, you're probably right. Just, don't feed the whole bag to the troba, okay? Just in case."

"Sure. You'd better tell Corrie that, though. She has it now." Jules remembered what he'd wanted to tell Zeb. "Corrie said she broke up with her boyfriend today."

Zeb stared at him.

"What?" He recovered his composure. "What does that have to do with me?"

Jules gave an exaggerated sigh.

"Don't play dumb with me. I've seen you with her. You're into her."

Zeb rubbed his face in his hands.

"It doesn't matter if I am. She's pissed at me because I won't tell her what I am." He waved his hands in exasperation. "Not that I know anything concrete. Krista thinks I should keep quiet, still."

"Krista—" *is paranoid*, Jules wanted to say, but he knew Zeb held his sister in greater esteem than Jules did, so he merely said, "Worries a lot. But this is Corrie we're talking about, here. She's cool."

"It's gone too far, now. Why would she trust me after this? It's not a great way to start something."

"Give her a little more credit, man." Jules shook his head. "It's your life. But I think Corrie can handle more than you expect." When Zeb didn't respond, Jules said, "You'd better go rescue your jellyfish before she feeds it all to the troba."

Zeb leaped upright and strode to the door. Jules stared after him. In his opinion, people thought too hard about feelings. If you liked someone, you showed them. It wasn't that difficult.

CORRIE

Corrie's phone buzzed with an email alert. She wriggled it out of her pocket and tore her eyes away from the relaxing troba to glance at the screen.

It was an email from her supervisor, Jonathan. Her heart sank. What did he want now?

Corrie, I received the list of applicants for the Tony Magnotta Award, as I am adjudicating them this year, and I saw that your name was not among them. Did you not apply last week? Remember to apply for all awards I send you. Funding in the lab is tight this year, and we must pull together to further our scientific goals. I'm afraid that without another award for you for September, you will have to take on extra teaching duties. This will take time that could be better spent in the lab. Please, don't miss another deadline.

Corrie dropped her head. She had completely forgotten about that award in the furor of cruises and analyses. She enjoyed teaching, but not at the expense of her project. And now that she was essentially working on two projects, her anemones and the creatures, she needed more time than ever.

First David, now this—if the troba hadn't shown up, Corrie would have gone back to bed and hoped that tomorrow would be brighter.

Zeb appeared, blinking in the light. He headed straight for Corrie and the tank and glanced around until his eyes fell on the bag of jellyfish. He looked visibly relieved. She nodded at him but didn't say anything aloud.

"We're almost on station," he said. "Ready for sampling?"

Corrie blinked at him. With all the hubbub of the troba rescue, she'd completely forgotten her sampling.

"No. Yes, give me a minute."

She raced to the lab and collected her equipment. When she raced onto the aft deck once more, Zeb had hauled out their dive gear. Corrie pulled on her dry suit without speaking. She wanted to talk to someone—David's phone call hung heavily on her mind, and the dispiriting email from her supervisor was no lighter—but there was too much tension between her and Zeb now to chat with abandon.

They collected anemone fronds and a water sample without fuss while Krista held the boat in place. Once Corrie had changed and they were on their way back to Spirit Island, Corrie flopped onto the deck next to the troba with a sigh of fatigue. Zeb wandered out and crouched down to look at the strange, horse-like creature.

"Is the troba still asleep?" he said in a tentative voice.

"No, it woke up earlier." Corrie waved at the troba gazing at them through the tank. "I tried some cream on it from your dad's locker. It liked it."

Zeb's eyes drifted to the container of devices and the jar of cream at Corrie's knee.

"Are you sure that's a good idea? What is it?"

"I don't know, hence the test," she said shortly. "I tried it on myself first to make sure it wasn't harmful. The sonar device wasn't, after all. Jules tried the cream, too, and it didn't do anything, but a sample size of two isn't exactly statistically significant."

"Try it on me." Zeb held out his arm. "Three is better than two, right?"

Everyone was lining up to experiment with strange ointments. Corrie shrugged. If Zeb wanted to join them in their endeavors, she didn't mind either way. She opened the jar and smeared a thin stripe onto Zeb's forearm, touching him for as short a time as possible. She looked at him expectantly.

"Well? Anything?"

Zeb frowned while he waited. Slowly, his face relaxed and his eyes closed. He tilted his head back and his mouth fell open with a sigh of contentment.

"Zeb?" Corrie's stomach clenched. He was clearly having

a reaction. She mentally kicked herself for trying out the cream on subjects without previous trials. Her antics certainly wouldn't have passed the ethics board at the university. "What's happening?"

"Did you feel this?" He rolled his head around and sighed again. "Everything is fuzzy and warm. No hunger, no worry, no itching. Is this how people usually feel? I could get used to this."

"Itching?" Corrie said, but Zeb was too immersed in his fuzzy, warm bubble to reply. Why had Zeb reacted to the cream, when she and Jules hadn't? And, while he and the troba were not similar enough to truly compare, they had both reacted with calm and peacefulness.

If Zeb was on the enhancer, it might be changing him somehow, not only in abilities, but in how he reacted to chemical substances. If he wasn't on the enhancer, as he claimed, and his body was different in some unknown way, that was even more fascinating. Corrie was intrigued despite her annoyance with Zeb. She glanced in the container, where the other jars waited for testing.

Zeb's face was blissfully smooth. He looked peaceful and happy in a way that Corrie had never seen on his face before, except underwater. It transformed him. She wished he felt able to show this side of himself more often, not only when under the influence of some unknown cream.

Corrie took a few notes on size and body features of the troba while she monitored Zeb. He didn't seem in danger, but things could change quickly. Zeb didn't speak until the dreamy smile on his face faded, some minutes later.

"Whoa." He passed a shaking hand over his eyes. "That was unexpected."

"You don't say." Corrie looked at him for signs that he knew what had happened, but he appeared as confused as she. "Looks like you and the troba have more in common than you think."

Zeb looked at her sharply. She gazed back, searching for signs of what he was thinking. He gave her nothing and she tightened her lips in frustration.

Zeb rubbed his face again.

"I'm starving." His eyes lit on something beside her. When she looked, the package of dried jellyfish crinkled beside her knee. "I'll take that back to the galley. We can bring it out when the troba looks hungry."

He leaned over and snatched it away from her, as if he were afraid that she would stop him. He stood with unsteady legs and stumbled toward the lab. Corrie frowned after him. He was always sure-footed. Was he still feeling the effects of the cream? She'd better follow him to make sure he was all right.

ZEBALLOS

The aftereffects of the cream had worn off, to Zeb's disappointment. It had felt amazing while it had lasted. He'd completely forgotten about his need for swimming and his hunger for jellyfish, which were both a constant in his life these days. His mind had been so clear and calm without their aggravating influence. He'd used to be like that all day, every day. What had changed? What was wrong with him?

Now that the effects were gone, Zeb's hunger was worse than ever. He wanted to tear open the bag of jellyfish and stuff the entire contents down his throat. His stomach cramped and he bent over with the pain. Hastily, he ripped open the bag and shoved his hand in. He managed to put five pieces in his mouth before his vision tunneled.

"Zeb!" Corrie's voice sounded far away. "Are you okay?"

He awoke on the floor of the lab, staring at the bottom grate of Corrie's tiny fridge. Corrie put her face near his.

"Zeb?" Her voice was panicked. "Zeb, are you there? Talk to me."

Zeb opened his mouth to speak, but pieces of jellyfish were in the way. He chewed and swallowed while he tried to sit up. Corrie's small hands wrapped around his shoulders with a firm grip. When the jellyfish had traveled down his throat—although they did little for the cramping still tightening his stomach with painful spasms—he leaned against a bank of drawers.

"I'm okay. I think." He closed his eyes and tried to control the spasms, to no avail.

"Are you in pain? Damn it, I didn't think the cream would do anything like that. The troba is still fine."

"It's not the cream. Not entirely. It's happened before." The words were out before Zeb could consider their import. He was too foggy to think clearly, and his stomach continued to give him grief.

"What do you mean? What's happened before? You keeling over? Why were you shoving jellyfish down the hatch like it's going out of fashion?"

Zeb shook his head with his eyes tightly shut. He couldn't answer that. He didn't trust himself to spin a story, not in his current state, and Corrie was too smart to be fooled by his lies. The only thing he could do was stay quiet. His stomach cramped again, and he grimaced.

"I don't know what to do for you if you won't tell me what's going on." Corrie stood. "I want to help, but you won't let me. I'll get Krista. Maybe she can figure it out."

Her rapid footsteps pattered into the galley and out of hearing. He clutched his stomach and waited. Surely, it would pass soon. Should he give in and go to a doctor? He'd always avoided them, just in case something showed up in bloodwork that identified him as not entirely normal. He wondered what the doctors had found when they'd examined his mother during her final illness. She had seen a few, he remembered, although they had given her no cures.

A chilling thought floated through his mind, as insidious and difficult to remove as an oil spill. Did his symptoms add up to something more sinister? What had his mother faced during her unknown illness?

What the hell was wrong with him?

KRISTA

Krista looked over when Corrie entered the wheelhouse. She'd been attempting to read some articles while driving through the open strait. The articles were important, but as dry as the Sahara, and she wasn't sorry for the interruption. Corrie looked pale, but she'd been out of sorts ever since Krista had boarded, so she didn't take much stock in that.

"What's up?" Krista threw the papers onto the counter.

"It's Zeb." Corrie looked worried. "We were testing some cream from your father's storage locker, and neither Jules nor I reacted, but Zeb went all funny, dreamy and spaced out. When that finished, he passed out for a moment. I left him sitting in the lab. I think he's hurting, but he won't tell me anything." Corrie composed herself. "I thought you'd have better luck."

Krista's face drained of blood as Corrie spoke. He'd passed out again? And what was this cream?

"Jules! Come drive for a minute," Krista yelled through the doorway. To Corrie she said, "I need to see the cream." At Corrie's affronted look, she added, "Please."

When Jules appeared, looking disgruntled, Krista raced to the lab while Corrie took the outside path to the aft deck for the cream. Zeb sat on the floor of the lab, leaning against the drawers with his eyes closed.

"Zeb." Krista touched his shoulder. "Talk to me."

"I'm fine." His words came out in a whisper. He cleared his throat and spoke louder. "A moment of weakness, a weird reaction to that cream. I'll be fine in a minute."

"You're not fine," she hissed. "You're getting into bed and staying there until you've recovered." *If he ever does*, a nasty voice in her head whispered. She banished the voice. "I'll skipper for now. Come on, let's go."

"No." Zeb's voice was firm and clear, and he opened his

eyes. Their pale irises shone with determination. "I'm fine. Leave it alone."

"It's for your own good."

"Stop trying to be my mother," Zeb forced out through gritted teeth. He lurched to his feet and his face paled, but he stayed upright with a hand on the counter. "I can make my own decisions."

Krista's temper flared. She wasn't trying to be his mother, but someone had needed to be in the early years. And now—it wasn't as if he were great at taking care of himself. He hadn't even figured out that he was exhibiting the same symptoms as his mother had shown. Who was going to look out for him if she didn't?

"You can hardly stand, and you have the gall to tell me you're fine? Trust me, I have no desire to be your mother, but it would be easier if you didn't act like a petulant child." She threw up her hands. "Dig yourself in deeper, then. Have fun. I just don't want to watch it happen."

She stormed out, but under her bluster, her heart broke a little. She didn't want to leave him stranded. But how else would he learn that he needed her?

CORRIE

Corrie met Krista coming out of the lab. Her face was stormy.

"He doesn't let you help either, huh?" she said. Krista huffed with annoyance.

"Stubborn ass. I have no idea where he gets it from." She flashed a look of complicity at Corrie, and she realized the other woman was making a joke. Corrie grinned despite the situation.

"We all have our foibles." She held up the jar. "Here's the cream we put on."

Krista's eyes narrowed.

"I recognize this," she said quietly. She took it from Corrie and turned it around in her hands. "Zeb's mother used it when she was ill. I have no idea what it's for."

"A painkiller, by the look of it," said Corrie. "Zeb was pretty blissed out for a few minutes, until he came down from the high. I wonder why only he reacted. A genetic predisposition? Like some people can't digest alcohol properly, or lactose. Maybe it's the opposite with Zeb, he can absorb and metabolize whatever compound is in the cream, and Jules and I can't. That's really interesting."

"Yeah." Krista seemed less enthused than worried.

Corrie narrowed her eyes. When would these people realize that Corrie wasn't the enemy here? Krista's suspicion was growing old, fast.

"Listen, about the cage and the troba," Krista said. Her topic change took Corrie by surprise, but since there wasn't anything they could do for Zeb, she supposed it made sense. "I think we should call Miles Callahan and make sure he's not behind it. He would be an idiot to tell anyone, but I don't trust him. How else would anyone know about the sonar device and the creatures?"

Corrie nodded. She'd been wondering the same thing.

"Let me call my roommate Adrianna. I think she has Miles' number."

A few minutes later, she and Krista were at the table in the eating space, staring at Corrie's phone as it rang on speakerphone. A rustle in the lab doorway alerted Corrie to Zeb's presence, but he only leaned against the doorway to listen. He looked pale under his tanned skin but steady on his feet. Corrie opened her mouth to say something to him—she wasn't sure what—but a voice answered, and she focused on the phone.

"Good morning, Miles Callahan's office. How may I help you?"

The woman's voice was young, smooth, and polished. Corrie replied.

"Hello. I'd like to speak to Miles, please."

"He's not available right now, but if I can take your name and number, I will let him know you called."

"It's actually quite urgent," Corrie said in a pleasant tone. "Please tell him Corrie Duval is on the line with an inquiry about his promise. I think he'll want to answer. I'll hold."

"I will check to see if he's free." The assistant didn't sound quite as collected as before. Tinny soft rock played through the speaker. Corrie looked at Krista.

"That did it."

The phone clicked and rustled.

"Corrie," Miles said. His voice was light and jovial, as if Corrie had called to invite him to a party. Corrie imagined him sweating with a fake smile plastered to his face. "How are you?"

"I'm disturbed, Miles." Corrie kept her voice friendly. "I've recently discovered a trap for unusual fish, that are lured into it by a replica of a certain device that your people were quite interested in a few weeks ago. It occurred to me that no one, save you and my friends, has any idea what that device does or how to replicate it. It was a big surprise, you can imagine."

"What are you saying?" said Miles. Corrie clucked her tongue.

"Come on, Miles. If it wasn't us that spilled the beans to this unknown entity—and we have an interest in keeping unusual fish a secret—then, by process of elimination, it must have been you. I confess, I'm disappointed. I thought we had come to an understanding."

"I didn't tell anyone," Miles said. Panic laced his voice. "I swear."

"Promises don't hold the same weight for you as they do for others. I'm not sure what's stopping us from releasing those documents that you are so keen to keep hidden." Corrie wondered at herself. When had she stooped to blackmail, like some movieland bad guy? Maybe she should be stroking a cat while she spoke to Miles.

"The only people who know are me and two employees of Tangled Net," Miles babbled. "I swear. Gavin is still on medical leave, and Flint wouldn't talk. Both are paid too well and have signed so many non-disclosure agreements, there's no way their lips aren't sealed."

Corrie looked at Krista, who sighed in frustration, and Zeb, who shrugged with defeat.

"All right, if you're sure. We're going to get to the bottom of this, though. If you have anything to do with it, we'll find out. If you have any information that would help—well, now you have my number. Goodbye, Miles."

There was silence on the line, so Corrie hung up and leaned back, breathing heavily from adrenaline like she'd run a race.

"That was incredible," Zeb said, shaking his head with awe.

"Did you like me channeling my inner Bond villain?" Corrie chuckled. "Kind of weird, kind of fun."

"Too bad he didn't know anything," Krista said. "He could still be lying, but I don't know. He sounded sincere. Panicky, you know."

"Now what?" Corrie said. She rested her chin on her hands. "How do we find out who's collecting creatures?"

Corrie retreated to the lab to process samples while they drove. She had too much to think about, and she let the events of the day pass through her mind while she pipetted and filtered.

"Guys?" Jules' voice floated from the bow when they had almost reached their anchoring bay. "Come see this."

Zeb walked by the open door. Corrie dithered for a moment, but curiosity won over her desire to appear indifferent. She tucked her tubes into a drawer and followed Zeb. Jules sat on the bow with headphones slung around his neck now that Krista was back in the wheelhouse. He pointed to the edge of Spirit Island.

"Check out that boat. Isn't that where the cage is?"

Corrie held a hand over her eyes to shade them from the sun and squinted in the direction where Jules pointed. A good-sized launch idled over the spot where the cage lay hidden under the waves. Two figures moved around the open area at the stern with ropes and a hook. The boat slid out of sight as the *Clicker* drove into the bay where they had previously spent the night. There was clanging from the windlass as Krista dropped anchor.

Corrie turned to Zeb when Krista came out from the wheelhouse.

"It's them," she breathed. "Finally. We need to figure out who they are."

"The boat's name is *Calypso*," Jules said. "I can look up records, see where it makes berth. Maybe we can find out who owns it."

Zeb tore his gaze away from the boat and looked at Corrie.

He seemed to search her face with his pale eyes.

"Can you do it?" she said. "Get close enough to find something out?"

Zeb nodded.

"Yeah, I can."

"Then do it."

Corrie didn't know what Zeb was or what he was taking, but if he could use it to benefit their cause, then it was time to let go of her hang-ups about his secrecy. They needed answers, and Zeb could get them, his way. Zeb looked comically relieved.

"What are you talking about?" Krista said in a repressive voice. Corrie waved her words away.

"Don't pretend you don't know. Come on, Krista. I've known for days that you've been covering for Zeb. I even wonder if you've been forcing him to lie about whatever it is."

Krista swelled up like a croaking frog.

"I didn't force anyone to do anything! Zeb's big enough and ugly enough to decide things for himself, as he was so keen on pointing out earlier. I don't know what you think you know…"

"Nothing! I know nothing!" Corrie yelled. She was tired of all this sneaking around. It felt good to get it out in the open, even if it meant an argument. Jules slunk away, clearly not eager to contribute to this fight. She focused on Krista. "Even though I've been in on the creature discovery from the beginning, and there's obviously a connection—either Zeb's on the enhancer or something even weirder is going on—no one tells me anything. You'd think that I'd earned enough trust by now!"

"You're telling me that your life is an open book?" Krista shouted. "That there's nothing in your past that you want to keep hidden? Everyone deserves their privacy. I knew this was a bad idea from the get-go, but Zeb wouldn't listen."

"How have I contributed to anything bad that's happened

to Zeb? We were all in the fight together with Matt, and Miles was the one who kidnapped him, not me!"

"You encouraged his obsession!"

"And you're suppressing it!" Corrie yelled. "No wonder he's telling you to back off. You can't control people. You can try, but it always backfires eventually. People don't like to be controlled. They don't like to be told what to do. They don't like to feel trapped."

Corrie breathed heavily. That cut a little too deep for her. She wasn't sure if she was even talking about Zeb anymore, or about herself. She and Krista stared at each other, both red-faced.

"You're going to have to get over it," said Corrie finally. "He's going to tell who he wants to. If you don't let him make up his own mind, he'll shut you out."

A splash turned Corrie's head. Red flippers disappeared into green water beside the *Clicker* where Zeb must have left to spy on the boat. Corrie swallowed. She hoped she hadn't sent him into danger.

ZEBALLOS

Zeb followed Jules down the side of the *Clicker*. Neither of the shouting women seemed to notice their departure.

"Not going to stay for the show?" said Jules. "They're fighting about you, you know."

Zeb shuddered.

"There's no way I'm getting involved in that. I'll get roped in eventually if I stay. Best to let them at it."

"Wise man." Jules jerked his head toward the galley. "I'm going to look up the boat's name, see if it has a home berth. Are you checking it out?"

"Yeah."

"Good luck. Don't be long, dinner's soon." Jules clapped him on the back and disappeared into the cabin.

Zeb pulled off his shirt and pants, slipped his flippers out of their hiding spot, and fitted them on his feet. Shouting drifted from the bow, and his heart beat uncomfortably.

Krista was the hot-headed one, not him. He didn't enjoy an argument the way she seemed to revel in them. He fought with her, sometimes, because it was inevitable with her as a sister, but his hackles rarely rose on their own. And Corrie, although she exuded lighthearted fun, had a backbone of steel that came out when she needed it. She could take care of herself.

Zeb took a deep breath and dived in. He was overdue for a swim, and his skin thanked him as it was caressed by the cool water. After the episode with the cream, he needed this more than ever. He pushed thoughts of the fainting episode from his mind. There would be time to dwell on the mysteries of his failing body later. It was more comfortable to ignore the evidence.

Anyway, he had creatures to save. His body undulated as he swam directly to the boat.

What was his plan? He had to hear what the two figures

were saying in case they let crucial information slip. He wanted names, plans, institutions, anything that would help him understand where they had come from.

He closed his eyes and opened his other senses. When he was close enough, the distinctive currents around the cage floated by his skin, along with the telltale signature of a boat on the surface. He opened his eyes and pointed his body up, careful to rise directly under the hull so that no onlookers would notice his form rising through the water. He pushed himself along the hull until he surfaced under the bow. Voices drifted toward him on the breeze.

"What a beauty." A man's clipped voice carried to Zeb's ears. "Another specimen D. I'm desperate to test a few theories on this one."

"I'm not getting this one to dissect, then?" a woman's light voice teased. "Where's my fun?"

"No doubt you'll have it soon enough." The man chuckled, then sobered. "At the speed Ryan wants results, there will be casualties. I swear, if that man phones the lab one more time to ask for a progress report, I'll give him a piece of his mind."

"No, you won't," said the woman. "You love this work too much. Where else would you be the first to study animals unknown to science?"

The man sighed.

"Yeah, you're right. But I still contend that Ryan should be satisfied with daily reports."

The two lapsed into silence. There were grunts and thumps, as if the two were pushing around something heavy. Zeb treaded water and listened hard. All he had so far was the first name of the boss, Ryan, and that these two worked in a lab, studying the creatures.

The woman breathed out heavily in a sigh of relief.

"What's the new theory you want to test?" she said conversationally.

"You read the most recent report, didn't you? Where they

described the man in the shark tank? They were sure he was on the enhancer made from the exudate of specimen A. The report said he was abnormally quick underwater and held his breath for a long time. Not very quantitative, but that's the data we have to work with. However, it also stated that he appeared to control the sharks in the tank. Although he was bleeding, and the sharks were due for a feeding, they didn't attack. Instead they circled him for a minute and then left for the opposite side of the tank. One stayed, but only to rub against the man in a friendly way before it left."

"Fascinating," the woman said. "What are you proposing?"

"Some kind of control mechanism," the man said with enthusiasm. "I have no idea how, yet. Chemical, maybe? Sound? How did he know how to use his new ability? I'll figure it out. Can you imagine, though? The implications?"

"Animal control?" The woman was silent for a moment.

"Who knows how it works, or whether it can translate to other animals. But if it could—pest control, removal of bears from cities, revolutionizing fishing practices, hell, even getting pandas to mate—the possibilities are endless."

"Incredible." The woman laughed. "One step at a time, though. Let's reproduce the results, first. Get this bad boy to the lab. Pass me the keys, it's my turn to drive."

Zeb flipped upside down and pushed off the hull to descend. The motor roared to life, and his mind whirled. These people wanted more than strength and speed. They thought that Zeb had controlled the sharks, and that they could figure out the secrets to doing so themselves.

But Zeb wasn't taking the enhancer. The scientists wouldn't find out what they wanted. They would only continue to hurt the creatures. Zeb's blood grew hot. They weren't harvesting a strolia to mass-produce the enhancer. They would keep taking and taking from the ocean until they had found every secret they could find, and still they would take more in their fruitless search.

Zeb swam fast and hard toward the *Clicker*. He had to do something. These people weren't going to stop. He needed to talk to the others. Maybe they would have a better idea of what to do, because he was drawing a blank. His expedition had given him only fear without any useful information.

A low moan paused his flight. He stopped and listened with his eyes closed, letting himself drift in the current.

The moan sounded again, this time sliding seamlessly up and down in tone. Zeb frowned. Was it a whale? If so, it was unlike any other whale he had ever heard.

His eyes popped open. Was it a creature from his mother's stories? He couldn't recall any tales about whale-like creatures that made sounds like this, but so much of what his mother had told him was lost from his memory. He had to investigate. What if he found something new?

It was difficult to tell in what direction the sound was coming from, but after a few turns, Zeb was certain of the way. He swam quickly but cautiously toward the sound. It was far enough away that he couldn't sense the source. An octopus slithered below him on the seafloor, but he ignored it.

The sound was closer, its ethereal moans prodding at his thoughts. It evoked emotions that he didn't understand, like catching a familiar scent on the breeze and having memories flood his mind. He couldn't grasp the memory, only the emotion behind it. It sounded like comfort and love, but he didn't understand why.

The notes changed into something higher pitched, more strident. Three short notes sounded, and then there was silence. Zeb sped up. Had the maker of the sound sensed his approach and sounded an alarm? Was he too late to see the creature?

He swam on through the green, but after a few minutes of

searching with his eyes and his other senses, Zeb conceded defeat. The sound maker, whatever it was, didn't want to be found. All Zeb was left with was a lingering feeling of melancholy from comfort lost.

CORRIE

Corrie left a silent Krista on the bow after Zeb splashed into the water. She had no interest in reaming Krista out further. She had said her piece. Either Krista had heard it, or she hadn't. It didn't truly matter to Corrie. At the end of the day, it was Zeb and Krista's issue to work out. She shouldn't have spoken out, not really, but Corrie hated to see people being controlled.

She had lab work to do, as always, but Zeb's absence and the questions about his secrets foremost in her mind brought her a brainwave. Was he hiding something in his cabin? It was a long shot, but Corrie was at her wit's end. Zeb wouldn't tell her anything, and she had no other way of getting information. Would she find a stash of strolia slime drug? It would explain so much.

Corrie nodded to herself. She would take a very quick look and be in and out before anyone noticed. It wasn't like there would be anything too private, since Zeb and Jules shared a cabin. She wouldn't see anything that Jules hadn't already seen.

With that thought to assuage her guilty conscience, she walked inside. Jules was busy in the galley, and noises from the wheelhouse hinted at Krista's whereabouts. It was now or never, so Corrie pushed the handle of Zeb's cabin and slipped inside.

It was identical to hers except for a man's shirt draped over the top bunk and a razor in a built-in cup by the sink. She closed the door with her heart hammering. She'd never sneaked into someone's bedroom before, and she felt the strain. She almost backed out, but after a deep breath, she pressed on. There might be answers here, and she wanted those above all else.

The only places to hide anything in the sparsely furnished room were four drawers built-in under the bottom bunk. The leftmost two had a jumble of boxers and socks in one, and tee shirts and shorts in the other. Corrie recognized one of the shirts as Jules', and she closed the drawers hurriedly. She wasn't trying to pry into Jules' life, only Zeb's. The distinction didn't make her feel any better about snooping.

The next drawer was stuffed with folded plaid shirts lying on top. Corrie carefully peered under the layers, but only clothing met her questing fingers. She closed the drawer, disappointed. There was one more drawer to check, then that was it. If Zeb had any evidence of secrets, it wasn't in his cabin.

The last drawer was sticky to open, and the creak it made when it finally jerked out nearly made Corrie's heart stop. When nobody came to investigate, she allowed herself to look in. Was the slime in here? She frowned with curiosity.

There were no clothes in here. Instead, the cavity held shells. There were sand dollars, clams, moon snails, sea urchins, and crabs. This must be where the moon snail shell in her cabin had come from. When had Zeb collected them all?

On the side lay a strange instrument. It looked like a curved recorder, but of a pure, translucent white. Corrie's fingers touched it, and the smooth yet porous surface reminded her of bone.

An opened bag of jellyfish nestled in the corner. Corrie picked it up. What did Zeb see in these? And, a better question, why did he like them so much that he had hidden them in his room for a midnight snack? A vision of Zeb passed out with pieces of dried jellyfish sticking out of his mouth came to her. She carefully pulled a piece of jellyfish out of the bag and placed it in her pocket. Maybe she could analyze it. Would its chemical composition tell her anything?

The thought of sampling reminded her of the cabinet behind the mirror. She eased the drawer closed to avoid squeaks and tiptoed to the sink. Inside the cabinet were toothbrushes, deodorant, soap, and two combs. Corrie ignored the one with longish brown hairs and picked up the other. There was one errant silvery hair stuck between the tines. She pulled it out and clenched it between her fingers. Maybe she would do something with this, maybe she wouldn't. Could it tell her whether Zeb was on the enhancer, if it had a similar composition to the slime? Or might it tell her what Zeb's story really was?

Corrie had played the odds for long enough. She crept to the door and pulled it open with a watchful eye on the hallway. When no one shouted at her, she slipped out and shut the door behind her. Her legs felt jerky and wooden as she walked quickly to the lab. No one was the wiser. She was fine. There was no slime, but she had a hair. And, maybe now, she could get the answers that Zeb wasn't willing to tell her.

Corrie was placing her samples in the fridge when Zeb's voice made her jump.

"Thanks for sticking up for me, back there," he said from the doorway. Corrie slammed the fridge shut and tried to wipe off her guilty expression before she turned. It took her a moment to realize what he meant.

"Oh, that. Yeah, your sister is a bit overprotective. Do you think she'll be off your back now?"

Zeb chuckled. It made Corrie smile to hear. A towel was wrapped around his middle, but his bare chest was wet, and he tousled his hair to shake water droplets out of it. Corrie's leg jiggled in her agitation.

"I doubt it, but it was a good try."

"Did you find anything?" Corrie tore her thoughts away from Zeb's abdominals and remembered the reason he was leaving puddles on her lab floor. Zeb looked grim.

"Yes, and no. There were two people on board, a man and

a woman, both scientists who work in a lab. They spoke about testing the creatures for something. It sounds bad, because they said they'd be dissecting them soon after. I don't know who they work for, except that their boss' name is Ryan."

"Not much to go on," said Corrie in disappointment. Zeb grimaced.

"There's more, but it's not good news. They think I'm on the enhancer, and that I was controlling the sharks in Miles Callahan's aquarium. They're looking for some compound in the creatures that will help them control animals." Frustration was etched over Zeb's face. "I swear, I'm not on the enhancer. They'll be looking forever for something that isn't there. They won't stop looking, so the creatures will never be safe."

Corrie rested her head in her hands. She wanted to be the one to study the creatures, damn it, not these scientists who had never heard of ethics or animal cruelty. Her second thought, as dispiriting as the first, was that the northern inlets she wanted to sample were even further away. She couldn't leave the creatures to be brutalized by these unknown people.

She looked at Zeb. He stared at her with earnest worry. He still swore he wasn't taking the enhancer, but either he was lying about that, or he was lying by omission about the real reason he could withstand the cold and hold his breath for so long.

Corrie had sent Zeb off to investigate the boat in the full knowledge he was using his abilities to do so. It was necessary at the time, but for how long could she ignore the elephant in the room?

"I don't know what to do about these people," she said. "Beside sticking around and trying to thwart them. Let's give it another day. I'll sample around the south end of Spirit Island."

Zeb's face was awash with relief. He was surprisingly expressive right now. Corrie wondered why.

"Okay, sounds good. Jules is trying to figure out the boat's owner. Maybe that will turn up something. And we can sabotage the cage better next time, to give us some breathing room."

"Good." Corrie nodded with a semblance of satisfaction, although her heart squeezed at the thought of the northern inlets.

Sleep was elusive that night. The morning brought gray skies, mitigated by Jules' excellent coffee and a heavenly omelet. Krista drove the short distance to their first station while Corrie pulled on her dry suit and all the rest, and Zeb tucked his feet into flippers and strapped on his diving vest. Sampling was uneventful, but it wasn't until Corrie followed a lazy lingcod on the way back to the boat that she remembered something. Once on board, she turned to Zeb.

"I brought some fish tags on this trip. I borrowed them from a friend in another lab, as well as a hydrophone. I want to tag some of the creatures. Are the same ones returning to the *Clicker* every time you turn on the sonar device, or are there new ones every time? How many are there? The tags should help us with those questions."

"The hydrophone," Zeb said slowly. "Is that for hearing whale calls?"

"Yes, exactly. We haven't seen any mammal-type creatures, so I don't know if it's worth bothering with—"

"Can we put it down anyway?" Zeb interrupted. "Just in case?"

Corrie narrowed her eyes at him. What wasn't he telling her? Her suspicion must have been obvious, because Zeb hastily elaborated.

"I thought I heard whale song down there, yesterday, but it wasn't any song that I recognized."

Finally, he was sharing. Corrie found herself smiling.

"Yes, of course. I'll grab it, then we can jump in. You can summon the creatures down below, then we can bring them to the surface and tag them there."

"Isn't it too soon to scuba dive again, since we just came up?" Zeb said. "And do you have enough air tanks? You don't want to run out, you need them for your anemone collection."

Corrie eyed him. He looked at her nervously. She liked him on edge. Until he spilled all his beans, he should feel uneasy. Maybe he would be tempted to divulge, if only to release the tension.

"We'll free dive," she said finally. "It was fun last time. Insanely cold—I won't go for long—but fun. I'll show you how to attach the tags, and you can do the work while I frolic."

Zeb's mouth turned up at the corners.

"Frolic?"

"Like a sleek seal." Corrie snorted at the idea and amended, "Or a beluga. We'll see."

Corrie caught Zeb's eyes on her body before they returned hastily to her face.

"Definitely not a beluga. Although they are surprisingly graceful."

"If I am a quarter as graceful as a beluga underwater, I will consider myself satisfied." Corrie jumped up. "I'll get changed. Meet you on the aft deck in five."

Corrie ran to the cabin and slipped into her bathing suit. Luckily, Krista was nowhere to be seen. She didn't want to revisit their argument yet. Hopefully, a little space would cool them both on the topic.

Corrie's mind drifted to Zeb's description of free diving at her party a few weeks ago. He'd woven such a story, painting a picture of an ocean of beauty and wonder and filling her with longing to be part of it. She'd caught a glimpse of that beauty during her first free dive with Zeb and Trip. Now she wanted more.

She raced to the aft deck with a detour to collect tags and the hydrophone. Zeb waited for her there, leaning over the bulwark and staring at the waves with an odd, yearning expression.

"I'm ready," Corrie said. Zeb turned with his face tranquil once more. "Here are the tags. You take this tagging gun and press it between the pterygiophores—the bones that support the top fin—and shoot the tag in. It's quick, but we'll need to bring the fish to the surface to do it."

Zeb turned one over in his fingers then nodded.

"Okay, got it. Let's swim down and call them, then draw them up with jellyfish treats. And the hydrophone?"

"Let's throw it over when we come back. I'll listen for a few minutes while I warm up."

Corrie rubbed her arms when a cool breeze touched her skin. Zeb looked at her.

"Are you sure about this?"

Corrie nodded resolutely. She wanted to experience diving again. It would be painfully cold, but that was what blankets afterward were for.

"I'll be fine."

"Just remember to take it slow. Last time, you almost ran out of air." Zeb frowned at the memory, his brow creasing with worry. "Don't overextend yourself."

"Yes, mother," Corrie said. When Zeb didn't smile, she relented. "Thanks for the warning. I'll take it easy."

Zeb set out the ladder and they stood on the edge of the boat. Zeb stretched his mask to place it over his head. Corrie put a hand on his arm to stop him.

"Stop lying to me," she said quietly. Zeb's eyes widened.

"I—what do you mean?"

"I know you don't need this." Corrie pulled the mask from his unresisting hands and dropped it on the deck. "When you put it on, it's a lie. You don't have to tell me everything, but I won't tolerate lying."

Zeb searched her face. Corrie stared back, unrepentant. It was true. They both knew he didn't need the mask, so what was the point in the charade? After a long moment, he nodded.

"Okay," he said quietly. "Okay."

"After you," Corrie said. "Since I need to conserve every second in that ice bath."

Without warning, like he'd been waiting for permission, Zeb threw the plastic bag containing the tags and gun into the water then dived into the gently rolling waves. Again, he executed a perfect dive, and Corrie felt awe, attraction, and envy in equal parts. She didn't bother trying to imitate his grace. Instead, she held her mask to her face and jumped in with a cannonball.

The cold was a living thing, attacking her with knives of sharp pain and filling her head with a pressure headache. She surfaced and gasped her reaction to the sky.

When she finally acclimatized, as much as she ever would, she noticed the tag bag tied to the ladder. Zeb treaded water in front of her, a grin on his face.

"Anytime you're ready."

"You're a jerk," she gasped. "I'm ready."

She took three deep breaths in a row to steady her shallow breathing. Then she took a final breath, filling up her entire torso, then thrust her head in the water and kicked clumsily downward.

Muffled silence filled her ears, accompanied by the pounding of her heart. She kicked furiously at first to resist the pull of buoyancy, but the force decreased as she descended.

A motion to her right made her start, but it was only Zeb calmly swimming next to her. His pale eyes, naked without their mask and pupils dilated until only a rim of pale iris remained, gazed at her in question. When he saw her looking, he gave her the okay signal. She responded but didn't cease her efforts to descend. She equalized her nose frequently, envying his ability to do so without holding his nose with his fingers.

Zeb stopped her once they were deep enough that the water was clear of phytoplankton. She looked around, enthralled. They were in a world of living greens, soft grays, and rusty browns. Stalks of kelp soared to an unseen surface far above, and a lingcod looked at her with lazy eyes from a sea star-encrusted rock nearby. It wasn't anything she hadn't seen dozen of times already while scuba diving, but it was different, now. She thought she understood what Zeb had been speaking of at the party. There was an immediacy to the sensations around her. The water was colder on her skin and saltier on her lips. There were sounds down here, sounds she had never heard before, clicks and groans and chirps. She had no idea what was making the noises. Her hair flowed in the mild current, and water passed over her scalp in a cool rhythm.

A school of fish approached her, and she squeaked in excitement when she saw their horns. She reached out to Zeb—everything was slow-motion underwater, but she found his arm eventually—and gave it a squeeze. He looked at her and smiled, his eyes bright. Then he swam toward the unicorn fish with a piece of jellyfish in his hand. It was a matter of moments before one of the fish broke out of the school and swam straight for Zeb. Corrie watched, fascinated, as he ran his hand along the fish's flank, held it firmly, then swam upward. Another three fish followed in curiosity, and Corrie trailed along.

On the surface, Zeb kept one hand on the fish and motioned at the bag. Corrie snatched the gun and passed it to Zeb, who lifted the fish's fin into the air and attached the tag. The fish didn't even wince and swam sedately back to its school once Zeb released it, and another took its place at Zeb's side. Zeb wore a look of patient concentration as he applied the tags. Corrie could watch his sure movements all day.

When the fish were all tagged, Zeb glanced at her with hopeful eyes.

"One more time for fun?" he asked. Corrie nodded and her heart squeezed. Despite the frigid cold, she wasn't done down there.

Zeb hardly waited for her answering nod before he flipped

upside down and disappeared.

She drew in a deep breath and kicked down once more. When she emerged from the cloud of phytoplankton into the clear water below, Zeb's eyes lit up. He pointed at her, then performed a deft twisting somersault in midwater. He turned expectant eyes her way.

It took her a moment to decipher his mime. When she realized he was inviting her to frolic like a seal, she let out a burst of bubbles in laughter. She twisted her body in a vain attempt to replicate his motion then shook her head with a smile.

He swam over to her and placed one warm hand on the back of her neck with the other on her stomach. Her muscles tensed. What was he doing? With a gentle pressure, he flipped her upside down and around in a somersault.

Corrie put a hand over her mouth to prevent any more laugh-bubbles escaping. Zeb grinned widely. Her lungs began to burn, and she tore her eyes away from Zeb to look up. She didn't want to leave, but she needed air. She kicked upward, the motion easier the higher she swam.

At the surface, Corrie released her breath and drew in gasping lungfuls until she was satiated. Was Zeb still down there? It was an incredible feat, no matter how it happened. She wanted so badly to know how.

She dived down as soon as her breath stabilized. This was too much fun. Her body was starting to shake from the cold, but she didn't want to stop yet. One more dive.

Zeb hovered above the seafloor with perfect buoyancy. When she reached him, he held out his hand. His face was like an open book, showing hope and bashfulness. Corrie looked down at the sea urchin shell that filled Zeb's open hand. Its delicate purple filigree was perfectly intact.

Corrie looked at Zeb and pointed at herself. *For me?* she tried to say. Zeb nodded vigorously and held it out further. She took it with tentative fingers and marveled at the intricacies of the shell. Thousands of tiny holes pocked the surface of the rounded form.

She glanced back at Zeb and mouthed, *Thank you.* He smiled again and brushed a floating lock of hair off her forehead. It was a futile gesture—her hair was escaping from its braid with reckless abandon, and the currents would push it back immediately—but the little motion struck a chord in Corrie.

Before she could examine this new emotion, shudders wracked her already shivering shoulders. Her body had decided that enough was enough and that it was time to get warm on the boat.

Zeb frowned with worry at the motion, but then his eyes traveled past her shoulders to something in the distance. They widened in shock.

Corrie whipped her head around, but there was nothing to see except green water and rocky seafloor. When she turned back to Zeb, he searched the waters behind her with pain and confusion in his eyes. What had he seen?

Her lungs burned again, and she thought irritably of Zeb's ability to stay down here for ages. She began to kick, but her movements were slow and uncoordinated from the shuddering that shook her entire body.

Zeb glanced at her ascent. Without a sign, he wrapped his arms around her torso and undulated his body in a sinuous motion to bring them closer to the surface. He was blissfully warm, and Corrie wished she wasn't too cold and oxygen-starved to enjoy the firm rhythm of his body against hers. She tried to banish the inappropriate thought, but his warm hands on her back didn't allow her. She held onto her sea urchin shell with a delicate grasp and rested her head on Zeb's shoulder.

ZEBALLOS

Although Zeb could tell that Corrie still chafed at not knowing his whole story, she seemed willing to return to a version of their previous camaraderie. She'd been downright playful under the water and had accepted his gift with a smile. Once they'd reached the surface, she'd disappeared into her cabin to change, but not before a chatty rundown of her excitement over tagging the strolias through chattering teeth.

He didn't like how cold she'd let herself become, nor how long she stayed under without air, almost to the danger point. She pushed herself hard to try to match his abilities, until he had to save her from the elements. He only hoped that he would be there to save her next time.

Regardless, it was wonderful to have someone down there with him. Scuba diving was a poor facsimile and only made him regretful and irritated. Free diving with another—well, he hadn't done that since his mother had died. His chest ached with the fierce joy of sharing the one thing in the world that made his heart soar. That it was Corrie he shared it with—well, that was a welcome benefit.

It was too bad she hadn't seen the flash of white at the end of their dive. He'd been certain at the time that he'd seen another glimpse of the pale woman he'd encountered a few weeks ago. He hadn't told anybody of that—it almost felt like a dream at this point, so similar was she to his mother—and he hadn't seen her since.

But Corrie had needed help to the surface, her cool body shuddering against his chest, and he'd forgotten the flash of white in his absorption of Corrie's head on his shoulder. By the time he'd swum her to the ladder, there was no point in chasing the phantom. Chances are it was long gone, if he'd even seen something at all. It could have been a discarded plastic grocery bag for all he knew.

Zeb toweled himself off, threw on his shirt and pants, then wandered to the galley. He found his phone tucked in a pouch near the table, and he slung himself onto the bench to look at it. He wanted to check whale noises online, to make sure the song he'd heard was something new and not an obscure gray whale call. He'd listened to the hydrophone for a few minutes with a shivering Corrie, but they hadn't heard a trace of any whale songs. There was a good database he'd found last year with local whale information, including audio clips. He started there and was immersed in the sounds with his eyes closed when he heard someone enter the galley.

"Not enough to swim?" Krista's voice cut through the chittering of a Dall's porpoise. "You're listening to whale noises instead of music now?"

Zeb's eyes popped open, and he regarded his sister warily. Her movements were stiffer than usual, but she seemed to be ignoring the blow-up on the bow. If she was willing to put it in the past, then he was happy to follow suit.

"It's soothing," he joked. "No, I'm trying to identify a call I heard this morning. I didn't recognize it."

"If you didn't recognize it, then what hope do you have that the Internet will have the answer? You're the resident whale expert here." Krista filled a cup with water and sipped it while she leaned against the doorframe.

"That's kind of my point." Zeb sat up in his eagerness. "I wanted to double-check, but I'm pretty sure it wasn't a song from anything we know." He looked pointedly at Krista. She rolled her eyes.

"Great, another one. Your logbook is going to be full soon."

Zeb leaned back, unruffled by Krista's lack of enthusiasm. She had never been on board with the creature quest, so he didn't expect her to be now. He wondered idly what the real issue was—why she didn't want him to look—but he shelved that topic for another day. Tempers were precarious enough currently. He wouldn't rock the boat.

"The closest one I found was a certain song of the Pacific white-sided dolphin." He opened the file and passed the phone to Krista. "Check it out."

She put her water glass in the sink then took the phone with a long-suffering look. The haunting sounds of a singing dolphin filled the room. When it ended, Krista swiped the screen.

"What other whales do you have on here?" She poked at the phone. "I lost it." Zeb rose to help. Krista's eyes were glued to the phone, and her brows contracted as she read whatever was on the screen.

"Whales aren't usually that concerning," Zeb said. "Here, let me help."

"Is this your bank statement?" Krista breathed. She held the phone up to show Zeb. Zeb's heart hammered. It was his banking app, showing an embarrassingly small number on the bottom line. He looked back at Krista. She said, "Please tell me you have more than one account."

"Why would I have more than one?" Zeb was genuinely confused. Maybe Krista's lawyer friends were loaded and needed multiple bank accounts, but he'd never had the means to consider that a necessity. Even the recent influx of funds from the inheritance had nested comfortably in his single account. At least, it had until the past few weeks had drained the money like water through a net.

Krista pressed her fingers over the bridge of her nose.

"Is this all the money you have?"

"Well, yeah."

Krista breathed deeply through her mouth, three times in quick succession, as if calming herself. It didn't work. Zeb cringed when she exploded.

"This is it? Why the hell are you out here? You don't have two sticks to rub together! You've run through all of Dad's money on this venture. What are you going to do now it's gone? You could have used it to do something positive with your life, instead of wasting it chasing dreams. You wanted to search until the end of the summer? You'll be lucky if you make it to the end of the week. I hope you've told Jules that he's almost out of a job. Have you budgeted enough for gas to finish Corrie's sampling, which you promised her? Hah, look at me talk about budgets like you even understand the concept. My mistake!"

Zeb's ire rose during this speech like a fierce burn, growing hotter and angrier. She'd never understood. There was more to life than money and climbing rungs on a corporate ladder. Her goals were so different from his that they weren't even in the same universe. He only wanted to *find* his place in the world, but Krista was determined to *make* her place there.

"I know exactly what I'm doing," he snarled. "There's enough for the week. Corrie will be taken care of. Jules knows it's a time-limited gig. I'll search until I run out of money. I'll make more, save up, and search again. That's the plan."

"That's ridiculous," Krista said. She shook her head in amazement, like he was the stupidest person she'd ever met and there was no point in drilling sense into him. Zeb clenched his fists.

"It's not your plan, it's mine. And it's not your life, it's mine. You don't have to like it. If I want to dig a hole for myself, I will. I know the risks. I'm not an idiot, even though you think I am."

"I don't—" Krista sighed and ran her fingers through her hair. "That's not it. Although you act like one."

"Why are you really against all this?" Zeb waved vaguely to indicate the whole creature-searching venture. "I just want to find my mother's people, my family. Is that so hard to understand?"

Krista gazed at him for a long moment.

"What am I?" she whispered.

She turned and left the galley, leaving Zeb feeling like a true idiot.

KRISTA

Krista marched to the cabin she shared with Corrie, praying that the other woman was elsewhere. She didn't have the energy to fight again. When she swung the door open, the space was blissfully empty. She closed the door and strode to her bunk to sit.

Zeb's flabbergasted face swam before her eyes. Had he really been that oblivious? Krista slammed her hand into her pillow. Men were so stupid sometimes. She hit the pillow again, but it didn't help as much as she wanted it to. She flopped back and stared at the bottom of the topmost bunk.

The irritating thing was, she did get it. It wasn't that she wasn't enough family for him, she knew that. If he were a normal man, he wouldn't be as obsessed with answers as he was now. It wasn't truly in his nature. Besides, there likely wouldn't have been secrets to keep.

But Zeb wasn't normal. Whether she liked it or not, finding more about his mother's family might help him know himself better.

Krista wouldn't have cared about that—what was in the past was past, and Zeb knew what his abilities could do, even if he didn't know why—but there was another reason she needed to support his search. His mother's symptoms in the early days of her illness were eerily similar to the blackouts and need for swimming that Zeb was exhibiting. Modern medicine had had nothing to offer Clicker. Maybe her people had something. Krista had to put aside her own feelings of rejection to help save Zeb's life, even if he didn't know that was why she relented.

She wouldn't tell him about the symptoms yet, though. There was no need. She didn't want to see him crushed again by the weight of despair. He'd only just started acting like his old self lately. There was no hurry. It wasn't as if they had any cure.

A crinkling noise drifted from the galley, and Krista wrinkled up her face, trying not to cry. Zeb was into the jellyfish again.

Her phone buzzed in her pocket. Krista pulled it out, glad for the distraction. The text was from Fiona.

Hey girl, hope your 'family emergency' is going well. ;) But seriously, get back here Monday early. The Finch account blew up. Partners are on the warpath and looking for people to take the fall. You need to show your best hard-working face.

Krista's stomach shriveled into a queasy knot. She had planned to be gone until Wednesday. She could cut it early— it wasn't like they were up north, with Vancouver days away— but her heart rebelled at leaving Zeb. What if he had another blackout? What if he needed her to figure something crucial out? What if the fight with the cage creators turned from a cold war into a hot one?

Thanks for the warning, she replied. She didn't know what she'd do tomorrow. She'd make the call then.

A knock at the door made her slide her phone into her pocket again. Jules poked his head through the doorway.

"Zeb wants to know if you're up for translating the notebook again," he said. "Why he doesn't ask you himself is a mystery, but there you are. I'll drive to the next station."

Krista nodded. She didn't have enough energy to come back with a quick retort for Jules.

"I'll come."

Jules disappeared and Krista heaved herself off the bed. When she entered the galley, Zeb's relieved face caught her attention. Krista guessed she had given him something to consider after all. He shuffled around the U-shaped bench to make room for her, getting closer to Corrie in the process. Krista gave Corrie a stiff nod, who warily nodded back. None of them mentioned any of the arguments that had preceded this moment, for which Krista was grateful. It was much easier to pretend they hadn't happened.

"Okay, let's keep going, starting here." Zeb pointed at the next page after their final translation. "I did a little translating on my own. It was a story about a rogue brigar."

"I read it," said Corrie. "Pretty tense stuff."

"What do you need me for?" Krista said. "If you're translating it yourself?"

"Because it took me an hour to do one page."

"Fine," said Krista. She took a breath and pulled the notebook toward her. Reading the Greek was another distraction from Zeb and from Fiona's pronouncement. She could use all the distractions she could get. "Let's go."

I don't know what bearing this tale will have on anything, only that every story may contain a hint for my search. I cannot leave any stone unturned, for his sake.

In the fortieth moon after the warm storms, the fish folk Zeef and Tazo led an expedition from the Center. Following the sunflow current, they traveled three days, swimming in the day and drifting in raft formation at night.

On the third sunrise, Tazo rose to the surface to feel the direction of the wind for guidance. It was also sunflow, and he leaped out of the water in a fit of high spirits.

A piercing noise assaulted his ears, the deafening, sharp sound of a whistle. Shouts accompanied the whistle, and Tazo knew he'd been spotted by a dry folk ship.

Tazo and Zeef consulted with their company. All agreed: the dry folk had seen a fish folk. The dry folk must perish. None may see Ramu's people and survive to tell the tale.

With strong kicks, the fish folk swam to the hull of the ship. Some braced themselves against the hull with bone spikes and supported others who hit the wood with powerful blows of their ligan tooth axes. Before long, a sucking hole appeared in the hull and the fish folk retreated. They didn't wait long. The dry folk absconded their ship in tiny rafts. The fish folk helped themselves to treasures from the sinking ship then overturned the rafts. Each warrior added a trophy tooth to his or her necklace that day, even Zeef's young daughter on her first patrol expedition.

"Sunflow? Fish folk?" Corrie blew forcibly through pursed lips. "These stories are fascinating. It's killing me, not knowing what culture told them."

"You and me both," Zeb muttered. Krista's lips tightened, but she pretended not to hear.

"Come on," she said. "Let's get another one out of the way."

I wish Clicker had told me this tale earlier, because it holds so much warning. But would I have listened? Probably not. She called it the love story of Peli and Martin, but I see only tragedy.

Many times have the wide-beaked birds flown since the pale folk Peli found her love Martin and lost everything for him, but her story is timeless, so listen well.

Peli longed for change, for a different path than her forebears, to swim farther than others. Her sisters tried to hold her back, but she would not be dissuaded. Finally, her sister Tega swam with her in the hope that an adventure would settle her.

They called their favorite yatulls and set off into the wild blue, where the harvest fields petered out and kin no longer surrounded them. They each took a kelp pouch of Ramu's grace with them, enough to last for a month of full vigor.

Peli adored everything about the open ocean: the wildness of the storms, the emptiness, the lack of disapproving eyes. Tega followed her sister with worry in her heart.

Days passed in this way. Sea creatures, the like of which the two sisters had only ever heard stories of, grew more frequent. Strange birds pierced their ears with shrill cries when the sisters surfaced.

"Land is coming," said Peli with shining eyes. "Land, Tega. We will finally see land."

"Why do you want to?" said Tega with a shiver. "That's where the dry folk live. Who cares?"

But Peli cared, and she urged her yatull even further toward the approaching shore.

On the day booming crashes vibrated their skin from waves hitting land, Peli turned to her sister.

"I will go ashore," she said. "You don't need to come. I want to experience everything, and the land will show me that."

Tega did not want to, but she followed her sister. They crawled onto shore and expelled the sea from their bodies. The air was harsh and dry, but Peli smiled in triumph.

"Now, we will meet the dry folk. We will have such a tale to tell when we return home."

Peli strode confidently to dwellings that ringed the bay. Tega crept behind boulders and watched. She did not have the courage of her sister. She watched and waited for many days, escaping to the sea when the air grew too harsh.

Peli was befriended by the dry folk of the bay. She learned their tongue quickly, in the way of her people, though it was strange. Before long, she had friends. She took a lover to experience everything the dry folk had to offer. The man, Martin, was besotted with his beautiful, strange new woman, and Peli, little by little, fell more in love with him. When she met with Tega on their infrequent visits, Peli tried to deny her feelings, but Tega was too observant.

"We must leave," she said. "Before it is too late. You have had your fun, but it is time to go home."

Peli was silent for a long while.

"I am home," she said finally. "Go back, Tega. Take pride in fulfilling your sisterly duty. You do not belong here."

"Neither do you," said Tega.

"But my heart does," said Peli sadly.

Tega swam away with a heavy heart. For years after, when rumor reached her of wandering pale folk, she sought them out for news of Peli. Finally, she received it. A strange, pale woman, wife of a fisherman named Martin, had died of a wasting disease, three wide-beaked duck flights prior. Tega grieved and told her tale until the end of her days as a warning to adventurous pale folk.

Krista closed the notebook with a snap that jerked the other two out of whatever reverie they'd sunk into. Her throat was scratchy from the recitation.

"That hit a little too close to home," Krista said with a significant look at Zeb. If he wasn't being careful around Corrie, why should she be? And the story was so similar to their father and Clicker, even of the wasting disease that finally finished Peli.

Zeb looked bewildered and sad.

"Are you talking about Zeb's mother?" Corrie said. She was too quick for Zeb's good. Krista desperately hoped that Zeb was right to trust her. Corrie hadn't shown any signs of betraying them, but Krista liked to hold onto her skepticism until she was certain about people. Too many were bastards, and it was safer to assume the worst instead of the best of people.

Zeb nodded mutely.

"So, we're pretty sure your mother came from this island culture where they swim a ton," Corrie said. She drummed her fingers on the table. "So much so, that they call themselves fish folk. And swimming for days on end? Was that an exaggeration for the story's sake?" She shook her head in confusion. "And, somehow, they know about these strange creatures. What's the conclusion? That there's an undiscovered island somewhere in the Pacific that has a sea-faring culture and people unknown to modern science, surrounded by populations of strange animals, like a mysterious Galapagos Islands?"

Krista stared at Corrie. How had Corrie managed to distill the crux of Clicker's mystery from the evidence she had?

"Yeah," Zeb said hoarsely.

"That's why you're obsessed, as Krista puts it," Corrie said with a half-glance at Krista. "It's your heritage. Makes sense. But also, holy cow. This is way bigger than anything I ever imagined. We're on the trail of an unknown people, like first contact with some Amazon tribe who have never seen any outsiders. Or maybe more like that island tribe who throws spears at anyone who comes close, so no one has ever met them. This is history-changing."

Krista glanced at Zeb, who looked at Corrie with panic in his eyes. Smug satisfaction flashed through Krista's mind at the vindication of her suspicious viewpoint, which was immediately swallowed by worry.

"You said…" Zeb faltered. Corrie rolled her eyes.

"I'm not going to tell anyone. I made you a promise, remember? But, wow, to be on the edge of something this momentous, it sends chills down my spine. Just the sheer cutting-edgeness of it, to think we're the ones discovering this, it tickles my science side to bits."

Krista sighed. Zeb was safe, for now. She hoped Zeb's faith in Corrie continued to be repaid.

"I'm done for now." Krista stood up. "We can try again later."

She left. The sound of their murmured conversation filtered through the door. Krista shook her head. She didn't want to discuss this anymore. Zeb's desire to find his mother's people, while necessary in ways he didn't even understand, hurt too much. Besides, she had other things to worry about. Fiona's message wormed its way through her gut, settling a dank cloud of unease over her. What was she going to do?

ALISTAIR

Alistair shrugged on his lab coat. Lunch had been a hurried affair—a hastily constructed sandwich in the early hours of the morning had been shoved gracelessly into his mouth in the hallway—but he didn't have time for a leisurely meal.

"Back already?" Britta asked from her position at the lab counter.

"Ryan's on my back again," Alistair said after he'd swallowed his final bite. "You'd think daily progress reports would be overkill, but he texts me every few hours now."

"You can't rush science," said Britta. She methodically laid out the equipment for their next activity. Alistair grimaced.

"We're going to have to," he said. "I'll grab the specimens."

He detached an aquarium from its recirculation tubes and rolled it over on a cart to Britta's counter. She handed him a thin metal unit that was plugged into the wall.

"I've adjusted it to the lowest voltage possible," she said. "It's still a decent kick, so it should stimulate them to excrete the substance, but it won't kill them."

Alistair snapped on a pair of gloves and poked the metal into the aquarium. The horned fish huddled together in the opposite corner.

"Can't run from this," he said quietly and turned on the unit.

The fish jolted as one. Alistair let the electrical current run for five seconds, then he turned it off and pulled it out from the tank. Britta wordlessly handed him a net. With it, he scooped one stunned fish and lay it on the prepared counter space. Quickly and efficiently, Britta scraped the thick layer of glutinous material off the fish's scales. Back in the water, the revived fish hid in a corner, and Alistair repeated their procedure with the rest of the fish.

When they were done, Britta held up a rack of test tubes

filled with excretions.

"Wow, that's a lot," she said. "We're getting better at this. I'll put it in the fridge, then I have a meeting with one of our divers. He checked out the cage this morning, so I'll get a report from him. I'll spin him some story about localized mutations if he saw something. Don't worry about cleaning up, I'll get Beth to do it."

Alistair waved and strode to the other room, his mind already on his next experiment. The excretions were interesting, but the way these creatures responded to sound was incredibly intriguing. The device they used to call the creatures to the cage was the basis of his hypotheses, of course, but the scope of what sound could accomplish went far beyond a simple attraction. He'd already done preliminary testing on a few of the specimens, but today he'd set up something special.

Alistair buzzed in with his keycard, opened the door, and nodded happily at the sight of four tanks, each with a different specimen encased inside. There was a cluster of Specimen A, the fish with horns, which swam in a small school within their tank. Specimen B was the hooked-fin shark. Specimen C, the water horse, and Specimen F, a sleek-furred otter-like creature with a dog snout, swam close to each other. Were they territorial or otherwise linked? Alistair planned to test that hypothesis another day.

"All right, my pretties," he crooned. "Time to dance."

He placed a small waterproof speaker in each tank. All four were connected to a central box, which was plugged into a laptop. When the speakers were positioned to Alistair's liking, he opened a program on the computer.

"Here we go," he said. He opened a notebook and spoke aloud as he jotted down some words. "First test, frequency at twelve hertz. Sound will emit for five seconds."

He clicked a button on the screen.

All the animals in the tanks paused their motions. One second into the sound, they all swam to the back of their respective tanks as one, as far away from the speaker as they could. Alistair laughed aloud.

"Amazing!"

The timer ran out and the sound stopped. The fish resumed their previous activities. Alistair scribbled in his book.

"All specimens responded. Instead of an attractant, this frequency acted as a deterrent. Must repeat later for confirmation."

He changed some settings on the program, his heart beating faster at the results so far. The animals' response was incredible. Ryan would be very pleased to hear about it.

"Next frequency, twelve and a half hertz, for five seconds."

The next two frequencies he tested didn't result in any straightforward behavior in the animals, but the fourth he tried exceeded his expectations. Every one of the animals jolted with surprise then started to flail and writhe in their tanks, clearly in pain. The horned fish in the Specimen A tank began to drip with thick excretions. When the sound stopped, they all resumed their swimming, although more slowly than before.

"Fascinating," Alistair murmured, his chest tight with excitement. What a powerful tool this sound could be. How could he use it to his advantage? Possibilities bloomed in his mind, and he jotted down his ideas in the notebook.

"All right, fishies," he said. "That was a good show, but a sample size of one is not statistically significant. Let's run that frequency a few more times."

The fish jolted as he pressed the button again.

Alistair was grinning when he entered the main lab. Britta waited for him.

"I thought you'd want to hear the diver's report right away," she said.

Alistair had been about to recount his triumph with the frequencies but paused. It wasn't like Britta to stop working. The diver must have had something important to say.

"Let's hear it," he said.

"The device had been tampered with—again—but the diver replaced it with a new one. I have the shop fixing this one for next time. But he swears he saw something down there."

"What kind of something?" Alistair appreciated Britta's slow, methodical way, but sometimes he wanted her to just spit it out. His brain ran too fast to appreciate a slow unveiling.

"There was a flash of white in the corner of his vision," she said. "He swears it was human shaped, but he couldn't figure out exactly what he saw. On the surface, the boat driver saw nothing, so it couldn't have been a person swimming." Britta shrugged. "I don't know what he saw, but he was adamant about it."

Alistair's mind churned. What could the diver have seen? Unbidden, the creatures in his tanks floated across his vision. They were strange, bizarre, and yet, similar to animals that swam in these waters. They were preposterous, unbelievable, but they were as real as he was. Was it too strange to hypothesize that other, more sentient creatures lurked in the depths? The spirit of acquisition burned his throat too tightly to speak. He needed it, whatever the diver had seen. And he would bet his lab that sound was the answer to catching it.

TRIP

Trip had needed this break. Her graduate studies were grueling. Summer had ceased to be a holiday ever since she'd started her undergraduate degree and discovered that engineering students took courses all year long. Years of habituation in grade school to expect a summer vacation had left in her a lingering dissatisfaction that only time away from her studies to bask in hot sun could cure.

A looming bridge threw a shadow over Trip, but the sun beckoned beyond and quickened her steps. A glimpse of the ocean reminded her of her night on the *Clicker*. Once she'd got over the seasickness—Jules was her savior, there—the journey had proved as entertaining as she could have hoped, certainly far more than a ferry ride. Diving to see Corrie's bizarre fish was a frigid highlight, but the real memories she'd made were of Jules.

Jules was clearly smitten with her. She knew she was an attractive woman, and others had made their feelings clear in the past, but none matched the earnestness and sweet adoration of Jules. She'd liked him from the start. Their minds were wired similarly, and he was easy on the eyes, in a rangy, skater-build way. It was awkward that he didn't live nearby, but Trip was resourceful. She wanted to see him again, and so she would find a way, simple as that.

A sign caught her eye. The "Culinary School of the West" was situated on her left, with views of the Lions' Gate bridge to the north shore. Her lips curved in a smile. Jules needed to see this. It was obvious he had talent, but he needed a push from someone who could see his potential more clearly than he could. Trip was good at prodding people in the right direction, and she prided herself on her astute observations.

She walked to the sign, positioned herself appropriately, and took a selfie with the sign visible behind her. She attached the picture to a message, and texted Jules.

You belong here.

She kept it cryptic yet to the point and pressed send. He could take from it what he wanted to.

She flipped through her recent photos out of curiosity, and a picture of the noise-emitter from the boat stopped her thumb. She zoomed in and stared at the controls for a long minute. Of course, how could she have been so slow? This was nothing more than a souped-up version of the sonar device that was creating the low frequency sounds underwater. The frequency could be modulated in this version using the dials.

She dug into her backpack, searching for the unit she'd taken from Zeb's box. A wire had disengaged from its connection, but she'd fixed it last night. It had been a simple soldering job, and the friend she was staying with luckily had a kit. Trip stared at the unit, which she and her friend had identified as a crude amplifier. Now that she knew what the device was, she understood that an amplifier was necessary to project the sonar signal with any volume.

She still didn't know what it was for, but that was a question for Corrie to ponder. She dashed off a text telling Corrie about her revelation. Before she pressed send, she paused. Zeb's ability to hear the frequency still troubled her, along with his other unusual traits. She added another line to her text.

See what Zeb can hear from this new device. You'll need the amplifier to send the signal further than a few centimeters, though. I have it with me, and it's fixed.

Trip thought for a moment, then sent another text to Corrie. *There's more that Zeb isn't telling you. Find out what.*

CORRIE

Corrie drummed her fingers on the table after Krista left.

"I don't understand how there could be an undiscovered island somewhere," she said. "There are satellites these days. Nothing can stay hidden. For that matter, why would nobody ever see any of these strange creatures until now? Surely, even if they stayed close to their home island—strange that none would undergo migration of any sort—some would get swept away and be caught in a fishing net or washed up on the beach. The odds are too low that something would have remained undiscovered until now."

"Unless something was keeping them there," Zeb said quietly.

Corrie narrowed her eyes at him. What was he trying to say?

"Care to elaborate?"

Zeb paused before replying. He kept his eyes on his hands while he spoke.

"Some of my mum's stories mentioned keeping the creatures in line, within a barrier of some kind. Vague references, for the most part, but still, maybe an explanation."

"How could they contain Sucker?" Corrie said. Zeb met her baffled eyes with a shrug.

"I'd like to know."

"She never told you where she was from?" Corrie was fascinated by this revelation of Zeb's unknown past. She knew where her parents were born, the year that her maternal grandparents had emigrated from France, and she'd even met one of her great-grandmothers before she'd died. To have her heritage fade into obscuring fog would be a frustrating shock. She could trace her diminutive height back to her great-grandfather, her nose along her paternal line, and echoes of her tidiness from the neat lines in a family bible, kept for generations. She liked to know where the pieces of herself came from that made up her unique whole. It was a grounding and a connection to her past. Did Zeb feel like an untethered buoy at times? He must, especially if his ancestors weren't mere potato farmers from Europe, but something else entirely.

Zeb shook his head. He clutched his father's notebook as if it were a life ring.

"Never, and I was too young to pester her about it. Too young and stupid to ask questions, to know how important it was. Too young to know she was dying."

Zeb scrubbed his face with one hand, as if to wipe away his thoughts. He took a deep breath and released it.

"What are we going to do about this cage?" he said.

Corrie's mind tore itself away from the conundrum of Zeb's ancestors and planted itself on their vexing problem.

"We need information, and we need time. Time to figure out what they are doing, and how to stop them."

"I can buy us time." Zeb sat up straighter. "I can wreck the cage again. They fix it quickly, but it will help a bit."

"Okay, good." Corrie jiggled her leg in thought. How could they get information? An idea wove together in her mind, and she smiled. "I know how to get information. The boat comes every day, right? If they're still there when we get back, Jules and I will chat them up while you sabotage. How efficient is that?"

"Very," Zeb said with a smile in his voice. "Let's get your station done, then head back right away."

Corrie stood and he rose beside her in the small space. The difference in height between them meant she was looking at his chest, which made it difficult to ignore his fingers unbuttoning his plaid shirt. She leaned over to grab the notebook and tuck it into a pouch on the wall to cover the warmth in her cheeks, then she walked toward the hallway.

"I'll get my suit on," she said.

Corrie and Zeb collected anemone fronds without mishap,

and she and Jules put the winch down for her water sample. Jules disappeared to the bow and Zeb to the wheelhouse once the water was on board. Corrie quickly filtered what she needed to and put the rest in the fridge for later. Her heart jumped at the sight of the *Calypso* on their approach to Spirit Island, and she ran to find Jules.

She found Jules on the bow with his eyes closed and an unfamiliar expression of glumness on his face. Corrie wondered if he was asleep. She had to wake him, though. The boat only came once a day, and they had to meet it. She touched his shoulder gently.

"Jules? I need your help."

Jules opened his eyes and an easy grin slid over his face at the sight of Corrie.

"What could the talented Ms. Duval want with me?"

"Your acting abilities," Corrie said. "And your small watercraft skills. Let's get the dinghy in the water. I'll explain on the way."

Jules jumped up.

"Sounds intriguing. I'm in."

Zeb helped them put the dinghy in the water while Corrie told Jules what they were going to do. Zeb's shirt was already off, and Corrie tried not to look at his distracting torso. Once she and Jules were in the little vessel and unhitched from the *Clicker*, Zeb dived off the deck in a high arc. Corrie shook her head in amazement at his athletic ability.

"How long do you have to practice to dive that well?" she said offhand to Jules.

"Your whole life," Jules replied. When he realized Corrie was looking at him for clarification, he shrugged. "He swims a lot. You know that now. I'm not spilling any secrets by saying that."

"Do you know what's really going on?" Corrie asked him. She didn't expect a real answer, but it couldn't hurt to try. Surely, Jules would know whatever there was to know. He and

Zeb were tight.

Predictably, Jules didn't have anything new to say.

"Who really knows that?" Jules shrugged. "Zeb will get around to it with you one day, not that there's much else to say. He's not a big talker, you might have noticed."

"Yeah, I got that much."

She and Jules shared an amused smile, before they both focused on the water ahead. The buoy for the cage was right around the next corner. Would the boat's occupants buy their act? Could they glean any useful information from them?

Jules prodded Corrie with a fishing rod.

"Better look the part," he called out over the roar of the outboard motor. "We're jigging for groundfish today, okay?"

"Got it," Corrie shouted back. She unhooked the lure from the reel and opened a jar of bait that was under her bench. While she squished a piece of weird goo onto the hook, she kept one eye out for other boats.

They rounded the corner, and Corrie's stomach jolted at the sight of the sleek white motorboat hitched to the cage's buoy. She glanced at Jules, who gave her a nod.

"Get your A game on," he said. She nodded back.

"Let's do this."

Jules slowed the engine when they neared and puttered toward the other boat. Two figures glanced at them as they approached. One, an older man with straggly gray hair and a lean, hungry look, frowned as they approached. The other was a thirty-something woman with shoulder-length light hair held back with a kerchief, who looked at them with interest.

"Hi, there," Corrie called out. Jules brought the engine down to a low rumble so she could talk. "How are the fish biting? We're fishing for the day, holiday on Bowen Island, you know, and I'd love to bring a fish home for dinner. How local is that? The place we rented even has a kitchen. I have no idea how to cook a fish, but that's what the Internet is for, right, Jamie?" This last comment she threw back to Jules, who took it in stride.

"Claire would burn a salad if left to her own devices," he said with a laugh. "But we'll manage. Anything biting?"

The other two looked taken aback by the barrage of words thrown at them, which was what Corrie had been hoping for. The woman shook her head.

"We're not fishing," she said. "Sorry, no idea what the conditions are like today."

Corrie gave an exaggerated glance at the buoy beside the boat.

"Oh, are you crabbing?" she said with excitement coloring her voice. "Jamie, check it out. Why didn't we rent a crab trap instead? I love fresh crab. But then you have to cook them whole, don't you? And alive? I don't know if I'm tough enough for that." She giggled. "I can hardly buy a whole chicken at the store, because it looks like a live one."

"What are we going to do if we actually catch a fish?" Jules said in an indulgent tone. "Honestly, Claire, it's lucky we don't have to forage for survival. Your soft heart would kill us in days."

"That's why I bring along my big, strong man." Corrie smiled sweetly at Jules, then caught the other woman shooting the older man an exasperated look.

"We're not crabbing," he said curtly. "We're researchers from Tellman Inc., working on a marine project."

"Oh, amazing," Corrie said brightly. "What's the project? I love the ocean. If I hadn't flunked high school biology, I would have loved to be a marine biologist." Jules coughed beside her, but she ignored him. "Killer whales are the best, aren't they? Are you studying whales?"

"Sorry, it's classified." The man walked over to the side of the boat near the buoy. "If you'll excuse us, we need to get to work."

"Try the point, where the kelp is," said the woman, trying to soften her companion's terse words. "Fish often congregate at the edge of kelp beds.”

“Awesome! Thanks so much,” said Corrie. She waved at the other two. “Good luck with your research. Come on, Jamie, let’s catch a fish. You can kill it.”

Jules grinned at her and let the engine roar. They zoomed away, and Corrie only let herself look back once. Both researchers were intent on their tasks and didn’t spare the dinghy a second look.

Once they were around the corner, Jules let out a whoop.

“You were on form,” he shouted to Corrie. Corrie laughed in relief.

“You too, ‘Jamie,’” she said. “They totally bought it. If you act ditzy enough, nobody ever suspects.”

Jules brought the engine back to an idle. He grabbed an oar, reached over the edge of the dinghy, and rapped the metal hull with a loud clang. Corrie stared at him in puzzlement.

“What was that for?”

“Give it a minute,” Jules said. He leaned back and put a foot on the bulwark. Corrie frowned, but didn’t press him further. He clearly wanted to surprise her with something.

A minute later, a splash of water across her legs made Corrie squeal. She whipped her head around. Zeb’s head bobbed in the water, and he looked pleased with himself. Corrie started to laugh.

“Is that why you hit the boat?” she said to Jules. “To tell Zeb we were near?”

Jules smiled.

“It worked, didn’t it?”

Zeb hoisted himself aboard in one sleek motion. He wiped his face and ruffled water out of his hair. Corrie put her hands up in defense.

“Like a big, wet dog,” she said.

Zeb’s mouth twitched in amusement, and he ruffled his hair more vigorously in her direction. She sent a gentle kick his way.

"Did you mess with the cage?" Jules asked, cutting through Corrie's laugh. Zeb nodded.

"Again. We'll see if it sticks this time."

"Let's get back to the *Clicker*," Jules said. He brought the engine back to life. "Corrie can tell you all about our adventures there."

JULES

Jules left Corrie babbling excitedly to a rapt Zeb and ambled to his cabin. He flopped onto the bunk and stared at the ceiling.

He felt spent. Last night had been restless, filled with dreams where he couldn't quite reach his destination, forever striving and failing. It had been exhausting. He couldn't fake cheeriness for another minute.

Reception was good where they were anchored, so he pulled out his phone to aimlessly scroll through social media feeds. There was a text waiting for him. How hadn't he heard that? Maybe the roar of the dinghy had covered it up. Jules' stomach gave a jolt when he realized it was from Trip.

You belong here.

The words were accompanied by a selfie of Trip, looking serious with a glint in her eye. What was she standing in front of? Jules zoomed in to read the sign.

It said, "Culinary School of the West." Jules stared at the words until his screen darkened, then he zoomed out to look at Trip's enigmatic face again.

What was she saying—that he belonged at this culinary school? Did she think he would have a hope of being accepted to something like that? Or—Jules' heart beat faster at the thought—did she mean he belonged beside her? Or both? Jules' mind ran wild through a fantasy of cooking a fabulous meal in a swanky apartment for an adoring Trip using incredible techniques learned from his day at culinary school.

The vision imploded before it could really get going when there was a knock on the door. Krista poked her head in.

"Hey, doofus. Make yourself useful and look up the people from the boat, will you?"

She closed the door and left Jules to simmer in his frustration and inadequacy. His fantasy had been just that—a fantasy. Too many obstacles stood in his way, and the largest one was himself. He'd never make it in, for starters. And how would he live, on what money? It was a dream. A beautiful one, but not real.

Reality was what he had now, and the sooner he learned to accept that, the sooner he could go back to his previous equilibrium. He'd been fine before Corrie's friends had planted impossible ideas in his head.

He looked up Tellman Inc. and found some employee pictures on the company website. Alistair Brown, the older man from the boat, and Britta Lawson, the woman, were both listed as scientists in the research and development branch of Tellman Inc. There were three Ryans that appeared in listings in the company, but only one, the Vancouver office director Ryan Stokes, looked like he would be in a position to manage the two in the boat.

There. Jules had found out information. He didn't know what to do with it, but hopefully the others would have some idea. Maybe it would satisfy Krista for one lousy moment, but he doubted it.

Jules flipped back to Trip's message, read it again, and looked into Trip's eyes. Did she really mean it? A tiny flicker of hope ignited in his chest. Maybe he wouldn't get into this school, but what was the harm in trying? None at all. It was as simple as filling out a form. As soon as the school replied with their rejection, he could continue as if nothing had happened.

Jules nodded to himself and opened the application. Quickly, before he could think too hard about it, he filled out his name and address. Under previous experience, he listed his favorite dishes. In the section asking why he was applying, he wrote, "Because I love cooking and want to go to culinary school." It seemed like a stupid question with an obvious answer, but he wrote it anyway. He didn't want to leave any field blank.

He reached the end of the form, then switched off his

phone. What was he doing? Filling out the application was a waste of time. He'd better tell the others about Ryan Stokes. Dinner was ready to come out of the oven, anyway.

He swung his feet out of the bunk, his stomach heavy with disappointment. In life? In his future? In himself? He wasn't sure.

KRISTA

Krista poured herself a beer in the galley to drink with dinner. Corrie was at the table and buzzing with excitement after her encounter with the researchers. Krista felt dull and slow in comparison and needed the pick-me-up to have a hope at enduring the other woman's elation.

She brought her beer to the table. Zeb was gazing at Corrie with fond amusement as she recounted her adventure one more time, expounded on the possibilities of what the researchers were looking into, and guessed how long destroying the cage would set them back. Krista settled onto the bench with a sigh and sipped her drink slowly. It slid down her throat with a warm promise of relaxation to come.

Jules stepped into the galley. Krista looked over at him.

"Find anything, doofus?" she asked him. "Or were you napping again?"

Jules' face tightened at her words, but he didn't respond directly to her. He held out his phone to Zeb, who took it with a questioning glance at his friend.

"They work for a company called Tellman Inc. As far as I can guess, the "Ryan" they talked about is Ryan Stokes, the head of the Vancouver branch. The man is called Alistair Brown, and the woman is Britta Lawson. They work in research and development, but the website is vague on details."

Zeb looked through the website on Jules' phone then handed it back to him.

"Nice work." Zeb looked at Corrie. "But what can we do with that information?"

Corrie's forehead wrinkled in thought.

"I don't know. Visit their offices? Ask around? Find out where they dock their boat?" She pursed her lips in annoyance. "Beyond sabotaging their cage, which is fighting the symptom, not the disease, I don't know how to get at them. How do we strike them at the source, so they stop for good? Is this a futile task?"

Zeb looked disheartened by Corrie's words. Krista sighed.

"Let me see what my colleague knows," she said. "She seems to know everybody and everything."

Krista pulled out her phone and tuned out the others' muted conversation. She opened her messaging app to Fiona's number.

What do you know about Ryan Stokes? Anything underhanded? I could be convinced to do nails again if necessary.

Krista didn't really want to get another manicure with Fiona—the polish fumes had made her head spin, and sitting in a chair doing nothing grated on her nerves—but she knew that Fiona wouldn't likely give her gossip without a trade, and girly activities were Fiona's currency. A moment later, Krista's phone pinged.

Off the top of my head, not much. He is best frenemies with Miles Callahan, though, so I wouldn't be surprised if they either shared or stole strategies from each other. But the price for that little nugget is karaoke night, FYI.

Krista groaned aloud. That was a high price for such a small bit of information. She'd never done karaoke, and for good reason. Why would she make a fool of herself in front of a bunch of drunks while singing? It sounded like nightmare fuel. She'd rather fall in a vat of fish guts than do karaoke night.

"What's up?" said Zeb.

"Nothing," Krista said. "Wait, yes. Ryan Stokes and Miles Callahan are tight. I think we can guess where Ryan received his information. Either Miles was lying—which I don't believe he was—or Ryan has a mole in Miles' office."

Krista's phone pinged, and she let the others exclaim over her information while she checked it. Fiona had written again.

You have to be here Monday. The proverbial fan is on. Partners are on the warpath, and if you don't show up, there won't be much I can do to help. Tie up that family emergency and be here bright and early, okay? I don't want to see you leave the firm.

Krista's stomach folded in on itself like a black hole of tension. She didn't want to lose her job. She'd worked too hard and come too far to jeopardize it. Yet, here she was, cruising around the strait while partners at her firm sharpened their knives, ready for a cut.

She glanced at Zeb. He gazed raptly at Corrie's monologue with a concerned expression on his face. Could she leave him to fend for himself against Stokes and his researchers? He had recently been kidnapped for his connection to the creatures. How could she leave him now?

Krista shook herself out of her dire reverie at Corrie's mention of the word "device."

"Trip said it's exactly like the sonar device on the boat," she was saying. "But instead of one tone, we can modulate it to produce different sounds. Kind of like a piano compared to a whistle. Way more flexibility. I don't know what for."

"But didn't Trip take a piece of that device with her?" Jules said. Krista whipped her head around to look at him. He leaned against the wall with his arms crossed and his face morose. It was an odd look on Jules. He looked different, older somehow.

"Yeah, she did," Corrie said. She slumped against the bench. "It's an amplifier to strengthen the signal. Well, it doesn't matter, anyway. I don't know how it would help."

They all fell silent. Krista worried the inside of her cheek with her teeth. What was the point in her being here, if there was nothing she could do?

CORRIE

Early the next morning, Corrie entered the galley. Zeb and Krista were at the table, and Jules leaned against a wall, coffee in hand. Corrie looked at Zeb.

"Let's do one more dive on the east side of Spirit Island," she said. It hurt her scientific heart to wait another day to sample the northern inlets, but she tried to make the best of her decision. "It will give me a baseline to look at when I finally get my low salinity data up north."

The others stood without comment. Jules slouched to the aft deck, and Zeb followed him. Krista threw back the rest of her coffee and moved to the wheelhouse, looking preoccupied.

Corrie took a deep breath and walked purposefully to the lab. Just because she wasn't sampling northern inlets didn't mean that she couldn't get good data. There were anemones here, and slightly different conditions. Every data point was helpful.

She collected her sampling gear while they traveled the short distance and then found Zeb on the aft deck. He wore only his swimsuit, flippers, and vest with tank. He looked at her with an expression of defiance and guilt.

"Give me a minute to gear up," she said, ignoring the elephant in the room. Or was it the manatee on the boat? She swallowed a giggle at her newly coined phrase and bent to retrieve her dry suit from its bag.

Zeb helped Corrie zip up her dry suit and lifted her vest onto her back. Before long, they stood at the edge of the boat where the railing opened. She glanced at Zeb's mask-free face, and he spread his hand to guide her into the water.

"After you," he said.

They found anemones quickly and without fanfare. Shortly after, she collected water with Jules and tried to ignore the second splash of Zeb diving into the sea once more. It was beyond aggravating, knowing that Zeb had a secret and wouldn't tell her. Was he really taking the strolia slime? And, if so, why wouldn't he share? She'd give anything to be able to dive under the water without fear of cold, without need for a tank of air, to explore that world unfettered by diving gear the way he did. What was stopping Zeb from taking her with him?

But if he weren't on the enhancer, what did that mean? How could anyone be like Zeb naturally? It would defy everything science knew about the human body. The translated stories from Zeb's father's notebook whispered in her mind, but she pushed them away. Surely, they were only exaggerated stories. Any other possibilities were too bizarre to consider.

"I guess we're going back to our bay," Corrie said to Jules when they had poured water from the Niskin bottle into her plastic jug for the lab. She couldn't shake the despondent tone from her voice. Sampling here was better than sampling at the pier at home, it was true. But sampling in the northern inlets would be better still. "I'll be in the lab if anyone wants me."

Jules only nodded, the glum look on his face mirroring Corrie's own. He'd been quieter this trip and more withdrawn. Corrie wondered what was bothering him. It couldn't be the same issue as her—surely, he didn't care where they traveled—but something was clearly bothering him. She opened her mouth to ask, but Jules had already turned to go inside. Corrie swallowed her question and walked into the lab with her samples.

While water was filtering and samples were incubating with reagents, Corrie ran some calculations on a piece of paper. They still had three more days of cruising. If they left tomorrow morning and drove at full speed to the northern tip of Vancouver Island, they might still be able to sample two or three locations before needing to turn around and come back to Victoria. If Corrie were willing to rent a car to haul her stuff from Campbell River, where Zeb lived and the *Clicker* usually docked, they could probably squeeze another sampling location or two with the extra time. It was tight, and that was assuming they left in the morning.

But how could they do that, while the creatures were still being captured and tortured? She and the others were the only ones able to take a stand for the creatures, since they and the researchers were the only ones who knew they existed, and the researchers clearly did not have the creatures' best interests at heart.

Her phone indicated that she had a new email. She clicked through and her heart dropped. It was from her supervisor, Jonathan.

Hi Corrie,

Where are you now? Have you sampled the Queen Charlotte Sound and Knight Inlet yet? I'm very interested to see those data, from two very different conditions. It is an important follow-through from your first cruise and, if the data show what we hypothesize they will show, will be worthy of a paper in a decent journal. Let me know what you have so far.

Jonathan

Corrie dropped her head. She had nothing but a series of samples from random islands in the strait. There was nothing interesting about them, no real differences in conditions that could prove or disprove her hypotheses, and she was wasting her golden opportunity to collect meaningful data that could not only further her career, but the field of cancer-reducing metabolites. What was she doing here? But how could she leave?

There had to be something she was missing, some key piece of information that they could use against the researchers from Tellman Inc. Corrie pressed fingers to her temples, closed her eyes, and sifted through everything she knew. There had to be something.

ZEBALLOS

Zeb slid through the cool water, finally free of the restrictive vest and tank after his dive with Corrie. Even that little bit of covering rankled these days. His skin stopped its ceaseless itching and reveled in the currents that drifted across it.

He hoped that a swim would flush away the despondency that draped over him like a suffocating blanket. They had hung around the cage for days, and they had nothing to show for it except a few happily released creatures. Zeb and the others were tiny fish in a sea of sharks, for which they had no defenses. Zeb felt very small and helpless, which angered him. Why was he always two steps behind?

He might as well check out the cage. It wasn't far. He could at least admire his handiwork after his sabotage earlier. That might improve his mood, if only marginally.

He struck out in the direction of the cage. The sensation of his body rushing through the water lightened his temper, and by the time he was within sensing distance of the cage, he was almost content.

That ended at the first hint of thrashing from above. Zeb frowned and sped up. There shouldn't be anything in the cage. He had messed with the sonar and trap opening so thoroughly that there was no way the researchers would have been able to fix them today. What was up there? He couldn't tell from the panicked commotion.

The green gloom finally gave way to the dim outline of a cage. Zeb slowed and peered forward.

Stuck between two bars was a dobar. It thrashed in a frenzy, its dark brown fur askew from rubbing against the wire. Its eyes were wild with trapped panic.

Zeb approached, but the dobar rolled its eyes and pumped its skinny tail even more fiercely. Zeb stopped. What could he do to help? The dobar needed to be freed of its entrapment, but the only way to do that was to bend back the flimsy bar that held it in place. If Zeb could get close enough, it would be easy for him.

He needed to calm the creature. Zeb closed his eyes and recalled the stronger calming hum that his mother had used on him when they were in a tight situation. Once, they'd hidden in a cave while a pod of transient killer whales had swum by. He'd nearly burst from terror and his need for air, but his mother had hummed to him, and he'd felt his fear wash away into the sea.

Zeb had no idea if it would work here, but he might as well try. He experimented with a few tones, then settled on what felt like the right pitch. He kept his eyes closed, but with every passing second, the currents that buffeted his body from the thrashing creature grew less.

When he could feel no movement from the dobar, he opened his eyes. He was careful to continue humming while he swam closer to the creature. It stared at him with wide eyes but made no move to dart away. Zeb reached out a hand slowly, so slowly, until it hovered over the wire. With measured movements, he bent the wire back from the dobar's body.

At the release of pressure, it was if a spell lifted. The dobar jerked its legs and shot off into the murk. Zeb barely had time to turn his head and watch the animal swim away before it disappeared.

That was another creature saved, but why was it here in the first place? Zeb examined the cage. To his horror, it was as unharmed as the first time he'd seen it. When Zeb looked closer, he realized that the cage was new.

The researchers from Tellman Inc. had been burned too many times. Now they carried a spare cage with them in case of sabotage.

Zeb curled his hands into fists. They thought they had won

today, but they hadn't counted on Zeb. With quick undulations of his body, he shot to the seafloor, grabbed a solid-looking rock, and swam to the cage once more. With powerful motions of his arm, he bashed the rock against the lock of the cage. When it popped open, he wrenched apart the doors and set to work with his rock on the sonar device within. When it finally quietened, he swam away with a pounding heart.

This couldn't go on. But what could he do?

The hull of the *Clicker* loomed above Zeb, eclipsing the gray light filtering from the sky. When his head burst from the calm water into frothy waves at the surface, Corrie's head popped over the railing.

"Zeb!" she shouted. "Hurry up. I have an idea."

Zeb hoped it was a good one, because he was fresh out of ideas. He cut through the buffeting waves with sure strokes and reached the ladder quickly. Corrie was hopping from foot to foot by the time he climbed onto the deck.

"Okay, the sonar device," she said without preamble. Zeb wandered to a towel he had left hanging nearby and dried his face. Corrie followed him, still talking. "The new one, the one from your father's storage locker. Trip said that it's made to produce different tones, different frequencies, depending on the settings. Right?"

"Right," said Zeb. He wondered where she was going with this. Her eyes were wide and bright with excitement.

"Right. So, why would your dad have something like that? He already had the usual sonar device installed under the boat, and it works great to call the creatures here. Why would he have something that can essentially do the same thing?"

"It must do something more." Zeb was getting an inkling of where Corrie was going with this.

Corrie jabbed a finger at him for emphasis.

"Exactly. But, what? If the usual sonar device frequency attracts creatures, what if that frequency means 'come' to them? And, if that's so, what if different frequencies mean different things? Is this a language, or at least a rudimentary communication system? Maybe the creatures can respond to more than a simple attractor. Most animals have pretty complex calls, for danger or attention or mating. Especially the social animals. Some of the work that's been done with wolf vocalizations is fascinating…"

Zeb let Corrie's words wash over him as he pondered their meaning. It seemed so obvious once Corrie said it aloud. The clicks, hums, and movements that he used to communicate with sea life were more than random, but he'd never thought much about it before. He'd communicated his thoughts easily to the ligan a few weeks ago, after all.

"I think you're right," he said, cutting through Corrie's recount of wolf howl research. "My mum taught me a bunch of calls. She was always a bit of a fish charmer."

"Yes!" Corrie beamed at him like a lighthouse in the dusk. "Yes, I knew it. And with this device, we can say whatever we want." A cloud passed over her face, and she looked at him quizzically. "Of course, we need the Rosetta Stone of creature language. Exactly how well versed in 'fish' are you? We need a translator."

Zeb shrugged with diffidence. He'd never thought about it much before. He did everything underwater based on intuition. What exactly did he know? What had his mother taught him, in her wandering, offhand way?

"I don't know. I'll have to think about it."

"Find something easy that we can test," Corrie said. "Say you wanted to say something to a strolia. How would you tell it to go away, or to calm down?"

Zeb frowned then closed his eyes. It was difficult above water to feel the rhythm of the waves, the special cadence of sound in his ears, and the movement of his body. He could practically feel Corrie quivering with excitement, so he tried to concentrate for her sake. Slowly, the sensation of the hum he would use to calm a creature floated to his conscious. He tried it out, although it sounded harsh and strange in the air.

"Is that it? Are you doing it?" Corrie gripped his arm. Zeb nodded, and she darted away. "I have to grab the frequency monitor. Hold on."

While Corrie rummaged in the nearby lab with bangs and muffled curses, Krista wandered out of the cabin with a mug in her hands. She looked at his towel-draped body with a raised eyebrow but didn't say anything. Zeb wasn't sure if he preferred this new, standoffish Krista, or whether he liked the old, nosy one better. He didn't have time to decide before Corrie was back with the monitor in her hand. She flicked it on and held the receiver to Zeb's chest.

"Okay, do it again." She kept her eyes on the screen.

Zeb felt self-conscious and acutely aware of Krista's eyes on them. Measuring the frequency of his hum felt like Corrie was studying him, which slipped too close into Krista's fears. Zeb wondered what the researchers would make of him if they ever found out that he was different. He shivered at the thought.

But this was Corrie. It was very different to be studied by a friend, someone whom Zeb knew to be on his side. He was in good hands. He wouldn't say no to more hands-on research.

At this train of thought, Zeb steeled his brain to focus on his task. He hummed the calming noise. Corrie tapped the screen with an eager fingernail then wrote a number in her notebook.

"Great, that's perfect. Try something else, something more complicated, maybe."

Zeb thought back to his interaction with the ligan, then he hummed and clicked sounds of thanks and appreciation. Corrie's eyes widened.

"Was the clicking part of it?" she said breathlessly. At his nod, she exhaled. "This is amazing. Do you think your mother's people used this to communicate with each other, or just the fish? Is this another language style entirely? Like the whistled language in the Canary Islands or the clicks in the Khoisan languages in Africa? Who are these people? Ahh!" Corrie ran her hand through her hair and clenched her fingers against her scalp. "I can't take the excitement."

Zeb's face opened in an involuntary grin. He loved Corrie's enthusiasm for everything. He might not show it like she did, but his own interest was intense. They were onto something big. He could feel it. His mother's secrets were behind steamy glass, and they were almost ready to wipe away the fog.

He'd never considered that the way he and his mother had communicated underwater was anything other than something she had made up. That it might be a language of its own from wherever she was from—his heart pounded in his chest at the thought.

"Do you want me to do it again, so you can write down the numbers?" he said. His voice was calm and didn't reflect the turmoil within. Corrie nodded, then she gripped his arm. Her warm fingers wrapped around his bare skin with tight intensity.

"Look at this." She pointed at the new sonar device that sat on a barrel against the cabin wall. Zeb leaned closer. There was a tiny metal rod welded onto a hinge. Corrie flicked it, and the rod tapped against a metal plate on the side of the device with a clear ticking sound. Zeb met Corrie's eyes.

"For the clicks," he breathed. Corrie's fingers tightened on his arm. They were so close that he could see green flecks in her hazel eyes.

She released his arm and stepped back.

"This device is everything a person needs to speak Zeballese," she said. Her eyes shone, and she held up the monitor to Zeb's chest again. "Do it again, and I'll add it to my new dictionary."

"Zeballese?" Zeb said. His mouth quirked upward. "You really need to work on your naming skills."

"You do better," she said with a laugh. "Or just make the sounds again. A rose by any other name, etcetera."

Zeb repeated the phrase, and Corrie noted the frequencies in her book.

"Does the length of time for each frequency matter?" she said, her eyes absorbed in the number on her page. "If I shorten or lengthen some, does it mean something different?"

Zeb ran a hand through his hair. He'd never given any of this much thought. It just was. He felt overwhelmed by this revelation, and aggravated that he remembered so little. Had his mother really taught him another language? Could he recover his memories to piece together enough phrases to be useful? He thought about humming a different way to create the same effect.

"I think it matters," he said finally. "I've never done it another way for the meaning."

"Okay, then I need a stopwatch." Corrie ran to the lab and back again before Zeb could blink. "Do it again now."

Zeb obliged, and Corrie had him repeat it twice more before she was satisfied with her notes. She bent over the new sonar device, now functional after Trip's make-do modification and a fresh battery, and fiddled with the dials and switches, then she looked at him with an expectant, hopeful gaze.

"Ready?" she said.

Zeb nodded, and Corrie pressed a button.

A faint hum emerged from the device. Without thinking, Zeb placed his hand on the top to feel the frequency better. Sound underwater was less about hearing and more about feeling the vibration. At the correct time, Corrie flicked the rod and a small tick sounded. When it was done, Zeb looked at Corrie. She was clearly waiting for his evaluation.

"You got it," he said. The sounds of thanks and gratitude spoke to him, clear as a winter sea. He shook his head in disbelief. "That's incredible."

Corrie jumped on the spot and whooped.

"Amazing! I can't even describe—" She walked in a tight circle while Zeb watched with amusement. She must not be able to contain herself. She stopped with a frown.

"I wonder if it plays the same underwater as in air, though."

"Probably better," Zeb said. "It was really quiet. Better vibrations down there. We could try it in water right now." He would never say no to another swim.

Corrie twisted her mouth in thought.

"Could we put the dinghy in? Then I could hold the monitor over the edge, and you could make the sounds. I won't last long in the water, otherwise." She made an apologetic face, which Zeb didn't understand. It wasn't her fault that he was abnormal. No one could last as long in the water as he could.

"The dinghy's a great idea. Krista?" He raised his voice to direct the words at his sister, who had been nursing her coffee while she stared out at the growing whitecaps and darkening sky. She was far enough away that she could ignore their antics, but he needed her help now. "Could you keep the dinghy steady for Corrie?"

Krista gave a silent nod after a moment's scrutiny during which Zeb held his breath. He didn't know where they stood right now. She used to be easier to read, but now he had no idea what ran through her mind.

Krista walked to the winch and swung the dinghy out with Zeb's help. Corrie leaped into it once it hit the water, and Krista leaned over the edge.

"Why don't we leave it hooked up to the winch?" she said. "No need to go anywhere. Water is water. You can do your experiments here."

She put a slight emphasis on the word "experiments," but avoided Zeb's searching gaze. He shook his head. He couldn't let Krista's weird mood get in the way of this. He and Corrie were onto something, and the implications were only starting to emerge from his imagination. The clicks and hums he used underwater really seemed to be a language of sorts. Maybe he could figure them out and replicate them enough for Corrie to learn the language and "speak" it herself using the new sonar device. The thought overwhelmed him.

"Come on!" Corrie shouted. She waved at him with one hand while she held onto the rocking dinghy with the other. "I want to try this. Don't make me wait. It's getting rough out here."

Zeb threw his towel to the deck and dived off the edge. The frothy water rose to meet his eager hands and he sliced cleanly through the green coolness. All was calm under the water, but when he looked up, the reflective surface was broken by high waves.

Corrie waved him over when he surfaced.

"How do you want to do this?" she said.

"Hold the device in the water and press the button," he said. "I'll listen down below."

He ducked under the waves and swam far enough under to avoid his head surfacing in the trough of a wave. Corrie's hands plunged into the water with the device between them, and she pressed a button.

Zeb frowned. He could hear it, but only just. He swam closer and the hum grew more distinct, then he popped his head out of the waves.

"It worked," he said. Corrie gave another whoop. He held up his hand, allowing his treading legs to keep him upright. "Ready to try it on a strolia?"

Corrie's eyes widened.

"Yes, oh yes! Bring it on. Hit the boat when you're ready, and I'll put the device in and play the sound on repeat."

Zeb held up a finger for her to wait then sank beneath the waves once more. The sonar device under the boat wasn't on, but he knew how to create that sound on his own. He hummed deep in his chest and waited.

Before long, three strolias swam out of the gloom. Zeb smiled to see that one had a tag from his efforts the other day. It and one other hung back, but the third was more inquisitive than most and circled him playfully. Zeb kept humming while he reached to the hull of the dinghy and rapped sharply on it. When Corrie's hands dipped into the water, he ceased his hum. Corrie pressed the button.

The strolia gave no indication that it heard anything. Zeb listened as well, but there was no sound. Was the device broken? He swam closer until faint vibrations hit his ears in a familiar pattern. It was quiet, that was all. He called the strolia, and the fish swam closer in its curiosity.

When the strolia was close enough, it paused midwater, clearly listening to the sound. When the sequence finished, the fish wiggled and finned in a tight circle. Zeb had swum with enough fish to recognize signs of happiness and playfulness.

He grinned widely. It had worked. The device had spoken to the strolia and been understood. Zeb thrust his body upward with powerful kicks and emerged from the waves with a spray of water. Corrie shrieked and Zeb laughed.

"It worked," he said with a grin, after he grasped onto the dinghy's side. "It worked."

Corrie laughed with disbelief.

"Amazing. Amazing! Wow, I don't even know what to say. Come on, we need to make our dictionary."

On the deck, Zeb could hardly get a word in edgewise, not that he tried to. Corrie babbled with excitement while a stoic Krista silently winched up the dinghy.

"Do you know what this means?" she said. "Anyone can communicate with the creatures, just like you. I can ask the strolias to stay still for their tags, just like you did. I need to rig up a belt for the device, then I can be hands-free. I bet I have something in the lab that will work. Maybe we can even get samples from the kroll, or the ligan, or—" Corrie's eyes widened. "Sucker. The octopus brigar thing."

Zeb chuckled, his euphoria from his swim still coloring his emotions, making him feel freer than usual.

"Good luck with that. They're particularly ornery."

"But still, a whole new world. In so many senses." Corrie stared into the distance, strangely lost for words. Zeb took his opportunity to speak.

"If you want to use the device, you'll have to get really close," he said. "It was too quiet down there. We could hardly hear it."

Corrie's eyes snapped back to his face.

"Trip has the amplifier. Of course. We need her back here now. But, do you know what this means?"

"No," said Zeb. It was too much. He could feel that it was big, but the implications overwhelmed him. What could Corrie see?

"We can talk to the creatures. We know how to attract them and how to thank them. What if we could warn them of danger in the same way?"

Zeb's thoughts were finally illuminated, like a ray of sun shining through a dark kelp forest.

"We could set it up to warn the creatures away from the cage," he finished for Corrie.

"Exactly." She beamed at him. "A simple, elegant solution."

KRISTA

Krista listened to Zeb and Corrie's conversation while she winched up the dinghy and strapped it in place. The weather was worsening, and a sloppy dinghy meant squished toes and busted equipment.

They had finally done it. They'd found a solution to the problem of the cage. They would send out a warning signal to any weird creature that swam by, and none would ever enter the cage again. Corrie and her science, as well as Zeb and his strange abilities, had come together to save the day.

Krista wondered again what she was doing on the boat. She wanted to be here to prevent Zeb from doing anything stupid, like sabotaging his future or getting into trouble, but so far he'd either rebuffed her help, stayed out of trouble by himself, or been saved without any help from her. All she was useful for was driving the boat, really. Everything else was out of her wheelhouse.

It was time to face facts: Zeb was a grown man who didn't need or want help from his protective older sister. Krista liked to be in the place where she could make the biggest difference, and it was becoming increasingly clear to her that the *Clicker* was not that place.

Fiona's warning loomed in her mind. *You have to be here Monday.* Krista wanted to be at the firm, proving herself, making a difference, working hard to move up to the really important cases. That was where she belonged. Not here, on this boat where she didn't have a role, but in the office and in the court. That was where she could influence the world most effectively.

She thought uncomfortably of her promise to Clicker to look out for Zeb. But what had the dying woman truly meant, when she'd extracted the words from her ten-year-old self? Zeb was grown, now, and had been for some years. Even if

Clicker were alive, Zeb's decisions would have been out of her hands long ago. Krista had fulfilled Clicker's final request, and now the decision lay in Krista's lap.

Krista cinched the final strap and straightened. She would go back to Vancouver, in time for Monday morning. Krista would leave and let Zeb handle his own affairs. That was the way he wanted it, and it was for the best.

It felt good to be free, even if the worry left a knot in her stomach. She didn't think it would ever go away, but the paradoxical lightness in her chest might make up for it. In a way, she felt more liberated than she had felt in years. Her brother could solve his own issues. She could cut herself loose from Zeb, and everything would be okay.

Corrie's voice pierced her thoughts with a mention of Trip and the amplifier. Krista interjected when Corrie took a breath.

"Let's head straight to Vancouver," she said. "Trip can come on board, take my place, and bring the amplifier with her. I need to get back to work on Monday."

Krista focused on Zeb looking hurt and tried to ignore the relief behind his eyes. She knew Trip was more useful than herself at this juncture. It was for the best. Whatever came of this, she knew that this was the right decision, for both of them.

It had better be.

Krista stared at approaching land over the *Clicker's* carved wooden wheel, which was so out of place on this old fishing vessel. She would have sworn her father hadn't had a lick of whimsy, except for this wheel.

Her bag was already packed and sitting on her bunk in readiness for her departure. She'd offered to drive to avoid contact with the others. She had no desire to endure Corrie's chatter, Jules was inexplicably jittery since Zeb's decision to head to Vancouver, and she didn't have much to say to Zeb that hadn't already been said.

Her brother decided to make an appearance as she turned the wheel to avoid an oncoming tanker. Zeb slunk in beside her, flipped open the folding chair, and sat carefully. She gave his taut expression a curious glance.

"What's eating you?" she said.

Zeb left a long pause, which Krista didn't break. He would speak when he was ready. She wouldn't pry it out of him, since he'd made it clear that he was his own man. He could ask if he needed her help—she wouldn't offer something that wasn't wanted.

"What do you remember about my mum's sickness?" he said.

Krista's stomach tightened as if in a vise, and she could hardly breathe. So, he had noticed. She had hoped to spare him the knowledge for a while longer. What use was knowing if he couldn't do anything to stop the illness' progression?

"You put it together," she whispered. He stiffened beside her.

"What do you mean? What do you know?"

Krista heaved a sigh before she spoke.

"I remember your mum swimming all the time near the end, multiple times a day, for ages at a time. Dad used to catch jellyfish for her and dry them out with that dehydrator. He kept it in the garage so you wouldn't see and ask questions. I only found it when I was looking for Christmas decorations." Krista didn't look at Zeb to gauge his reaction, but instead plowed ahead. "She came over faint a lot, but she never wanted you to see, so I took you to another room when it happened. That cream you found, I don't know what she used it for, but it was always on her night table." Krista drew another shuddering breath, then released it with a sharp exhalation. She didn't look at Zeb, couldn't look at Zeb.

He was silent beside her for a long time.

"Is there any point?" he said finally, his voice hoarse. "In seeing a doctor?"

"I don't know," Krista said. "It didn't help your mum, and I doubt they've been researching her symptoms in the meantime. I don't know, Zeb. I don't know what to do."

An ache in her fingers made her look down. The knuckles were white with their death-grip on the wheel. She loosened her hands and shook them out, one at a time.

"If there are no answers on land," Zeb said softly. "Then there might be answers with my mum's people. I have to find them, Krista."

"I know." She blinked a few times then finally risked a glance at him. His jaw was tight, but his eyes determined. Krista nodded. If Zeb could still hold onto hope, then so could she. "What can I do?"

Zeb drummed his fingers on the dash with his eyes on the sea ahead and his brow creased.

"Take the notebook," he said, his pale eyes on hers once more. "We need to know what it says."

"I can't translate it," she said in protest, then the solution came to her. "But I can read it aloud and send you the audio."

"Yes," he breathed. "Exactly. We need to know whatever Dad did, whatever he was hiding. He knew way more than he ever let on. And, if we're quick enough, maybe we can get some answers."

Quick enough. The words hit Krista like a slap to the face. How fast would Zeb worsen?

Zeb stood, then he turned to Krista with a concerned expression.

"Don't tell Corrie, okay? I don't want her looking at me like…" He trailed off.

Krista nodded grimly.

"I won't say anything. And put the book in my bag. I'll do everything I can to get to the bottom of this, if it's the last thing I do."

TRIP

Trip pulled the hood of her raincoat closer around her head. The wind threatened to blow it off, which would expose her hair to the rain that pattered on the sea by the dock where she stood. She didn't mind getting wet—she wasn't that fussy—but the bedraggled wet-rat look could wait until after Jules saw her again. Impressions were important.

She had been surprised at Corrie's phone call but interested to see how the device worked in action, now that she had figured it out. She was done with Vancouver, anyway. The city in the summer sun was a joy, but in driving rain was simply dismal. She might as well be working if she couldn't enjoy the beach.

She was just as happy not to take the ferry, with its line-ups, endless waiting, and militant rows of chairs. It always worked out that some sniveling kid was yelling over the music of her headphones in the seat in front of her. No, another journey on the *Clicker* suited her just fine.

Jules was a bonus. Trip let a slow smile creep over her face. She wouldn't fight it, when another opportunity to see him again was dropped in her lap. She liked to embrace whatever the fates threw her way, and she had no issue embracing Jules. The thought made her smile wider.

Her eyes scanned the sea past a rocky breakwater and narrowed when they spotted a blue fishing vessel. Yes, there was the *Clicker*, fighting valiantly through the waves toward the harbor. Trip's smile fizzled, and she dug into her bag for the seasickness medication she'd bought as soon as Corrie had called. Jules' home remedy had worked wonders last time, but she needed the big guns to deal with this wave action.

The *Clicker* came around the breakwater and stopped crashing unpleasantly through every crest. Trip swallowed then steeled herself. She could do this. The drugs would work.

She was going to have a great time with her friends and potential flame. Her stomach wasn't going to get in the way of an excellent journey across the strait.

As the boat drew closer, a familiar figure stood at the ready on the deck. Trip's brave grimace turned into a real grin. Jules pushed floppy hair out of his eyes and waved at her enthusiastically, and she nearly laughed aloud. He was like an eager puppy, so happy to see her and excited to show it. It kindled a warmth in her belly that no rain could dampen.

Trip lifted her hand and wiggled her fingers in a small wave. Once the boat had drifted into dock and Jules had leaped down with practiced motions and secured the lines, he loped toward her.

"Hi," he said breathlessly. He pulled up short when he drew near, clearly wondering how to greet her.

"Hi, yourself," she said in a neutral tone to tease him. "Can you grab my bag?"

His face fell at her coolness, and Trip relented. She couldn't let him hang too long, so when he grabbed her bag she leaned forward, cupped the back of his head, and delivered a long, deep kiss.

He responded fervently, and Trip eventually had to draw back.

"As much as I would like to continue this conversation," she said. "It's really wet out here. Can I come aboard?"

Jules' eyes were dreamy, but he made a visible effort to focus and grinned at her.

"Your chariot awaits. I made some special tea for you. It's a wild ride out there."

Trip reached into her bag, sliding her hand over his side as she did so. His stomach clenched under her accidentally-on-purpose touch, and she smiled inside. Her hand plucked out the seasickness medication to wave in front of his face.

"I'll drink your tea to cover all the bases, but I planned ahead. I hope you have a good meal in the works for tonight."

Jules' smile was genuine and infectious, and Trip kissed him again, quickly, just to taste that happiness on her own lips.

CORRIE

Corrie gave Trip a hug after Krista had left and she entered the galley, despite her soaking raincoat.

"Trip! I'm so glad you could come. Come in, take off your coat. Jules, where's that tea you made? You'll need it when we get moving. That was good thinking, bringing a raincoat in June. It was so sunny when we left Victoria."

Trip pulled out the amplifier from her bag, and Corrie paused her words.

"Is this what you were looking for?" Trip said with a teasing smile. "Where's the rest of it? I can put the device together now, before it gets too rough. It will only take a minute."

"Yes!" Corrie looked over at Zeb. "Where is the new sonar device?"

Zeb wordlessly passed it to Trip. He shrugged sheepishly when he caught Corrie's inquisitive glance.

"I'm eager to see it fixed," he said.

Without another word, Trip sat on the bench and pulled both pieces toward her. She eased them together, then with a screwdriver plucked from a side pouch of her bag, she screwed them tightly. With a few twists of loose wires, the connections were complete.

"Mmm, I should keep a screwdriver in my purse," Corrie said quietly. "Right next to my keys and lip chap."

Trip snorted.

"It's come in handy more times than you'd think. And, come on, if Adrianna can keep sedatives in her bag, I can carry a screwdriver around. You probably have fish food in yours."

Corrie laughed.

"No, but it's a good idea. Maybe some dried jellyfish for the strolias, just in case."

Zeb shifted beside her but said nothing. Corrie remembered

that he liked the strange snack as well. He stared at Trip's deft fingers until she held up the completed device.

"There you are," Trip said. "In working order once more. You should probably test it to make sure."

Corrie glanced at Zeb, who looked at her with the same expression of anticipation.

"You think?" she said.

He nodded and turned to Jules.

"We need to get gas. Can you fill up while Corrie and I test the device?"

"What, are you two going swimming?" Trip stared at them with incomprehension. "There's a gale out there, in case you haven't noticed. It's freezing, and there are whitecaps everywhere."

"The gas station is behind the breakwater," Zeb said quickly. "And we'll only be a minute."

"I have to try it out," Corrie said. She had to know if it worked at greater range, and they had worked on their dictionary for the past hour. She had memorized at least ten "phrases" and was desperate to try them out on a real creature. She only hoped they could summon a strolia, and not a brigar or ligan. "I need to know that it works."

"Your ice bath," Trip said with a shake of her head. "I'm staying on the dry boat. Jules and I will keep warm."

She threw Jules a glance at this comment, and Corrie was amused to see Jules flush and grin. He had been noticeably low since Trip had left, and it was nice to see him happy again.

Trip followed Jules to the wheelhouse, while Zeb went outside to untie the *Clicker* and Corrie went to change into her swimsuit. There was another reason she was so eager to jump in the ocean again, despite the unappealing steel gray of the water that promised bone-shattering cold.

She pulled off her sweater and remembered Zeb's words from pizza night at her house. His low, smooth voice had slid into her ears with seductive ease, speaking of the wonders of diving without scuba gear. She couldn't shake the draw that his words had instilled in her. Now that she'd been down a few times herself, without tank or dry suit or regulator for air, she understood a little of what he had said and wanted a bigger taste. It was uncomfortable to hold her breath, it made her colder than she'd ever been in her life, and the water was too murky to see very far, but she couldn't let go of the longing to try it again. And now that she could communicate with the creatures below, she couldn't wait to jump in.

Corrie wrapped a towel around herself and hurried out of her cabin when the dock slid past her window. Zeb met her in the hallway.

"We'll stay in here until we know where the attendant is," he said. "Then we can climb down the ladder quickly without anyone seeing. We'll have about five minutes before Jules has to move the boat."

"I won't last longer than that," Corrie assured him. "Way too cold."

Zeb gave her a half-smile.

"Of course. That's fine. If it works, it should work quickly." His smile traveled to his eyes. "Do you think you can keep the shrieking to a minimum when we jump in?"

Corrie whacked him on his upper arm then laughed.

"I'll do my best. It's near impossible, though. Hey, can you handle hot water, if cold is fine for you? What temperature do you shower at?"

Corrie was genuinely interested in the mechanism by which Zeb could withstand the cold, but as soon as the words left her mouth, they sounded suggestive to her ears, especially given their current state of undress. Zeb didn't appear to react, which made it easier to keep her own countenance solemn. Zeb shook his head.

"I don't mind the warmth for a while. I'm not a big fan of hot tubs, but a warm shower feels good." He looked out the window when the engine spluttered into silence, and a shout of greeting drifted through the open doorway. "It's time."

Corrie let Zeb go first to scout for any onlookers, but the pounding rain had driven everyone indoors. Corrie was tempted to let it do the same to her when she felt fat drops splat on her bare shoulders, but she steeled herself for the plunge. It was only going to get worse before it got better, so she needed to grit her teeth and accept it.

Zeb quietly placed the ladder over the edge with a minimum of clanging. With one more glance around, he shed his towel and swung himself over the side to clamber down the ladder with the new sonar device in one hand. His torso immediately dripped with rivulets of rain. Corrie shook her head at the path her thoughts were taking her.

"Get your head in the game," she whispered to herself. She tucked her towel under an overhang, yanked her mask onto her head, and followed Zeb over the edge.

The breakwater stopped the worst of the waves, but it still wasn't what Corrie would classify as calm seas. Before she reached the final rung of the ladder, frigid water splashed over her calves with biting intensity. She bit her tongue to avoid yelping at the pain signals that her frozen nerves were sending her.

"It's easier just to jump in." Zeb's voice was pitched low to avoid carrying to the attendant, but she could hear him clearly enough. "So I've heard."

"Don't be a jerk," Corrie gasped. She took a deep breath to work up her courage. When that failed, she tried another one then mentally berated herself and deliberately let go of the ladder to force her entry.

If jumping in was easier, then she didn't want to feel the pain of a gradual entry. Sharp knives attacked every part of her skin with equal ferocity. Her head instantly tightened in a vise of discomfort. She kicked to the surface and took a gasping breath. Her lungs wanted to scream out in agony, but she forced herself to hold onto the last rung of the ladder and draw in shallow breaths, one after another. She glanced at Zeb, who tread water next to her with concern in his face.

"It's never going to get comfortable," she panted. "We might as well go now."

"If you're sure," he said. "Deep breath, don't forget."

Corrie let out a huff of incredulous laughter—her lungs had no intention of expanding in this temperature—but she tried a few experimental breaths to prepare. Zeb sunk below the surface. Corrie took one final breath, trying to fill up her entire torso, then followed him.

The howling wind shut off like it had a mute button and was replaced by the muffled stillness of underwater. Despite the cold, Corrie's heartrate slowed at the reduction of sound and movement. Waves rocked her gently instead of splashing in her face, and the deeper she sank, the less she felt them. It was dark under there without the sun to send shafts of light into the depths, but it was a moody dimness, not a frightening one.

Zeb waited for her in mid-water. He held out his arm to her, and she grabbed it briefly to steady herself. He nodded to the side, where a single strolia swam in circles while watching Zeb. Corrie pointed at Zeb's chest to ask if he were humming, and he nodded.

She let go of his arm and took the device he presented to her. It was fastened with zip ties to a Velcro strap that was long enough to go around her waist, and she attached it around her middle, rather proud of her inventiveness. She looked at Zeb's pale eyes, clear without a mask in the way, and he nodded toward it.

There was no time to argue—Corrie could feel the breath in her lungs like a timer ticking down to zero—so she set the device to the "I am a friend" signal and pressed the button.

Within a few seconds, the strolia swam closer and stayed there. Encouraged, Corrie tried the "let's play" signal. The strolia responded by swimming upside down and in a circle. Corrie grinned with delight and looked at Zeb, whose eyes were bright with joy. He flipped in midwater and swam in a circle, perfectly copying the strolia. Corrie held a hand over her mouth to keep her laughter from releasing precious bubbles of air.

Corrie didn't want to stop this—she wanted to do somersaults like Zeb, too—but the cold still knifed through her skin and her lungs were starting to burn. They had a job to do, and she wouldn't leave without completing it. Her fingers twisted the correct dials for the "danger" signal, and she pressed the button.

Both Zeb and the strolia stiffened. A second later, the fish darted away and disappeared in the gloom. Zeb lost his smile, but he nodded at the device's success. He made the scuba diving signal for "up" and Corrie gladly kicked to the surface. She barely had enough breath, but she didn't need Zeb's help making it to air, so she must be getting better at gauging the oxygen she had left.

Zeb's head emerged from the waves a moment after she gasped to the surface. The ladder was far enough away that she needed to swim, which wasn't easy. Her limbs were heavy and sluggish from a lack of circulating blood. Zeb must have seen her flailing attempt at swimming, for he swam underneath her, wrapped her arms around his neck, and kicked to the ladder in a few swift strokes. When she let go to grasp the ladder, she had a fleeting moment of regret that she wasn't still clutching Zeb's solid body.

Trip ran out when Corrie climbed stiffly over the side of the boat. She wrapped a towel around her friend and dragged her to her sleeping cabin.

"I can't believe you keep doing that," Trip said as she helped Corrie dress. Corrie's fumbling fingers were more of a hindrance than a help. "You're not Zeb, you know. Hypothermia is a real thing."

"I'm becoming aware," Corrie said between chattering teeth. "I'd kill for a hot drink right now."

"Luckily, the sane members of this boat are way ahead of you. Come on, Jules has something in the galley."

When Corrie was safely ensconced on the bench, wrapped in a blanket with a steaming mug of tea before her, Trip squeezed in beside her and folded her in a hug.

"Someone has to keep you warm," she said.

Zeb wandered in, wrapped in a towel and rubbing his wet hair. At the sight of Corrie in Trip's arms, a frustrated look briefly passed over his face. Corrie wondered what it was caused by.

"Why the long face?" she said. "We figured out the danger signal. We can scare away the creatures now."

Zeb smiled. He was handsome in repose, but he suited happy.

"Yeah, we did. Let's get to the cage and install it."

JULES

Jules wiped his hands on a tea towel and spoke to Zeb.

"I talked to the gas attendant. We can stay here until we're ready to go. There's another spot to tie up, and it's always quiet when it's raining."

"Okay." Zeb looked out the window. "We should get going soon, though. The weather's only getting worse. Let me get changed and cleaned up, check the currents, then we can head out."

"Aye aye," said Jules. Zeb ducked out of the galley into the hallway. Trip and Corrie were still huddled together on the bench, but Corrie's color was back, and she'd stopped shaking.

"You're looking warmer," he said to her. "I guess Trip's hugs are good at making people feel better."

He glanced at Trip and was rewarded by an arch look.

"Wouldn't you like to know," she said.

Jules was about to reply when movement out the window caught his eye. He peered closer.

"Who is out in this weather?" he said in bafflement. "Other than crazies like us." He narrowed his eyes as the figure loading a nearby motorboat with supplies turned its hooded face toward him. "It's the woman from the cage. Britta something."

"What?" Corrie scrambled to the window. After a moment, she cursed. "There she is. Are they going to the cage again?"

"Looks like it," Jules said.

They watched Britta heaving boxes from her cart into the boat. Jules squirmed. Surely there was an opportunity here.

"Their boat is right there. There has to be something we can do." He sighed. "But, what? It's not like I can knock her out or something. The boat is right there, and there's nothing I can do. Totally useless."

Jules was so pathetic. He could feel it in every pore, the

futility of everything he tried. There was a golden opportunity here, and he was squandering it because he couldn't think of anything clever to do, and he didn't have any abilities that would count for anything. Britta and the boat would roar away, and he would lose another chance.

He felt Corrie's inquisitive gaze on his face, and he turned to look at her. She tilted her head in question.

"I hope you don't believe that you're useless," she said. "You need to give yourself more credit, even if others don't always." Corrie's eyes narrowed, and Jules wondered if she were thinking about Krista, like he was. "What do you want to do? How can you change this situation, using the skills you have?" She lifted a finger to point at him. "And don't go saying you don't have any skills. We all know that's not true."

Jules turned away from Corrie's too-clear gaze and rested his eyes on Britta once more. His sluggish brain churned over the possibilities. It was kind of Corrie to say he had something to contribute, but she didn't really know. He wasn't good for much.

Britta loaded the last box into the boat and paused for a moment, perhaps to catch her breath. Then she leaned over the outboard motor and pulled out the gas gauge. Apparently satisfied, she screwed it into place before trundling the cart back up the dock.

A ghost of a notion flitted through Jules' mind.

"I might have an idea," he said slowly. As soon as the words left his tongue, he regretted them. "I don't know if I can do it in time, though. It probably won't work."

"I bet it will," Corrie said. "I know you have it in you to jump in when we need you. Remember when you grabbed the cleaning lady on Kurina Island? You didn't think, you just did it. That was brave. You can do it again. Just don't think too hard about it."

Jules wavered for a moment with indecision. Trip and Corrie remained silent while he watched Britta turn at the end of the dock.

If he didn't do this now, he would chastise himself for weeks for not manning up when his friends needed him. And Trip was watching. What would she think of him if he chickened out now? He didn't have much to offer. He didn't know why she was interested in him anyway. If he could bolster his image in her eyes, and help his friends at the same time, then that was a risk worth taking.

Jules wriggled off the bench.

"Corrie, do you have any tubing that I could use?"

Thirty seconds later, Jules jumped onto the dock with a roll of tubing and a gas can in one hand. He pulled the hood of his raincoat over his head, which had the dual benefit of hiding his face from watchers as well as keeping him dry.

He walked with purposeful strides down the gas station jetty, past another alley, and down the dock where Britta's boat was tied. It wasn't the *Calypso*, but he was sure she had loaded gear into this boat. He glanced around, but no one was in sight. The parking lot was hidden behind many boats and an administrative building. Jules knew he had only minutes to complete his task, if he were lucky, so he quickly leaped aboard and leaned over the motor. His nimble fingers twisted the gas cap off in moments, and he stuck the end of Corrie's tubing into the tank.

He set the gas can on the deck and crouched beside it. Corrie's tubing was clear, and as he sucked the end of the tubing, the gas visibly traveled up the loop and flowed toward his open mouth. Just in time, he shoved the end into his gas can and listened to the splash of liquid with satisfaction.

When his can was halfway full, his phone beeped with a text. He pulled it out of his pocket. The message was from Trip.

She's coming.

Jules' heart gave a jolt, and he yanked the end of the tubing from the motor. With trembling fingers, he screwed the cap back on, rolled up his tubing, and heaved the gas can off the boat.

There was nowhere to go on the dead-end dock. He would have to pass Britta and her cart if he wanted to escape. Jules pulled his hood low on his head and tucked the stinky tubing under his arm, where it might not catch Britta's attention. He hoped his gas can could be explained by the gas station nearby, although why he would be hauling a can instead of driving his boat up to the station was inexplicable.

Jules' long legs carried him swiftly down the dock, but the rumbling of a cart grew steadily louder. He ducked his head low. Britta had seen him clearly when he and Corrie had pretended to be a vacationing couple fishing for the day. If she caught sight of his face, there would be no hiding.

"Excuse me," a voice rang out. Jules jumped and stood clear of the cart while keeping his face low. The wheels of the cart rolled past his feet without stopping. When Britta turned onto the dock where her boat was tied, Jules let out his breath in a long sigh. His legs wobbled, but he forced himself to walk with measured steps toward the *Clicker*.

On board, he tucked the gas can out of harm's way and gave himself a moment to lean against the cabin wall and let his hammering heart return from thundering to merely agitated. One big breath later, he entered the cabin and made his way to the galley, where Trip and Corrie had retreated.

"Did you do it?" Corrie blurted out when he made his appearance. Jules lifted his hands with mock dismay.

"Did you doubt me?"

"Never," said Trip firmly. She walked over to him and whispered in his ear, "Stop being so sexy. You're getting me all worked up."

Jules couldn't help his wide grin. He was proud of himself for taking the leap, if only to prove to himself that he wasn't entirely useless. But Trip's reaction, that was the icing on the cake.

He loved a good cake.

ZEBALLOS

Zeb finished checking the charts to plan their best approach to the cage, then he walked to the galley.

"Can you grab the lines, Jules? We're ready to leave."

"Zeb," Corrie called out. "The researchers are leaving, too."

"What?" Zeb raced to the window in the galley and looked out. Sure enough, Alistair and Britta were puttering out of the marina in the *Calypso*, bundled up against the rain but looking determined despite it.

His chest burned with anger at the sight, the two looking smug and untouchable. He didn't want them to get their grasping hands on another creature. It was more important than ever to install the new sonar device and destroy the cage once more. Maybe, if he were persistent, they would finally get the message. His rational side objected, but his angry side roared in approval.

He looked at Corrie. This wasn't his decision to make—it was hers. And after looking at the charts and doing some quick calculations, Zeb had an unwelcome truth for her.

"We can chase them and set up the device," he said. "But if we do, we won't have enough time to go up north."

Zeb clenched his jaw as he waited for Corrie's answer. He wanted to follow the boat without a thought for anyone else, but this was Corrie's cruise that he'd promised her, and already she'd given up so much sampling time for the creatures.

Corrie closed her eyes. When she spoke, her voice was quiet.

"This cruise is a once-in-a-lifetime opportunity for me to get data that would elevate my science project from decent to game-changing. My hypothesis is sound and going north would give me the evidence I need to move forward." She opened her warm brown eyes and gazed into his. "But I won't stand by when our creatures are being hunted, mistreated, and dissected. We need to stop this."

Zeb's heart swelled at the determination in Corrie's voice.

"Then we'd better get moving," he said with crisp finality. "Get the lines, Jules."

When the boat was moving, the others squeezed into the wheelhouse with Zeb and watched rain splatter against the window. Once they passed the breakwater, the storm hit them hard. The *Clicker* rocked up and down and slammed against every wave with a jarring thud. Waves crashed over the bow and sprayed the window until the wipers could hardly keep up. Zeb gritted his teeth and pushed the boat faster. It was a tough old vessel. It had handled worse.

Trip looked nervous but wasn't throwing up yet, so that was a blessing. Zeb didn't feel like scrubbing the wheelhouse today. Corrie gripped the dash with white knuckles and winced with every thundering crash against the waves. Jules didn't look overly agitated—he'd been in worse weather, just like Zeb—but he looked concerned about what awaited them at their destination.

For the most part, they were silent as they fought through the storm across the strait. When they drew nearer to the bay where Alistair and Britta had set the cage, Zeb slowed.

"Jules, take the wheel. Anchor in the neighboring bay, as out of the wind as you can. I'm going to mess with their cage for starters. We can install the device later, when we have more time."

Corrie's mouth opened, but he didn't give her time to protest. He pushed an unresisting Jules toward the wheel and slid past Trip into the hallway. He shed his clothes with practiced effortlessness and threw them into his open cabin, then raced to the life ring where he stored his flippers. After a moment's hesitation, he grabbed a wrench from the toolbox inside the lab door.

The boat's movements would have made anyone else

stumble, but he'd been traveling on the *Clicker* since he was a child and could maneuver a tossing deck in his sleep. The air outside was thick with salt spray and smelled divine to Zeb. He didn't wait for a steady moment, instead launching himself over the edge in a frantic dive.

The smell of the sea transformed into the taste of salt on his lips. His frenzy calmed into a deep sense of purpose. He would get to the cage and destroy it right after they set it up. Then he would have a whole day to install the sonar device so that no creatures would get caught ever again and the researchers would be none the wiser. They had a plan, and it was a good one. It was up to him to carry out the first step.

The distant roar of a motorboat startled Zeb, and he paused to listen. Were Alistair and Britta repositioning their boat in the storm? Another roar, distinct from the first, made him frown. Who would be out in this weather?

He shook his head and resumed his progress toward the cage. It didn't matter what was happening up there. He had a mission that needed completing. He angled his body to swim deeper, out of the incessant pull of wave action that affected him even at this depth. The storm was whipping up into a decent one, strange for this time of year. He hoped Jules managed to find a safe place to anchor.

Another roar started. Three boats out in this weather? What was going on? One of the rumbles drew near, so Zeb cast his senses in its direction. Two disturbances in the water below the boat made him pause. If he wasn't mistaken, there were two scuba divers in the water. Why would anyone be diving in a storm? At least they had propellers, judging from the speed at which they were traveling. That would help if they were trapped by the waves.

If people were willing to risk their lives diving in this weather, that was their lookout. Zeb has his mission. He undulated his body faster, in a direct line to the cage, with the wrench tight in his grasp. The researchers wouldn't capture a creature, not today.

CORRIE

Corrie stared, flabbergasted, as Zeb threw himself over the edge of the boat. She turned to the others. Jules had his mouth set in a tight line as he navigated the increasingly stormy waters. Trip stared back at her with a bewildered expression.

"What the hell?" Corrie said. "What was the rush?"

"He got angry," Jules said absently. "When he saw the boat. He wanted to save his fish."

"Yeah, but there's plenty of time." Corrie frowned. "How could you tell he was angry?"

Jules shrugged.

"I don't know, he goes kind of tense, and quiet."

"More quiet than usual?" Trip said. Jules' mouth quirked.

"Yeah. The tells are there, they're just subtle."

"Okay, fine." Corrie felt miffed that Zeb had taken off, but she would get over it. At least he was safe from the storm under the water. She was more nervous about the *Clicker*.

Jules, to his credit, steered them expertly into the moderately calm bay, which was sheltered from the wind by a peninsula of land. With some panicked help from Corrie, he managed to anchor the vessel. When the engine was off, the three of them stood, panting, in the wheelhouse.

"Come on," said Jules at last. "Nothing more we can do here. Might as well get a late lunch going."

Trip followed Jules into the hallway with her hands on the walls as the boat tipped and rolled. Corrie glanced in the direction of the cage. The buoy wasn't visible from their vantage behind the point, but it wasn't far around. The sight of another motorboat made her frown.

"What's another boat doing out here?" she said loudly. Trip and Jules joined her at the door, and they watched the motorboat bobbing like a child's toy in the water. As they watched, two scuba divers with propellers jumped overboard.

In the distance, another boat appeared, with two more divers.

"I recognize those boats," Jules said. When Corrie turned to look at him, his face was pale. "They were right next to the researchers' boat. They must be together."

The answer fell into place in Corrie's head. Her stomach dropped at the realization.

"They knew we were coming," she whispered. "It's an ambush."

"Zeb's still down there," said Trip with a worried frown. "Do you think they'll find him?"

"I don't know, but it wouldn't be good if they did," said Jules.

"We need to warn him," said Corrie. Her brain spun in a frenzy of ideas and half-baked plans, each wilder than the next. The most likely one slotted into place, and she snapped her fingers. "Where's the new sonar device? I'll warn him. That amplifier works great. I bet he'll be able to hear the signal loud and clear."

"I'll put down the ladder," said Jules, and he raced off.

Trip rushed to the galley and returned with the device. Corrie grabbed it.

"I turn this," she murmured. "And right here, plus a click. Okay, that should say "danger." Let's give it a try."

Corrie tucked the device under her arm and lurched down the hall toward the aft deck, where Jules waited next to the ladder. He held out a lifejacket.

"Since Zeb's not here to save you if you fall," he said. "It's rough out there."

Corrie peered over the edge with a firm grip on the railing. She swallowed. The ladder rose and fell three rungs with every wave. She nodded her thanks to Jules, her throat dry, and slid the lifejacket over her coat. Rain pelted her face and ran in rivers down her hair, but she wrapped the device's Velcro strap around her arm and held on with whitened fingers to the rungs of the ladder.

When the first wave struck her leg, she hissed at the cold. She gritted her teeth and stepped down another rung, then pressed the button on the device and reached down as far as she could into the water.

Her breath came in a fast pant as she tried to manage her fear and coldness. How long should she let the signal repeat? Would Zeb notice it?

"I see his head," Jules yelled. "He heard!"

"But the boat is between him and us," Trip shouted over the wind. "Do they have a net?"

"He doesn't know there are divers," Corrie yelled. "How can we warn him about that?"

"Bring him back to the boat," Jules shouted. "With the device!"

Corrie hauled the device up and turned dials with shaking fingers to signal "come." She tried to ignore the waves that crashed into her and soaked her from her waist down. She held the device underwater again.

She would hold it there for as long as she could manage before her freezing fingers slipped off the ladder. Would Zeb hear the call? Would he be able to escape the divers before they saw him? Corrie's teeth chattered from cold and fear.

Then, she saw it. A lone strolia rode a wave near her, drawn to the siren call of the device. Her frantic brain worked overtime, and she gasped when a thought struck her. Would it work? Could she afford not to try?

She climbed down one more rung and waited with her hand out. The strolia passed again, closer this time. She waited some more, her hand trembling. The strolia appeared again, and Corrie knew it was now or never. Slowly, gently, she reached toward the fish. With one swift movement, she jabbed her hand out and wrapped it around the horn of the strolia.

The fish flopped in a spasm of terror, but Corrie lifted it out of the water. She hooked her arm around the ladder's rung and used her hand to grab the wildly thrashing tail. With a grimace of distaste, Corrie opened her mouth, stuck out her tongue, and licked the fish from tail to slimy gills.

She threw the strolia out as far as she could to avoid the poisonous horn and hoped fervently that a brigar wouldn't decide to make an unwelcome appearance.

"What the hell are you doing?" Trip screamed above her. Corrie looked up.

"Helping Zeb. Grab me my flippers, mask, and dry suit."

Jules disappeared without a word. Corrie looked at her outstretched fingers. They weren't trembling anymore. In fact, she didn't feel cold at all. Was that another side effect of the strolia slime? She'd meant to give herself speed and strength underwater, but not feeling the cold was a welcome bonus. She wriggled out of her pants, lifejacket, and coat. They would only add drag to her body, and she needed all the speed she could get. She tossed them up to Trip, who looked too bewildered to say a word. There were no hallucinations, which Corrie credited to the fact that she was partly in the water. There was no point in tempting fate by emerging and seeing flying spiders or whatever her brain would dream up.

Jules reappeared with her requested items. She held up her hand to catch them.

"Just my flippers and mask, Jules," Corrie called out. "Apparently, strolia slime turns people into Zeb in the water. I'm going to find him and warn him."

"We'll follow in the dinghy," he shouted back.

"Be careful!" Trip said, then they disappeared.

Corrie awkwardly fitted on her flippers and mask, strapped the device around her waist, then took three steadying breaths. One last breath, then she clamped her mouth shut and let go of the ladder. All she had was the sonar device, the strolia slime coursing through her body, and her wits. She hoped it was enough to find Zeb and bring him to safety.

Corrie swiftly paddled below the waves. Once she was deep enough, she let her flippers do the work.

It was amazing. The water felt cool, almost too cool to be completely comfortable, but eons away from the biting pain she was used to. She sliced through the water with ease, and it wasn't only because of her flippers. Her legs felt stronger, as if the water held less resistance than usual. It was an incredible experience, and Corrie understood Zeb's desire to swim better than before.

She couldn't dwell on it, though. She had to find Zeb and tell him about the divers so he could escape. She didn't know what the end goal of the ambush was, but letting them capture Zeb wasn't a good idea. At best, they would haul him in for damage of personal property. At worst, they would study or interrogate him to find out what he was using to gain his abilities. Zeb insisted that he wasn't taking strolia slime, and Corrie had almost been convinced that he was telling the truth, but now that she felt the effects, she had a hard time believing it. The researchers would be keen to test long-term reactions to the slime, if nothing else. Maybe the people from his mother's stories ingested strolia slime constantly to survive so much exposure to the ocean.

Her lungs burned. If Zeb were taking the enhancer, then either he had really practiced his breath-holding, or he was using another substance to increase his lung capacity. She pointed her body skyward. The surface of the water roiled like a shaken pool of mercury. She burst through the barrier, gulped a deep breath, and looked around to orient herself. The nearest boat was straight ahead.

She sunk below the waves again, hoping the driver hadn't spotted her. This time, she needed to turn on the device. If she signaled "come," would Zeb get the message? There was only one way to find out. She pressed the button and struck out toward the boat once more.

She swam for less than a minute before a figure loomed out of the dimness. She let out a bubble of distress and stopped short, but it was only Zeb. She rushed forward and hugged him fiercely. He clutched her tightly and drew her to the surface. She followed, unresisting.

When they could speak, Zeb shook his head in disbelief.

"What are you doing, Corrie? It's too cold for you."

"I licked a strolia," she said. His face cleared with understanding. She frowned to let him know that she thought he had, too, and his expression clouded as he understood her accusation toward him. "We can talk about it later. We need to get out of the water. There are divers everywhere, with propellers. We can't let them see us. That's why I came to get you."

"We should go under, then." He glanced at the boat when they rose on a wave crest. Without another word, he sank below a trough, and Corrie followed.

At a depth low enough to avoid wave action, Zeb took her hand firmly in his and drew her in the direction of the *Clicker*. She kicked beside him, anxious to get aboard and put this fiasco behind her.

Zeb stopped in midwater. His face, so expressive underwater, registered confusion and fear. Corrie's stomach dropped, and she scanned the water before them. What had he seen?

A high-pitched whine drifted past her ears. Immediately after, a diver emerged from the murk. He held a propeller in one hand and a long speargun in the other. Without hesitation, he aimed at Corrie and fired.

Zeb thrust sideways in a flurry of motion, dragging Corrie with him. The spear sailed harmlessly past. Zeb let go of her hand and raced toward the diver with rage in his eyes. The diver scrambled to reel in the spear cord and reload the gun, but Zeb kicked forward with powerful strokes of his legs. He was only a handspan away when the diver turned on his propeller and zoomed out of sight.

Another whine made Corrie's head turn. She looked frantically into the darkness. Out of nowhere, another diver roared straight at her, speargun at the ready. She squeaked—unnoticed but for a bubble released from her mouth—and dived sideways.

The diver zoomed past but continued to train his gun at her. A flash of anger filled her brain. They couldn't just come and start shooting at any random swimmer. For all they knew, she was totally innocent. Whatever happened to sitting down and discussing their differences?

She kicked toward the diver in a zigzag pattern to stay unpredictable. She ignored the low hum that began to vibrate in her ears. When the diver looked ready to fire, she dived down and immediately shot upward, straight to his propeller. Her unnaturally powerful motions sent her careening into the machine, knocking it from the diver's grasp and sending it sinking to the seafloor.

Satisfaction filled Corrie, until she glanced at the diver. He looked frightened but determined. The speargun pointed directly at her stomach.

She watched the diver's finger close on the trigger with dreamy detachment, as if he moved in slow motion. She gathered her limbs for a great push upward but knew it was too late. The best she could hope for was that the spear would avoid vital organs. In the stretchy vastness of time while she tried to move and the diver pulled the trigger, she wondered vaguely how her life had led to this moment of underwater battle for legendary sea creatures.

An immense head crashed into the diver. Corrie had an impression of dark green scales and unfathomable length before she was bowled over by the pressure wave of the creature's passing. Was it an eel? A massive snake? Corrie's head cleared as she pulled herself out of an uncontrolled somersault and kicked her way to the surface.

Her brain finally clued in that a ligan had saved her. Zeb's giant sea serpent was here. Corrie fought for air at the surface, her adrenaline-soaked body and pounding heart needing more oxygen than the stormy waves allowed her to gather. Above the howling wind and crashing waves on the nearby shore, she heard faint shouts and the incessant roar of motorboats. She had no idea what was happening up there, but there was no time to find out. Zeb was still down there, with speargun wielding divers and a terrifying ligan. Corrie was pretty sure the ligan was on their side—it had taken out her diver, after all—but still. Its mouth would easily bite through her entire torso for a snack. She needed to help Zeb.

One last breath, and she sank below the tumultuous waves. She couldn't see anything, and for a moment she panicked. Where were the divers and the ligan? Where was Zeb? The ocean was too huge to search for him. She was only one person on borrowed abilities.

Corrie fumbled with the device, still fastened to her waist by the trusty Velcro belt. She twisted dials in the signal for "come," pressed the button, and waited. Would Zeb hear her? What if he were hurt, and couldn't swim her way? She hugged herself while she tried to keep panic at bay.

A shape loomed below her and Corrie nearly screamed aloud until she recognized Zeb's white-blond hair. He sat astride the ligan, his face filled with joy and a wild light.

The ligan was even more terrifying head-on. Corrie pulled herself into a tiny ball in an instinctual attempt to appear small and inconspicuous. It didn't work, and the ligan swam right for her. Corrie closed her eyes.

An arm wrapped around her stomach and dragged her through the water at great speed. The arm gathered her in and hugged her against a torso. Scaly skin rasped her bare thighs, but the tight arm across her chest and a comforting warmth against her back held back the panic. She opened her eyes.

There was nothing but rushing darkness and the head of a horrifyingly huge serpent before her, so she turned to look behind. Zeb smiled reassuringly and squeezed his arm around her stomach. She didn't know what they were doing or where they were going, but Zeb was there, so it would be all right. They would figure it out, together.

JULES

Jules threw the toolbox into the dinghy then raced over to grab the emergency kit.

"Your friend is insane," he yelled to Trip. "What is she thinking?"

"When she knows what she wants, she won't stop until she gets it," Trip shouted back. "Should I unstrap this dinghy?"

Jules waved his agreement and darted into his cabin. He still had the slingshot he'd made to throw slime balls at the giant octopus Sucker. He wrenched open a drawer and tossed clothes aside until he unearthed it. On the way out, he grabbed rags and the gas can from beside the engine room door, then lurched outside across the tilting deck.

He tossed equipment into the dinghy and waved at Trip to stand back while he winched the vessel into the roiling water. Trip looked down with trepidation.

"We're really getting in that tiny cork?" she said.

"This is nothing," Jules said with a nonchalant gesture at the heaving water. "You should have seen the swell a few years ago. I drove this dinghy up and down mountains to get to the *Clicker*." Jules shook his head at the memory and glanced at Trip. Her eyes were wide, surrounded by dripping locks of hair while she braced herself against the railing of the boat. She looked vulnerable and uncertain, and Jules reconsidered his plan. "You should stay. It'll be dangerous."

"Forget that." As if Jules' words had lit a fire in Trip, she zipped on Corrie's lifejacket and flung herself onto the ladder. "Last one down gets to massage the other's shoulders when this stress-fest is over."

Jules grinned and followed her down the ladder. That was a contest he didn't mind losing. He unhooked the dinghy, started the engine, and they roared away from the violently rocking *Clicker*.

The dinghy was even worse. Trip held on with both hands to her bench seat, and water sprayed her face with every third wave. The little vessel shuddered as it jolted over the chop. Even though Jules knew how sturdy the boat was, it still felt like it would shatter with every impact.

"What's the plan?" Trip shouted back. Her hair dripped onto the lifejacket, but her eyes were bright with excitement. "Pick up Corrie and Zeb, or show these bastards what we've got?"

"If you see the others, we'll get them," said Jules. "But I don't know how we'll spot them in this chop, and Zeb can stay under forever."

"Plan B it is." Trip reached down and grabbed the gas can. She threw Jules a curious look. "What did you have in mind?"

Jules smiled wickedly.

"Follow my instructions. The plan might seem crazy, but don't worry—boats don't blow up as easily as the movies would have you believe."

Trip wedged herself in the bottom of the boat while Jules drove and shouted directions at her. She was clever, and Jules barely had to outline his idea before she had grasped it and started to assemble what they needed. Jules concentrated on keeping the boat upright. He peered ahead at the nearest motorboat, whose driver was throwing a buoy out of her vessel. His eyes widened as he realized what she was doing.

"They have a net," he yelled at Trip. "They're trying to catch Zeb and Corrie. We need to get the net out of the water."

Trip looked over the bow. She turned to Jules with a fierce expression.

"Then you'd better pour on the coals. I'm ready."

Trip braced herself against the bench and the hull so that her hands were free, then she loaded the slingshot with a gas-soaked rag. Jules brought them closer to the boat with the net. Trip aimed and released.

The rag dropped into the ocean. Trip cursed and loaded

against swiftly.

The next rag flew past the driver and into the boat. Trip yelled with delight and took a flare in one hand. Jules roared toward the boat while Trip struck the flare's head until it flamed with a brilliant light. She wound her arm back, waited until the dinghy was on the crest of a wave, and tossed it in a high arc.

The flare landed directly in the boat. The driver screamed with alarm, but Trip didn't hesitate. Another gas rag went into the slingshot, flew into the boat, and was followed by a third.

By the time Trip ran out of ammunition and Jules drove away, the boat was filled with flames. The driver shrieked and threw the rest of the net overboard, then she leaped to the wheel and zoomed to the nearest shore.

Jules whooped with relief and amazement.

"That was epic!" he yelled. Trip turned and shot him a wild, fierce look of pride.

"We rock," she shouted. "One boat down, three to go."

Jules looked around. One boat was still attached to the cage buoy, and another was on the other side of the bay, but the nearest boat flew over the waves toward the net left drifting in the current.

"The net," Jules called. "Let's haul it in. We don't want Zeb and Corrie getting caught in it."

"Onward!" Trip pointed to the net's buoy like a defiant figurehead. Jules gunned the engine, heedless of the waves. His heart thumped wildly in his chest, and he felt more alive than he'd ever had. Trip was right: they rocked.

They reached the net before the other boat. Trip did her best to yank the net into their dinghy, but it was heavy and slow-going. Jules wanted to help, but without his guidance into the worst of the waves, the dinghy would capsize. The other boat approached, heading directly toward them through the pounding rain.

"I can't get the net in the boat!" Trip shouted, her voice

close to panic.

Jules leaned forward and snatched another flare from the emergency kit.

"I'll do my best to hold him off. Damn it!" he said when a wave caught them almost broadside. In his distraction, he'd let the dinghy turn sideways. Trip pulled harder at the net with a grimace, but there was so much of it. Jules struck the flare against the hull, once, twice. The third time, it caught, and he squinted against its overwhelming brightness.

The roar of the other boat's engine was loud enough to drown out the wind in Jules' ears. He was a terrible shot, but there was nothing for it—he had to throw the flare. It was now or never.

He heaved it skyward. The brilliant flame arced through the air, end over end. It landed with a hiss in the remorseless ocean. Jules' stomach dropped.

The boat was almost on them. Was it planning on ramming their dinghy? With the net half in the water and causing drag, Jules couldn't drive them out of the way in time. Should they jump for it, or would that be suicide?

The other vessel's motor sputtered and died. The boat drifted to a stop and turned broadside to the waves, threatening to tip with every impact.

Jules gaped. Had this been the boat he'd siphoned gas out of?

"You saved us!" Trip shouted at him with glee, then she screamed at the other driver. "Take that, sucker!"

The other motorboat tilted sideways. Jules blinked. The waves weren't coming in that direction. An enormous, green tail whipped out of the water and slapped against the bow of the boat. It swung around until the waves were hitting it broadside and threatening to tip it into the cold ocean.

Jules' blood ran cold through his veins. The ligan was here. Jules was in a tiny dinghy with a gigantic sea serpent swimming below him. The metal hull of the little vessel now appeared woefully, laughably inadequate. Sure, it kept out water, but it could be chomped in half at any moment.

This was a mistake. Jules wasn't brave. He shouldn't be out here, battling boats and racing over terrifying sea creatures. He should be cutting lawns for pensioners and delivering pizza. He wasn't cut out for this.

The ligan bumped the boat once more, and the driver inside yelled with fright. Trip looked at Jules while she hauled the net, hand over hand.

"Is that the giant snake?" she called out. "I think it's helping us."

Jules swallowed and looked at the other boat again. The ligan was bigger than any animal had a right to be, and it was terrifying beyond measure, but Trip was right. It focused on the enemy boat, hitting it around in the water like a bath toy. Jules drew in a shaky breath then squared his shoulders.

"Let's trade places," he said to Trip. "Keep the bow pointed into the wave, and I'll haul the net in."

YARO

Yaro had been on stormier dives before, but this job was the strangest. Tellman Inc. paid him well enough that the company culture of *don't ask, don't tell* didn't usually bother him. The number of non-disclosure agreements he had signed before his first day of work had caused his hand to cramp. This was the most he would ever get paid as a commercial diver, though, so he'd massaged the kinks out and happily suited up.

They'd been briefed before they had left. Yaro still remembered the squirming feeling in his stomach when they'd been shown photos of the strange creatures. They weren't natural. Had they been bred by Tellman Inc.? He didn't ask, and they didn't volunteer the information.

If he pretended that they were just weird fish, he could ignore the greater implications. It wasn't his business to know, and that was fine. It was the other directive they had been given that bothered Yaro.

They had orders to shoot a man on sight, using spearguns. That didn't sit well with Yaro. He'd taken part in a few questionable jobs in his tenure at Tellman Inc., but they'd all fallen short of bodily harm to another person. The other divers took the news in stride, but Yaro couldn't calm his churning gut.

And who was this guy? They expected him—and possibly others like him—to be swimming in the ocean, with no thermal gear, air tanks, or any of the equipment needed to survive in these waters. How could this man achieve the impossible?

Was that why Tellman Inc. wanted him so badly?

Their orders were to bring him in alive, if possible. Injured was an acceptable outcome. Questions had burbled up in Yaro's throat at this announcement, but he had swallowed them like the good employee he was.

And now he was underwater, with a propeller for speed and

armed with a speargun the length of his leg, looking for the strange man and his friends. If Yaro did find the man, the speargun would only allow one good shot before he'd have to laboriously reload it, so he hoped his aim would be true. It would be even better if the man didn't show up at all.

He was technically diving solo, with the requisite pony tank strapped beside his regular one. He'd jumped in with a colleague, but because of low visibility and the combative nature of their assignment, they needed to be self-sufficient. Yaro was equipped with a wristband sonar device that gave a very rough indication of what was in the direction it was pointed at. It made Yaro's head ache to figure out the visual output, but he tried his best.

He kept a steady depth and held onto his propeller while he traveled a search pattern. He glanced at the monitor on his wrist occasionally, but it didn't give him anything he couldn't already see—namely, that there was nothing near him.

Maybe the man would get away, and Yaro could go home and forget this strange assignment. He would prefer that, even if they were reprimanded at work for not completing their task. He could weather that storm.

There was a blip on the screen. Yaro looked more closely. Was something swimming toward him? He tilted his wrist, trying to get a handle on what the screen was telling him. The blip bobbed in and out of sight on the screen.

Yaro rolled his eyes and looked forward. He didn't know how to trust his monitor, but he knew what his eyes saw. Slowly, slowly, a figure emerged from the gloom. It was Dirk, the diver he had entered the water with. Dirk's eyes were wide and frightened, and he gave the hand sign to swim together.

It was against protocol—they were supposed to spread out and cover as much ground as possible—but Yaro didn't mind. A buddy to dive with would alleviate some of his unease.

They fell into place beside each other. Yaro glanced at his monitor once more, out of habit, and was surprised to see another blip. Was it a fish, or seal? Or had they found the mysterious pale-haired man? Yaro tightened his grip on his speargun.

The blip traveled toward them faster than any human could. Yaro's shoulders relaxed. It must be a seal. And, soon, they would run out of air and have to surface and leave this assignment. He couldn't wait.

A seal-like shape emerged, but there was something wrong about it. It was too long and oddly colored with a squashed face. Yaro barely had time to process the seal because of the figure astride the animal's back.

A woman clung to the seal as tight as a limpet. Her long white hair and the greenish-brown strips that surrounded her like clothing flowed in ribbons beside the seal's streamlined body. Her strange, exotic face held a look of intense concentration.

Before Yaro could dodge sideways, warn Dirk, or react at all, the woman and seal barreled into Dirk. The seal bit his arm, releasing bubbles of air that expanded as they rose, and the woman yanked at the hoses of his regulator. Yaro only had time to register the panicked horror on Dirk's breathless face before the seal dragged him to the depths, out of sight.

Yaro's regulator wasn't delivering nearly enough oxygen to support his heaving breaths. He put air in his vest and rose to the surface as fast as he safely could. The woman would come back for him, he knew it. His name was the next on her list.

He filled his emergency float with air. It was an orange inflatable tube that was taller than the highest crest of this stormy sea. The longest minute of Yaro's life passed while he waited to be dragged below the surface by teeth embedded in his flipper. He took frantic glances below his feet with his speargun at the ready, but the darkness revealed nothing. The lead boat finally puttered close to him, and he waved it down.

Once he'd clambered aboard, Yaro managed to force out

his tale.

"She wasn't normal," he finished in a babble. "She's more than whatever the man is supposed to be. I'm not going back down there."

The two scientists aboard the lead boat looked at each other expressively. The man leaped to the radio. After a crackling exchange, he uttered a command.

"We need to get this one alive. Bring out the echo nets."

ZEBALLOS

When Corrie started squirming, Zeb knew it was time to bring her to the surface to breathe. He hummed to the ligan, which rose swiftly up.

The signals were flooding back to him the more he used them. Half-forgotten phrases floated from deep in his memory. Despite the divers attacking them, the ambush, all of it, his heart lifted every time he called to the ligan and it responded. It was like pieces of himself returning to him that he had forgotten he'd lost.

The air was a chaotic mess that buffeted Zeb's senses like a hurricane. Noise assaulted him, engine rumbles and screams and crashing waves and the incessant wind whistling in his wet ears. The motion of rolling whitecaps made him clutch the ligan more firmly between his legs. It stayed put, just below the surface, while Corrie gasped for oxygen. Zeb's eyes adjusted to focusing in air and he looked around.

During brief interludes when they rose high on a frothy crest, the seascape hove into view. Two boats circled in the near distance. Another was driving toward the shoreline, carrying a cargo of leaping flames. Zeb blinked at that, but his attention was drawn to his dinghy. Jules and Trip bobbed in the rollers, the dinghy threatening to tip at any moment, although Jules was a good driver and wouldn't let that happen. Trip was hauling in a long net, but the final boat raced toward them.

Zeb's eyes widened. Was it going to ram the dinghy? Anger flashed through his system. Not on his watch. He squeezed Corrie around the middle.

"Ready to go?" he said into her ear.

She nodded once. Zeb leaned to the side to put his face in the water, then he hummed his intentions. The ligan sank into the waves. Then, with a tremendous undulation of its long body, the serpent lunged forward. Zeb only barely hung on by squeezing his legs together as hard as he could, and Corrie's fingernails dug into his encircling arm.

The ligan raced toward the boat. Engine noises approached then died, and Zeb sensed the shape of the vessel above him. The ligan humped its body upward and bashed the hull against its body, right behind where Zeb and Corrie clung.

The jolt snapped Zeb off the ligan. He held onto Corrie tightly and swam down, away from the thrashing serpent. The ligan would perform its task better without them getting in the way. Jules and the dinghy were near—maybe he should take Corrie there, get her out of the water. She was doing great, thanks to the strolia slime, but it wouldn't last forever, and her breaths were still limited. She could help Trip with the net while Zeb corralled the ligan, and they could all escape this madness.

Corrie twisted in his arms and pointed with a frantic finger jab. Zeb turned his head.

A sleek creature, like an elongated seal, darted past. Zeb's heart hitched. It was a *yatull*, the steeds of his mother's stories. And astride the yatull was a figure from his dreams.

It was the pale woman he'd seen in that early morning swim, two weeks ago. Zeb would recognize her anywhere, from the ragged dress of kelp-like fronds she wore, to the dispassionate expression on her face, to her too-long feet that wrapped around the yatull's flank. He'd almost given up ever seeing her again.

She gave Zeb a brief, piercing glance, then tucked her head in to make her shape more streamlined. Zeb froze for a moment. Then, he grabbed Corrie's hand and dragged her alongside him as he swam with powerful undulations, following the pale woman.

After a moment of hesitation, Corrie's deadweight lifted as she swam beside him. Her scuba diving flippers, while huge and unwieldy, gave her extra power, and she kept up with his more experienced strokes.

Zeb didn't have any real hope at catching the woman, whose steed was many times faster than he could ever hope to be, but he was in luck. The yatull has stopped below. Zeb was elated, until he descended to where the visibility cleared and realized why.

Both the yatull and the woman were attacking a scuba diver. The man thrashed midwater in an attempt to regain his air source, but the woman was relentless. She tore his mask off and ripped away his tank. Her attack was done with an expression of pure concentration. Zeb would have understood rage better. It was as if she had a task to do, and she was methodically seeing it done.

The yatull snapped a powerful jaw around the man's thigh. His mouth opened in a silent scream with bubbles streaming out of his mouth. The seal-like creature tugged him downward, with a swift, jolting motion, the woman following behind. She threw Zeb one last, clear-eyed glance, before she disappeared into the darkness.

Corrie looked at him with horror. Zeb was sure his own face reflected her expression. She pointed up and started to swim. Zeb followed her, his mind reeling. Sure, the divers had been shooting at them. He had certainly felt angry enough to attack them, especially after they'd shot at Corrie. But the cold-blooded strike by the woman, and the yatull dragging the diver down to certain death, left him shaky and queasy.

On the surface, Corrie turned to him.

"Who the hell was that?" she gasped while treading water. A wave splashed over them and she sputtered. "Should we be worried? Or is she on our side?"

"I don't know."

Zeb didn't know anything. That's how this whole thing had started, because he was fumbling for answers in the dark. The woman might have answers, but would she be willing to give them to Zeb?

"The boat that the ligan attacked is down," Corrie said when they crested another wave. "But the other two are positioning themselves so that we're between them and the shore. What are they doing?"

"Jules and Trip are still getting the net on board," Zeb said. "Let's get the ligan and get out of here. We can pick up Jules and Trip with the *Clicker*."

Zeb sunk beneath the waves into the relative calm of the ocean, and Corrie followed. They descended until the wave action diminished, then Zeb hummed a call to the ligan. He motioned to Corrie to do the same with her device. The ligan would likely hear his sound, but it couldn't hurt to use the amplified frequency as well.

The ligan's head loomed into view, and Zeb relaxed in relief. Then, a deep, thundering sound vibrated his whole body. He curled into a fetal position, trying to protect himself from the noise that was everywhere, painful and unendurable. It thrummed through his head and chest, threatening to burst his eardrums with the pulses.

When it didn't stop, he cracked open one eye. Corrie looked at him with alarm—the sound clearly wasn't affecting her— while the ligan thrashed behind her. Corrie's signal must have gathered the nearby creatures to them, because a small school of strolias twitched in agony below them, and a kroll danced with pain to his left.

With the part of his brain that was not wholly consumed with crushing agony, Zeb wondered what was happening. The boats must be emitting a signal, something that would incapacitate their prey. Why hadn't they used it in the first place? Maybe they wanted to get him in their sights, first. Now that two of their boats were down, they needed every advantage they could get.

A strain of sound entered Zeb's conscious. It was faint, but the little he could hear was a balm for the barrage of noise that the boats emitted. He opened his eyes further and uncurled his body.

Corrie floated in midwater with the new sonar device strapped to her waist. She positioned the speaker right at Zeb, and her face spoke of nervous anticipation. Zeb realized that she must be using the calming signal, and he gave her a thankful wave. Behind her, the ligan's thrashing slowed, and the strolias and kroll appeared to be less distressed than before. The calming sound didn't stop the noise—nothing could cover the vibration that rattled Zeb's very core—but it made it bearable.

The ligan uncoiled and shot toward one of the sources of the sound. Zeb's head whipped to watch it until it disappeared into the murk, then he closed his eyes and followed the serpent's progress with his other senses.

The ligan exuded cold anger and grim determination. The boat, somehow still afloat without its engine and after its previous encounter with the giant serpent, couldn't have known what hit it. The shape of the boat disappeared from Zeb's senses, until a huge splash told him that the ligan had rammed it completely out of the ocean, where it had landed on its side, taking on water in the stormy seas.

The sound lessened enough for Zeb to function, and the creatures once held captive by the noise fled to deeper waters. Corrie swam toward the surface for a breath of air. Zeb was about to follow her when he saw a flash of white. He hesitated, then dived after it.

CORRIE

Corrie needed a breath, but what scared her more than anything was a sluggish feeling in her legs and knife stabs of cold all over her body. The strolia slime had run out, and she was stuck in the middle of a freezing storm. She surfaced and drew in a few lungfuls of air before a wave enveloped her again. At least Zeb was with her.

Zeb's head hadn't surfaced. She stuck her face into the water and peered down, but the flash of his white hair didn't materialize.

Now she was really frightened. Jules and Trip were somewhere near, but the chances of them seeing her in these waves was lower than she wanted to contemplate. Her body started to shudder, and another wave crashed over her head and left her gasping. She fumbled with the sonar device to produce a "come" signal, but after a minute was forced to admit defeat. Where was Zeb? Why wasn't he coming?

She had no dry suit, no lifejacket, and no one who knew she was there. Suddenly, her priorities shifted from helping sea creatures to saving her own life. She struck out for shore, fighting whitecaps and her leaden limbs. The trees retreated with every stroke she took, and she started to seriously panic. Was she going to die out here?

An engine's roar cut through the whistling wind in her waterlogged ears. Her heart leaped. Was she saved? Could she be so lucky?

It wasn't the dinghy, but beggars couldn't be choosers. Corrie waved frantically, and the boat headed straight for her. She wondered briefly if they meant to run her over, but the bow sliced beside her and the engine puttered to idle. A hand reached down, and she gratefully grabbed on with all her waning strength.

Corrie collapsed on the deck of the motorboat. Her head

banged against the driver's seat with every slam against the waves. She tried to hold it steady, but her body's shuddering didn't leave her enough motor control to fine-tune her movements. Britta Lawson glanced at her from her position at the wheel, and a scuba diver sat in the seat beside her. His wide eyes told Corrie that he'd seen things down below, but after he glanced at her he kept his eyes ahead.

Alistair Brown held onto the side and looked down at her from his position near the stern.

"You," he said. "It's all coming together, now. Why are you so invested in these creatures? What do you know that I don't? You might as well tell me. We'll find out sooner or later." He waved at the only other boat still afloat. "You even have the boss personally overseeing operations, since things have escalated. Trust me, we'll get answers."

Was Ryan Stokes here? Corrie opened her mouth—to say what, she didn't know—but her voice dried up at the sight behind Alistair.

The pale woman crawled silently over the stern, beside the motor. Her brown clothing glistened wetly like kelp, and she moved with a flowing grace that shifted with the rocking of the boat. Her eyes were fixed on Alistair.

Corrie needed to distract Alistair, and she needed to do it now. If the pale woman were on her side, then maybe she could help with Corrie's current threat. Corrie burst into a babble of words, forced through chattering teeth.

"You won't get anything from me! Why are you trying to find the creatures? And hurting them, too, there's no call for that. Trust me, I'm all for studying the creatures, but there's no need for cruelty. Did you apply for a research permit from an ethics board? I doubt it, because those take ages to come through, and you've just started. The press would have a field day with this, wouldn't they? People would be up in arms—"

Corrie stopped mid-sentence. The pale woman, while Corrie had distracted Alistair, had crept up behind the man and slit his throat with a long, white knife. Alistair flopped sideways with the motion of the boat, his arteries pumping blood out of a hideous gash on his neck. The woman stepped over him, her face no more troubled than if she'd fileted a fish.

Corrie froze with shock, then she doubled over and emptied the contents of her stomach onto a deck already wet with rain, seawater, and blood. Shuddering wracked her body from mind-numbing cold and the shock of seeing death before her eyes. She tried to stand, to put some distance between her and the woman, but her legs wouldn't respond.

Britta must have sensed something was wrong, for she looked back. Her eyes swept over the carnage, and her mouth opened in shock. The pale woman was on her in two steps, but Britta was made of sterner stuff than she looked. She ripped off the diver's pony bottle and swung it at the pale woman. It struck her stomach, and the woman spit water over her opponent. Britta used the distraction to pull a gutting knife from a pocket beside the driver's seat and slice the pale woman across the chest.

Blood bloomed along the cut. The pale woman, her expression finally registering emotion, drew her lips back in a silent snarl and lunged for Britta. Britta hit the white knife away and stabbed the pale woman deep in her gut.

Corrie gasped, and the pale woman doubled over. Britta relaxed her stance, clearly feeling secure now that she'd dealt such an injurious blow. With one swift jab, the pale woman whipped her white knife up and out.

Blood spurted out from the slice across Britta's neck. She looked surprised as she crumpled to the floor. The pale woman stumbled, staggered, and finally toppled over the edge of the boat.

The diver, who had taken over the wheel when Britta had stood up, looked at Corrie with a green-tinged face for a long moment.

When an engine roar cut through the howling wind and

rain, Corrie and the diver turned their heads. Corrie blinked.

The other boat was helmed by a grim-looking man who looked familiar. Where had she seen him before? A picture on Jules' phone swam before her bleary vision. That was Ryan Stokes, Alistair and Britta's boss and the reason they were all in this mess. Was this mission important enough for him to be involved?

"Is this one of them?" Ryan shouted to the diver. "Good, so this trip wasn't a complete loss." He glanced at the bodies shifting near Corrie's legs. "Terrible. Tie her up and bring her back to Vancouver. She'll help us with this setback."

Without waiting for a reply from the gawking diver, Ryan turned the boat and thundered away.

The diver cursed under his breath.

"Callous bastard," he said. He glanced at the bodies then looked away quickly. "That's it, I'm done. I can't work for something like this anymore." He looked at Corrie with weary eyes and said hoarsely, "Can I take you to your friends? The ones in the dinghy?"

Corrie wrapped her arms around herself, trying not to think of what had just occurred.

"Yes, please."

ZEBALLOS

Zeb followed the woman by using his other senses. The visibility was too low in this summer storm to see much. She swam directly for a boat with a puttering engine. Zeb was surprised when she climbed aboard and disappeared from sensing.

He surfaced but could only see glimpses of what was occurring on the boat when he crested a wave. Alistair Brown stood near the stern. One glimpse showed him that the pale woman stood behind Alistair, then the next wave revealed that Alistair had disappeared and the pale woman stalked toward the bow. Britta stood, then a wave obstructed his view. Zeb cursed and sank below the surface. Maybe he could climb on board himself and see what was going on. Would the woman talk to him there?

When he reached the hull of the boat, a body dropped into the ocean. The pale woman's hair floated around her face, which held a grimace of pain. Zeb's eyes widened at the trail of blood that flowed from a deep wound in her stomach. What had happened up there? Had Britta attacked her?

He swam over until they were an arm's span apart. She opened her eyes. They stared into his, as pale as Zeb's own, and his heart squeezed at the memories of his mother.

This woman was older than he was, by a decade, maybe. The paleness was the same as his mother's, and the facial features were similar, but she was clearly someone different. With a start, Zeb saw her chest move in short breaths, and he realized she was breathing the water. Was that even possible? He couldn't remember his mother ever doing it. Why not?

The woman clicked, and hummed, and moved her hands and body in pained yet graceful motion. Like a dream, Zeb slowly understood some of what she said to him.

Help me. Take me deep. I don't want to float.

She held out her arms, and Zeb gathered her in his own and swam to the darkness below them. He didn't know what she meant, but he was damned if he wouldn't do what she wanted. Maybe, with prolonged contact, she would say something that would help him understand.

Who are you? He tried to say. His hums were halting as he tried to remember the frequencies. *Who am I?*

She took Zeb's necklace in weak fingers and turned it over, then she smiled with the first emotion Zeb had ever seen on her face. She touched Zeb's cheek.

I knew your mother. I wish I could have seen her again. She said something that Zeb didn't catch. *The sickness is hard to avoid. I wish you the best.*

What sickness? Who are you? Where are you from? In his impatience, his frequencies jumbled together. He tried to rein his frustration in.

The woman's face spasmed with pain.

Take me below. When I die, I don't want to float.

You can't die. Zeb finally had all the answers he could ever want, here in this woman. She couldn't die on him, not now. He looked down at her wound and was horrified at how much blood leaked out of the gash. His hand left her side to press against her stomach, but she swatted it feebly away.

I am almost done. Do not keep me from joining Pelu.

No. Zeb could hardly force the clicks out. *No.*

The woman gave a last spasm of pain, then her body relaxed in his arms. Zeb shook her gently, then harder. Her head flopped back and forth, but her expression of serenity remained.

Zeb released the body. Without his direction, the pressure of water at this depth pulled her down. She floated away from him with her hair drifting around her peaceful face. Zeb watched until she disappeared into the darkness of the abyss.

His heart felt empty, cold. She was gone, and it was like losing his mother again. The old wounds, healed so long ago, opened fresh and raw, more painful with the knowledge of what was lost and what could have been. He wanted to sob, to rail at the skies, but he couldn't do that down here. He pointed his body in the direction of the *Clicker*.

From deep below, the song of an unknown whale thrummed through his body. The notes pulsed through him, speaking of sadness and loss with a familiar cadence. It reminded him of his whistle, but deeper and under the water. It was almost as if his mother were singing to him from beyond the divide.

He almost turned back to investigate, but his lungs reminded him that it was time to surface. He thought bitterly of the pale woman breathing water. Could he do the same? He was almost tempted to try, but the consequence of failure would be fatal. There must have been a reason his mother had never tried it with him.

As he pushed onward and upward, he wondered. Was the pale woman the only one, or did others now sing for her loss as they gathered her body from the depths?

How could he find out?

CORRIE

The diver had delivered Corrie to Trip and Jules in the dinghy as promised. Once Corrie had clambered from one boat to the next—needing all the help she could get from Jules since her limbs hardly worked anymore and the waves rocked the vessels terribly—the diver nodded and took off toward the shore, where the burning boat had beached. Corrie didn't know what his story was, but she didn't care right now. He had helped her, and that was enough.

"You're practically hypothermic," Trip said once she'd wedged Corrie in the bottom of the boat to safeguard against the wave action. "Get back to the *Clicker*, Jules!"

Jules didn't need telling twice. He let the engine open to a full roar, and they crashed away through the waves. It was a rough slog, and Corrie banged her head twice on the hull and was soaked with spray more times than she could count. Numbness set in, which Corrie felt should worry her more than it currently did.

"We're almost there," said Trip. She rubbed Corrie's hands between her own and shared a concerned glance with Jules. His mouth tightened and he pushed the engine harder.

"I'm fine," Corrie said. It came out slurred. That was weird. Whatever, Trip would get it. "What about Zeb?"

"Zeb will be fine," Jules said. "Don't worry about him."

They finally reached the *Clicker*. Jules leaped onto the ladder while Trip kept the boat facing the oncoming waves, her lips set in a thin line. When the hook appeared above them, Corrie stared at the metal, silhouetted against the swirling gray sky.

"It's like we're fish," she murmured. "No bait, though. What would someone use to catch a Corrie?"

"An all-expenses-paid science cruise, apparently," Trip replied. She grabbed the hook and fastened it to the dinghy.

"Stay there. We'll winch you up."

Trip climbed the ladder and disappeared over the boat's edge. A moment later, the shifting and jolting of the ocean gave way to the swinging of the dinghy on a cable. Corrie smiled sleepily.

"Like a hammock," she whispered. "A pillow would be nice, though."

On deck, Trip pulled her upright.

"She can't walk," Trip panted. "Help me get her to her cabin."

Jules grabbed her under the arms and Trip took her feet.

"I'm fine," Corrie mumbled. "This is silly."

Trip stripped her down in the cabin while Jules warmed water in the kitchen. Once Corrie was in dry clothes and bundled in every blanket Jules could find on board, she felt like an enormous caterpillar. The thought made her smile, then her body started to shudder.

"Thank goodness," Trip said. "She's finally shivering again. Pass me those towels you warmed in the oven, Jules. And the warm water. Can you crank up the heat any more in here? We need her to breathe warm air."

Corrie still couldn't feel her hands or feet by the time Jules gasped at the window.

"What the hell?"

Trip spun around and pressed her face to the tiny window. Corrie wriggled her blanket-clad body to see.

"What's going on?"

Her question died on her shivering lips. Ryan Stokes' motorboat had taken off toward Vancouver. It was far away but still recognizable.

Tentacles surrounded it. Massive arms the color of an angry bruise on one side and a dead-flesh white on the suction cup side waved in the air. Corrie hardly had time to gasp before the arms crashed onto the boat, tiny as a toy in a monster's bath. Pieces of vessel broke and splintered, then the arms relentlessly drew the broken bits down. A figure waved frantic arms in the water before it, too, was wrapped in tentacles and pulled to the depths. In the space of a few seconds, the motorboat had vanished, along with Ryan Stokes and the last of those pursuing the creatures.

Corrie had seen too much in the past hour to feel more than a dull numbness at the loss of life to Sucker. She sat back against the bench and closed her eyes. Trip's warm arm curled around her shoulders and they rested together without speaking. Jules busied himself in the galley while they waited for Zeb.

Where was he? Now that Corrie was out of danger, she could devote some thought to Zeb's fate. The four motorboats were either sunk or beached. Had he met a diver down below who hadn't received the memo that the battle was over? Had Sucker been hungry enough to nab Zeb as well?

Did the pale woman have friends that meant Zeb harm?

Jules' face grew more and more grim as time passed. Trip glanced at the clock frequently. Corrie focused on moving her fingers to gain feeling and tried to ignore the cold pit in her gut. Something was wrong. He shouldn't have been gone this long. But how could they search for someone deep underwater?

A clanging thump on the hull made Corrie's shoulders slump in relief. Trip passed a shaking hand over her eyes, and Jules let out his breath in a whistle.

"Finally," he said and darted to the door. Moments later, he returned with a dripping Zeb in tow. Trip threw him a towel and he rubbed his head and torso.

"Sorry I took so long," he mumbled, not meeting anyone's eye. "I needed to do—something."

"I'm just glad you're back," said Corrie, but privately she decided he needed to tell her what he was doing, later.

"You missed a lot," Jules said. "While you were galivanting with fish or whatever you were doing." Zeb's face spasmed with emotion, but he mastered himself quickly. Jules continued. "Trip and I disabled some of the boats, Corrie almost died of hypothermia—"

"What?" Zeb's attention zeroed in on Corrie. "What happened? I thought you were on strolia slime."

Corrie shrugged, only now remembering that he had left her. The memory stung. Why had he abandoned her?

"It wore off. Right after you left me."

Trip's eyes widened, then she glared at Zeb. To his credit, Zeb looked distraught, with more emotion on his face than Corrie could ever remember seeing above the water. He kneeled beside her and took one of her freezing hands in his. It was surprisingly warm, and Corrie had a flash of annoyance that he didn't get cold.

"I'm so sorry for leaving," he said quietly. His pale eyes searched hers, distress pouring out of them. "I thought you were—" He bent his head over her hands for a moment then lifted his face again. "You were like me, for a while. I forgot you were different. I'm sorry."

Corrie rubbed her thumb over his knuckles.

"Apology accepted. But you'll have some making up to do."

"Anything."

She smiled and squeezed his hand then withdrew her own. He stood.

"There's more," she said louder to include the others. "The pale woman slaughtered Alistair and Britta on their boat."

"What?" Zeb looked like someone had slapped him in the face. Trip gasped, and Jules put out his hand to steady himself against the wall.

"Yeah," Corrie said. She closed her eyes at the memory, but visions of splattering blood and vicious wounds popped her eyes open again. She swallowed at the sudden queasiness. Why was she wrapped up in this? She'd never even seen a dead body at a funeral before today, and now she was a witness to murder. "Britta stabbed her—she's probably dead."

"Yes, she is," Zeb said. Corrie fixed her gaze on him, but he looked out the window to avoid eye contact. Was that what he had been doing after the battle? Dealing with dead bodies? Corrie's scientist mind wondered how big the cloud of blood would grow underwater, if someone were bleeding out. Her stomach rebelled, and she quashed the thought.

"Did she have a vendetta against them?" Jules said. "And Sucker took down Ryan Stokes' boat. Was it acting as cleanup crew? Did the pale woman order it to kill the rest of the group?"

Zeb looked as overwhelmed as Corrie felt. She snuggled deeper into her blanket. She was still cold, but sensation coursed through her extremities once more. Painful sensation, but it was better than the numbness. If only she could warm up the cold pit in her gut.

"I'll get changed," Zeb said. "Then I'll take us back to Victoria."

TRIP

Corrie had dragged herself to her cabin in glassy-eyed silence while they traveled back to port. When Trip checked on her, she was sound asleep. Trip supposed it was natural—it took a lot of energy to warm up from Corrie's ordeal, and she was probably exhausted. Trip was an odd mix of tired and wired. Too much had happened to process. People had died out there, but it felt conceptual, like she'd read about a tragedy in a book. Maybe later she would understand it more deeply, but for now, she took refuge in the lighter side of things.

Jules looked like he didn't know what to do with himself, so she helped him in the galley while they were underway. It was the most work she'd ever done making toast, but it brought up both their moods, and partway through they were both chuckling. Trip held onto the toaster with one hand while Jules juggled butter, a dull knife, and the open fridge door.

"We were amazing out there," she said. Jules beamed at her.

"We were, weren't we? You were fierce, like an avenging angel."

Trip laughed.

"I've never been called an angel before."

"Really?" Jules' naked surprise warmed her heart. She rubbed her foot against his calf, since it was the only part of her that wasn't holding down equipment. He smiled at her and spread butter on the toast. "I don't believe it."

He chased the toast around the counter as it slid with the rocking boat. Trip laughed at his antics.

"Thanks for flying with me," she said. "You were a natural."

Trip expected him to brush off her comment or make some self-deprecating remark. In her short time knowing him, it seemed like what she should expect. Instead, he gave her a piercing look, then smiled faintly.

"Thanks."

Trip already liked Jules, but that simple acknowledgement of her compliment sent warm tendrils of attraction through her body. She shifted closer to him.

"This was a crazy day. Do you have anything to drink on this boat? I want to unwind, and I want to do it with you."

Jules leaned forward and pressed his lips to hers. She closed her eyes and opened her mouth to receive him. His initiative made for a welcome change.

A soft crunch made Jules break off the kiss. He glanced down and grimaced.

"There goes the toast." He looked back at her with apology. "Sorry, that ruined the moment."

"Never mind," she said. "There will be more moments."

KRISTA

Krista heaved a huge sigh while she shrugged on her jacket against the rain outside. It was seven in the evening, and the day had been grueling, but she was still employed. Fiona had been right to tell her to come back today. Krista was almost certain that her presence had allowed her to keep her job.

She wondered how Zeb and the others were doing then shook her head. Zeb would be fine. He could look after himself, and he had good people behind him. She trusted him.

Although, an occasional text wouldn't hurt.

She put her brother from her mind when there was a knock at the door. Fiona popped her head in.

"I hope you don't have plans, because I'm taking you out for a drink to celebrate our gainful employment." She smiled sweetly and reached out for Krista's arm, and Krista let herself be guided out of her office. She had no plans, beyond ordering takeout and putting her feet up on the couch with her cat on her lap. Drinks sounded like more work, but she couldn't deny Fiona after her timely warnings and help.

"Where did you have in mind?"

Fiona's eyes sparkled, and she looped an arm through Krista's as they sauntered down the hall.

"A quiet little place where we can talk. Don't worry, you're in good hands."

Fiona led them to a nearby bistro that Krista had seen but never bothered entering. The lights were dim, the atmosphere subdued but convivial, and the bar well-stocked. When they were settled in a corner table, an oil lamp lighting their faces with mysterious shadows, Fiona slipped her purse onto her chair arm and sighed in relief.

"We dodged the bullet," she said while wiggling her fingers at a server. "We still have jobs. That cut was a doozy."

"You didn't have anything to worry about," Krista said

with a wave of her hand. "You're in everyone's good books, and talented to boot."

Fiona gave her a self-satisfied smile.

"You flatter me. But no one is immune when the ax is hovering."

The server appeared, and they ordered drinks. Krista asked for a craft beer that she liked, but Fiona ordered Chardonnay. When the server disappeared to the bar, Krista took her opportunity to say something she'd been meaning to mention for a week.

"Thanks for staying quiet on the documents you gave me, about Miles Callahan," she said. "I know you need to act on them sometime, but I appreciate the breathing room."

"I'm still dying to know why. Haven't I earned your confidence?"

"You have, but it's not my secret to tell." Krista sighed and stared at her fingers. She hoped Zeb found whatever he wanted to find, and soon. It wasn't fair to keep those documents vilifying Miles Callahan a secret. A criminal needed to be brought to justice. "Maybe one day soon."

"All right, I won't pry anymore." Fiona twisted her lips like the words were sour. "Strange words out of my mouth, right?"

Krista chuckled, and Fiona leaned forward.

"You're smart, Krista. Smart and hard-working. It's a combo that will take you far." She gazed intently into Krista's eyes, and Krista found herself not wanting to blink to break the moment. "But do you want to go farther?"

Krista frowned. What was Fiona getting at?

"What do you mean?"

"Don't take this the wrong way, but you still have rough edges that need to be polished out." Fiona put up a conciliatory hand when Krista puffed with indignation. "Don't get your panties in a twist. Everybody does, at some point. But those rough edges will cause you to snag on the ladder to the top. They'll get in your way."

The server came with their drinks, and Krista fumed silently while she waited for her to leave.

"Is that why you brought me here? To insult me?" She gripped her beer glass with a tight fist. Fiona laughed lightly, totally unconcerned by Krista's mood.

"There's that fire. If we can direct that appropriately, there will be no stopping you. If we don't, you'll either burn up or fizzle out. I can help you channel it. Do you want to be a raging forest fire, a wet blanket, or a well-directed flamethrower?"

Fiona sipped her wine, her eyes on Krista's face. Krista swallowed the retort that had been building on her lips and thought about what Fiona was saying. She did feel stifled at work. Her natural tendencies to stand her ground and lash out at wrongdoings were being eroded away by pandering to senior partners and trying to not clash with colleagues. She assumed that it was the only path. Could Fiona show her something different?

"I don't understand," she said finally.

Fiona clapped her hands like a little girl.

"Yes, I know. That's why I'm here. I like you, Krista. I think you have potential, and I think I can help you make the most of it. If you're willing, I'd like to polish you up."

"What would that involve?" Krista said, her eyes narrowing in suspicion. "If you think that getting your nails done every week counts for something, I'm highly skeptical."

Fiona laughed richly and glanced at her fingers, currently blood-red.

"Nails are just for fun. I'm talking about networking and people skills."

Krista sighed and took a gulp of her beer. She didn't particularly like Fiona's "skills" in that regard. It made her seem two-faced and untrustworthy. Krista valued unaffected sincerity in others and had no desire to appear otherwise.

"I don't want to smile and preen for others," she said as delicately as she could manage. Even now, not saying what she really meant stuck in her craw. "Pretending to be something I'm not, it doesn't feel genuine."

"Not all networking has to be a pretense," Fiona said, exasperation coloring her words. "Sometimes, it really is enjoyable to find out about other people."

Krista threw her a disbelieving look, and Fiona chuckled.

"It might not seem like it to you, but you can fake it until you make it. Sometimes, I have to show a different face to someone. Yes, it's not genuine." She put her palms flat on the table and stared at Krista. "But do you want to be a stickler for your strict moral code over the small stuff? Or do you want to make a difference in the big league? My way, you can win far more often and hit the bastards where it hurts. Is that worth a little pretense?"

Krista stared back into Fiona's honey-brown eyes. She did want to make her mark on the world. Too many rich men steamrollered their way through life, taking what they wanted and leaving behind trails of destruction. In her line of work, it was often literal destruction, of forests, shorelines, or human health. Some days she felt that she was making a difference, but other days she was overwhelmed by how little she could accomplish. Her tiny drops wouldn't fill the bucket fast enough to make a difference.

Did Fiona think that Krista could turn her tap on faster?

Fiona must have seen the indecision in her eyes, because she pressed her advantage.

"We're already at a disadvantage against them. We're not rich, and we're not men. There is no shame in using every tool at our disposal."

Krista wavered. It still felt strange—going against her long-held values went against the grain—but she could see the truth in Fiona's words. Maybe this was a skill she needed to learn. Fiona's comment about her rough edges still rankled. Maybe it was time to change that.

"I don't know," she said, doubt coloring her voice. "You

don't think I'm a lost cause?"

Fiona's eyes brightened, and she rubbed Krista's shoulder.

"Never," she said. "I have it all planned out. There's a networking event next week. We can talk schmoozing strategies before, then you can put your lessons into action. This will be great." At Krista's skeptical look, Fiona chuckled. "It'll be fun, I promise."

Fiona held up her wineglass and they toasted. Krista wondered what she had fallen into, but her stomach tightened with anticipation. It was a new challenge, and Krista always rose to the occasion. If she were learning how to network, then she'd be damned if she wasn't the best networker she could be.

CORRIE

Corrie wasn't surprised at Trip's decision to drink in the galley with Jules. Trip didn't like to dwell on things. She liked decisive action, and she liked distractions. Now that the action was finished, drinking with Jules must have seemed like a good way to distract from the upset of the day. She could hear them from her cabin, playing some noisy card game. Neither sounded like they were winning, but from the laughter floating from the eating space, neither of them minded.

Corrie couldn't shake off her ordeals that easily. She'd assured Trip that she was fine when she'd come to check on her after her nap, but the slice of the pale woman's knife across Alistair's throat played over and over in her mind. Every time, she felt the nausea rise again, and she had to steel herself against throwing up.

There was nothing to distract her in the cabin. She wanted to talk to Zeb and ask him the questions that needed asking, but she was too tired. Bone-deep weariness planted her body on the bunk and forbade her limbs from moving. She wondered if she would fall asleep again, but every time she closed her eyes, the white knife flashed.

She watched the second hand on the clock in her cabin tick around and around, too tired to care how boring it was. Finally, she swung her resisting legs out of bed and shuffled to the door, still wrapped in her blanket. If her brain wouldn't allow her to sleep, then she might as well get answers.

Zeb looked surprised to see her when she hobbled into the wheelhouse, bracing herself against the walls at each wave. The sea was still stormy, but far calmer than during their battle at Spirit Island.

"Are you okay?" he asked.

"Wow," Corrie said. "What a question. I don't know when I've been less okay."

"I'm sorry." Zeb looked contrite. He hopped off his chair and opened the folding seat for her then grabbed the wheel quickly when it threatened to turn. "Of course. Are you warm enough? Do you want some food?"

"No, thanks." She sat and closed her eyes. "I'm just tired. And confused. What the hell happened today? I mean, I know what Alistair and Britta—" She took a moment for the bile to settle at the memory of their blood spilling over the deck. "What they wanted. But where does the pale woman fit in? What the hell was she?"

Zeb was quiet for long enough that Corrie eventually opened her eyes. He looked sad and lost. His finger traced the edge of the wheel.

"She looked a lot—" Zeb swallowed. The rest of his words came out in a hoarse whisper. "Almost exactly like my mum."

Corrie stared at him, her mind kicking back into gear after its frozen numbness.

"Holy crap," she breathed. "What—what does that even mean? Holy crap."

"Yeah," he said. "I don't know. The creatures, her, me, it's all tied together, and I need to know how." He leaned back and rested his head on the wall, looking drained. "I don't know how to find out more."

Corrie's brain was still whirling with possibilities.

"She wasn't normal," she said. At Zeb's grimace, she backtracked. "Sorry, that didn't sound great."

"No, you're right," he said. "She wasn't. Neither am I."

"You're telling the truth about the slime, aren't you?" Corrie exhaled sharply. Zeb wasn't taking strolia slime to be able to swim in the ocean. He was just like that. How?

Zeb nodded with a pained look.

"Okay, how was the pale woman different?" Corrie poked her fingers out of her blanket cocoon and started marking ideas off each. "One, totally pale all over. Just like your eyes and hair. Two, did you check out her feet? Super long toes and webbing." She scrubbed her face, but gamely went on before she could think too hard about the implications. She bent over to look at Zeb's feet. When she came back up, he looked at her with a baffled expression.

"Well?"

"Yours look pretty normal." She checked herself. Words mattered, and Zeb didn't need to feel alienated. "I mean, they look about the size I would expect them to be. Also, when Britta punched her in the stomach, she spat up a bunch of water, just like we would gasp out air. Do you think…"

"She can breathe water?" he said. "Yes. And before you ask, I never saw my mum do that. I can't, either."

"Have you ever tried?" Corrie asked. It was a reasonable question. She'd never tried because she knew she couldn't. If Zeb believed the same thing, why would he risk drowning?

"No, I never thought to." He fidgeted with his fingers for a moment, then placed one palm down on his lap and looked Corrie squarely in the eye. "I'm going to lay it all out for you. Nothing hidden anymore, okay?"

"Finally," Corrie said. "Yes, hit me." Maybe now they could get to the bottom of all this mystery. She sat up straight. Zeb stared at her, worry and determination warring in his face. Determination won.

"Dad found Mum in the village of Zeballos, on the west coast. She couldn't speak English when they met and would only make hums and clicks. That's why he called her Clicker, and the name stuck. She was soaking wet and looked in distress, so he took her aboard and made her comfortable. By the way he told it, he took to her right away. Like, love at first sight, although he'd never have used those words. He brought her home, and she learned to speak English within weeks. She never said where she had come from. It was something she would never discuss. They married, had me, and she taught me how to swim."

Zeb's face cleared at the obviously happy memories.

"We could swim so fast and so deep, and we'd never get cold. I can hold my breath for ten minutes with ease, and she could do longer. We had our own private language down there, based on hums and clicks and positioning of the body." Zeb frowned. "I always thought she'd made it up between us, but now I guess she knew it from before. It used to bug Dad that we were so tight. He would try to laugh it off, but I know it bothered him. When she died, he closed like a clam and I lost him, too."

Corrie wiggled out of her blankets and reached to put her hand on his. He stared at it for a moment. When the quiet had stretched on for long enough that Corrie was confident Zeb had finished his revelations, she spoke.

"Wherever your mother was from, this pale woman obviously came from there, too. Maybe there is an isolated tribe of people who had to adapt to huge evolutionary pressures in a short time and underwent major physical changes. I have no idea what would cause that, but it's the best theory I have. It's really too bad that we couldn't talk to the woman."

"I tried," Zeb said in a low voice. "She died too quickly. All she said was that she knew my mother, once she'd looked at my necklace." With his free arm, he pulled it out of his shirt and over his head. Corrie grabbed his hand and pulled it and the necklace toward her. The shell was carved in exquisite detail out of a white, almost translucent bone. When Corrie flipped it over, purposeful-looking scratches marred the smooth underside. Corrie squeezed Zeb's fingers in her excitement.

"That's incredible. This was your mother's? It must be some symbol, or family totem. That gives a lot of evidence for our theory. We just need to find another pale person to question."

"If only it were that easy." Zeb slid his hand out of hers and rubbed his face. Corrie contemplated him while ideas percolated in her mind.

"I think we need to study you," she said finally. "Some answers might be in your physiology, your DNA. But I'm only a grad student who studies anemones and bacteria. I think we need to find someone who can look at your blood, genes, anything, and see if there is something obviously different. I'm beside myself with curiosity to see what the difference is. What kind of pressure could induce changes like that so quickly?"

Zeb paled.

"That idea doesn't thrill me." He sighed. "It's Krista's worst nightmare, honestly. Me under the microscope. I have to say, after the past couple of weeks, I'm starting to see her point."

"No, I get it." Zeb had been kidnapped for someone thinking that he knew about the creatures. What would an unscrupulous person do if Zeb's true identity were uncovered? Corrie drummed her fingers on her lap while she thought. "We need to find someone trustworthy. And then give them an anonymous sample. I think it can be done."

Zeb blew air from between his lips.

"I guess so," he said finally. "Maybe it will show us something. Since I can't get any of them to talk to me."

Corrie understood that "them" were the pale people. Her heart ached for Zeb. It must be beyond frustrating to have that mystery in his life with no way of finding out more. She was practically going crazy with curiosity, and she didn't have nearly the same stakes in this whole venture that Zeb did.

"Okay, great," she said. "I'll text Adrianna, get her to bring a syringe when she comes to pick up Trip tonight. We can get some blood, hair, cheek scrapings, the works. I don't know what we'll need, so best to get it all."

Zeb grimaced.

"There's something else, since I'm spilling my guts tonight. I've been trying to give the impression that Dad left me a boatload of cash, and that money is no object. That's not true. Dad was a fisherman-turned-charter operator, and I crewed on his boat. One hundred percent blue collar, here."

"When you wear a shirt," Corrie said with a wry smile. "I was starting to guess that. Thanks for telling me. It doesn't matter to me, though."

"It will," he said. "We can't go north anymore. There's not enough time—you knew that already—and not enough money for the gas to get there and back. It turns out my budgeting skills aren't as sharp as I thought. I need to get a job for a while."

Corrie's heart fell. This was a huge blow. She had so little to show for this cruise, only endless samples around the same small island. She had no idea how she would use the data to show something useful. She had been counting on the northern inlets, and choosing to help the creatures instead had been a heart-wrenching decision. She'd consoled herself with the hope that they would be able to sample a few rivers partway up Vancouver Island in the last few days of her cruise. Now, Zeb was saying that they were through? What would she tell her supervisor?

She tried to marshal her face into something resembling understanding, but knew she was failing miserably from Zeb's guilty gaze.

"Okay," she said. What else was there to say? "I guess that's it, then."

"We can sample around the Gulf Islands some more, if you like," Zeb said. "There's enough gas for that. Probably." He fidgeted with his fingers again. Corrie shook her head.

"I don't even know what to do with the samples I do have from Spirit Island. No, it's best if I head home now, since we're going to Victoria already. Adrianna can give me and my stuff a ride home when she picks up Trip."

Zeb's face fell.

"I'm sorry," he said. "I didn't mean to make this end early. I just—all this creature stuff cropped up and got in the way of your science. I'm sorry. And then the money…" He looked out the window, his mouth tight.

"I chose to help the creatures, too," Corrie said. She reached forward and rested her hand on his forearm. Zeb dragged his eyes away from the window and stared at her hand. "You don't have to take all the blame for that." She leaned back. "As for budgeting, don't get me started. One time, in undergrad, I spent all the money from my student loan by October—it was supposed to last until January—and I had to eat ramen for months. Luckily my friends at the time threw a lot of pizza parties, otherwise I wouldn't have seen meat or vegetables until Christmas."

Zeb's face relaxed as she recounted her exploits at university. They weren't her finest hours, but he needed cheering up and she had plenty of material to entertain him with. His eyes started to smile, and he even chuckled at one anecdote. Corrie mentally patted herself on the back.

She was in the middle of a particularly unflattering story about what she found in her apartment after coming home from the bar one night, when Zeb's eyelids fluttered, and he swayed in his seat. Corrie frowned. She might not have noticed, except that the storm was easing and the waves minimal in the narrow passage they drove through. He drifted sideways but caught himself before he fell to the floor. He looked bleary and puzzled when his eyes opened fully.

"Are you okay? What just happened?" Corrie stood up and shuffled closer to his chair. Zeb passed a trembling hand over his face.

"I don't know," he said. "I felt funny for a minute. It's gone, now."

"Is it like when you keeled over after putting the cream on? Do you often feel faint? That can be a sign of lots of conditions. Have you seen somebody about it yet?"

"I'm fine." He waved her off. "I feel good now, don't worry. It's happened two or three times, that's all."

"That's a lot." Corrie frowned. Why was Zeb brushing this

off, and looking so nonchalant about it? "Is this another secret of yours? I thought you were spilling your guts tonight."

"Just something weird I'm working through, health-wise. I promise, I'm looking into it." He gave her a half-smile.

Corrie felt satisfied that Zeb wasn't hiding something else that she should know. She held on tighter to the arm of his chair when a wave rocked the boat. The heat from his side radiated through his thin shirt, but she tried to ignore it. She hitched her blanket up higher on her shoulders and sighed.

"I guess I'll go pack my lab equipment."

Zeb looked downcast again.

"I really didn't mean to cut this short."

"I know, I'll miss our cruising, too." Corrie smiled and picked up his hand in her small one. He squeezed it, like he didn't want to ever let go. "Come and visit Victoria sometime?"

Zeb nodded, his pale eyes intense as he gazed at her.

"I'd like that."

JULES

Jules flopped onto his bunk, unable to keep a stupid grin off his face. Trip was amazing. Better yet, Jules felt like he had the ability to conquer the world when he was with her.

He recalled their evening with a contented sigh. They'd all been somber after the battle—Corrie, especially, since she'd seen the pale woman murder the others—but Trip's idea to relieve their tension in a bottle had suited Jules to a T. Corrie had stayed in her cabin, for some reason. Granted, it was easier for Jules to shake off the shock and horror, since he hadn't actually seen the bloodshed, but he still felt Corrie would have benefited from a stiff drink.

He hadn't minded alone time with Trip, though. They'd poured each other drinks, and played dice, and laughed until their sides ached. A game of cards had ended when Trip had started tossing her cards in the air, one by one, and then it had been a race to throw the whole deck to the ceiling. When they'd stood to find something to eat, Trip had drawn him toward her and let him push her against the wall as the boat rocked beneath them. There, Jules' lips had become far better acquainted with Trip's mouth.

A text from Adrianna had halted their pursuits, but Trip had pressed herself to him one last time.

"I'll see you soon," she had murmured in his ear.

Then she had disappeared to her cabin to pack, leaving Jules both frustrated and lighter than air.

Corrie was rummaging around in the lab, and Zeb was in the wheelhouse, so Jules quietly slipped into his cabin.

For the first time in a long time—longer than he could recall—he was excited for what the future might hold. Zeb hadn't promised him any more money after this week, so he would have to find a job back home. Who knew what that might be? It didn't concern him right now. He didn't know where his relationship with Trip might lead, especially since she lived in Victoria, but he didn't dwell on the practicalities. They would figure something out. She wanted to see him again, that was the important thing.

Jules dug out his phone and flipped to the culinary school application. He checked through the answers, but everything was filled out. Jules stumbled at the end when he realized they required an application fee. He checked his bank account. The paltry sum would just cover it, and Zeb would pay him more at the end of the week. Jules transferred the money before he could get cold feet.

His finger hovered over the screen. His breathing quickened and he stared at the orange "Apply" button. Then, before he could think any more about it, he tapped his finger. The screen loaded to a page thanking him for his application.

He breathed as hard as if he'd run a race. Had he really just applied for culinary school?

CORRIE

Corrie packed up the lab with a heavy heart, although she kept her movements brisk and purposeful. If she slowed to have a rest, she would never get up again. Every part of her ached with weariness, and it was only the thought of her snug bed at home that kept her moving.

She slid racks of test tubes into a large, plastic container. Was this the last time she would cruise on the *Clicker*? The thought added another weight to her already leaden heart. She had only been on the boat for a total of eleven days, but it felt so much longer. After everything she'd experienced, it could have been months. She knew Zeb didn't have the money to go north, but maybe she should keep sampling around here. Was she leaving too soon?

No, she decided. She would only be staying for sentimental reasons, not for the science. The questions she had wouldn't be answered by anemones around the Gulf Islands. It would be best to get home and start processing what she did have. Hopefully, she could cobble together a report out of the data. She cringed inwardly. What was she going to tell her supervisor?

Maybe he would buy a story about engine malfunction. This week was a bonus, anyway. Neither her supervisor nor Corrie had expected this. If she didn't get any data from this cruise, there was no harm done. It was as if it had never happened.

Corrie stared at a pipettor as she considered the thought. This week had definitely happened. There was no way she could forget what she had seen, what she had felt, what she had learned. Zeb's heritage, his connection to the pale woman, the brutal murder of Alistair and Britta... The memory of their blood on the deck threatened to bring up the toast she had numbly shoved into her mouth after the ordeal. She jammed the pipettor into a box and opened a drawer.

Maybe she could forget it, with time. She'd have to. It wasn't like she could see a counsellor about it. They would be obliged to report the murder. What would that diver say? Would he mention her involvement to police? Would he say anything at all?

Her future felt precarious, but there was nothing she could do. She vowed to buckle down for the rest of the summer and focus on her work. She needed to apply for awards, process all her samples, try to make sense of the data, and there were her teaching duties in September since she'd forgotten to apply for funding. There wouldn't be much time to pursue the creature inquiries.

The thought saddened her, but the sadness was shot through with relief. Her curiosity burned like the sun in its intensity, but, at this moment, all she felt was overwhelmed. Too much had happened today to ignore. People had lost their lives over these secrets. They had jobs, families, lives to live, and they had been snuffed out in the space of a heartbeat, with no greater thought than blowing out a candle. Was learning the mystery of the creatures worth being part of that?

Corrie wasn't sure, but she knew she wouldn't find the answer tonight. She needed sleep, and space, and time to think. She resolutely closed the last container. Leaving tonight was sensible.

She wished she knew why leaving felt so wrong.

Zeb poked his head in the door.

"Adrianna's here," he said. He looked around the packed-up lab, and his face tightened, but he made no comment on the clear counters and tidy boxes.

Corrie nodded and followed him to the eating space. Adrianna stood up from the bench when she saw Corrie and enveloped her in a crushing hug.

"I'm so glad to see you in one piece." She pushed back and searched Corrie's face. Corrie tried for a smile, but it didn't feel very convincing. "Are you okay?"

"Maybe tomorrow," she said. "Let's get Zeb's samples and then go home."

Zeb submitted to Adrianna's needle pokes and cheek swabs with patient resignation, although his eye twitched when Corrie put the vials into a plastic bag and labeled it "Specimen A." She tucked the bag into a lab cooler, some of Zeb's nervousness rubbing off on her. Finding out more about what made Zeb different could only be a good thing, right? She would be careful. No one would ever know that Specimen A was him. She'd told Adrianna that Zeb had traces of the strolia slime in his system, and she wanted to know how a human body reacted at the cellular level. She wasn't entirely sure that Adrianna believed her, but she was kind enough to avoid prodding for answers today.

Zeb helped load her equipment onto a cart and into Adrianna's car. Trip was already waiting in the passenger's seat.

"I'll give you two a minute," Adrianna whispered to Corrie. "Take your time." To Zeb she said, "Take care of yourself, Zeb."

Zeb nodded, and she ducked into the driver's seat and shut the door. Corrie walked closer to Zeb, who stood at the driver's side taillight, looking lost and unsure what to do next. Corrie impulsively took both his hands in hers. His warm fingers wrapped around hers firmly, as if he couldn't bear to let her leave. She let her eyes travel up the plaid shirt on his chest and trace his lips, before they met his forlorn gaze. She smiled despite her mixed emotions at leaving.

"Don't be a stranger, okay? This isn't over." She shook his hands gently for emphasis. There was more to learn about the creatures and Zeb's place among them, and she wouldn't let him search alone.

Zeb searched her face intently. He must have found whatever he was looking for, because his face softened.

"Okay." He took a deep breath. "Okay."

When she let go of his hands, he released hers reluctantly, but she only wanted the mobility to fling her arms around his neck. He was tall enough that she had to rise on her tip toes, and she tucked her chin into his neck.

After a second of tense hesitation, he wrapped his own arms around her waist with a firm yet gentle pressure, like she was fragile, but he would never let go. It felt right to be encircled in his warm arms.

"Take care of yourself, okay?" she whispered in his ear. "Just remember, you're not alone."

He squeezed her a shade tighter but didn't speak. With regret, she sank onto her heels and released his neck. It was too cold without his heat, and she shivered through her parting smile. His face was a mix of emotions that she couldn't decipher. He looked much more like his underwater self with his heart on his sleeve.

She slipped into the car and shut the door. She wanted to stay, but it wasn't for the best. Memories of blood flashed in her vision again. She needed time and space, and she could only get that at home, even if it meant leaving a forlorn Zeb to himself. She hoped she was doing the right thing.

Jules was with him, she reminded herself. He wasn't alone.

Adrianna put the car into reverse and sped out of the parking lot.

"It sounds like an eventful trip," she said. "Is everyone still in one piece?"

"I'll get there," Corrie said. She leaned against the headrest and closed her eyes. "Sleep, and food, and a distraction from the mess that was today, that's what I need."

"What are you going to do with Zeb's samples?" Adrianna asked. "Your lab isn't equipped to handle them, is it?"

"No, and I don't have the skills or the materials I need to do them justice." Corrie yawned and slid deeper into her seat. "I need to find someone who can, with the moral compass to not ask questions. Good luck to me."

Adrianna was silent for long enough that Corrie slipped into a doze. She jolted awake at her friend's voice.

"I might know someone," Adrianna said.

Corrie opened her eyes and sat up. She leaned forward and gripped the back of Adrianna's seat.

"Really?"

Adrianna glanced at Trip, whose eyes widened.

"You don't mean…" she whispered. Adrianna nodded.

"I do."

Corrie looked back and forth between her friends.

"Who is this person? Better question, can they be trusted?"

"Yes," Adrianna said quietly. "Oh, yes."

ZEBALLOS

Zeb wandered back to the *Clicker*. His mind was a mess, jumping between the mysteries of the pale woman, the death and destruction of today's battle, and the shock of Corrie's early departure.

Corrie's body had pressed against his as she said goodbye, soft and warm and so small that he could have wrapped his hands under her thighs and lifted her with no effort...

His body was in no clearer state. His stomach ached with hunger, his arm itched with his need to swim, and the rest of him felt empty with yearning for Corrie's closeness. He could have kicked himself for not checking his bank account more closely. Krista was right—in some ways, he was a child pretending to know how to make his own decisions. The future spread out in front of him, and it wasn't pretty. He'd have to dock the *Clicker*, go home to Campbell River and get a job— whatever he could find—and set aside his search until he could afford to do more. Corrie was conspicuously absent from his foreseeable future, and the realization gnawed at him like a sea urchin on kelp.

He was both terrified and elated that he'd revealed everything to Corrie, but he couldn't help the overwhelming trust he felt in her presence. He knew, right to his core, that she wouldn't do anything to hurt him. She had chosen to help the creatures of his world over her science. On top of that, she'd risked everything when she had licked that strolia to follow him into the water and warn him. If that wasn't an ultimate test of her dedication, he didn't know what was.

In the galley, he shoved a handful of jellyfish into his mouth then grabbed his whistle from his shell drawer. Jules was asleep already with a hint of a smile on his face. Zeb couldn't do anything about Corrie's departure except mourn her loss, and the jellyfish were a poor substitute for whatever he was craving, but he could swim.

The dark water received him into its embrace, almost as welcoming as Corrie's spontaneous hug. The coolness calmed his heart and washed away the turmoil of his thoughts. Everything was simpler down here, here where he could think properly. And if he didn't feel like thinking, there were water currents to feel, phosphorescence to see, and the pressing stillness of the ocean on his eardrums.

Zeb let his body twist slowly around while he swam along the breakwater's edge. When the loose boulders of the breakwater gave way to the open strait, he headed out to sea.

His eyes were closed, but his fingers ran over the holes of the whistle. Its curved smoothness was as familiar as an often-recalled memory. He'd never thought to play it underwater—his mother had taught him on land—but his suspicions about the origin of the whistle and the pale people made him want to experiment. He brought the end to his mouth and began to play.

Strange, haunting sounds burst forth from the whistle. It was halting, since Zeb didn't waste air on playing. Instead, he gathered water in his mouth and forced it through the mouthpiece. Despite the patchiness of the sound, it was unmistakably the same noise as the strange whale calls he'd heard earlier in the week.

The pale people were here, and they played callo whistles.

Hope kept Zeb playing for a few minutes. Surely, if the pale people were near, they would investigate what sounded like one of their own. When no one came within range of his senses, Zeb let the whistle drift out of his mouth.

He curled into a ball midwater, his face twisted with grief. He was almost sick with longing for answers from the pale people. Was five minutes of their time too much to ask? Five minutes, to learn where his mother had come from and who he was? What would it take to get them to talk to him?

Want to be in the know?

Subscribe to Emma Shelford's newsletter, where you'll receive a free book, news about new releases, cover reveals, and giveaways exclusive to the newsletter. Be the first to know!

emmashelford.com/signup

Want to stay in touch on Facebook instead? Join Emma Shelford's Fantastical Lair, where we share our book reviews and our love of all things fantasy.

facebook.com/groups/fantasticallair

If you have a moment, I would love a review on your favorite retailer (see emmashelford.com for links). It's a wonderful way to support an author, as reviews makes a huge difference for a book's visibility. I whole-heartedly appreciate every single review!

Emma Shelford

ALSO BY EMMA SHELFORD

Nautilus Legends
Free Dive
Caught
Surfacing
More to come

Musings of Merlin Series
Ignition
Winded
Floodgates
Buried
Possessed
More to come

Breenan Series
Mark of the Breenan
Garden of Last Hope
Realm of the Forgotten

ACKNOWLEDGEMENTS

My fearless editors braved the waters of *Surfacing*: Wendy and Chris Callendar. Christien Gilston of Chris Gilston Design produced a wonderfully mysterious cover. Dr. Danielle Winget read the manuscript for scientific accuracy. Alayna Siddall and Brianna Wright answered my fish and whale questions. And, last but never least, thanks to the members of Emma Shelford's Fantastical Lair for help brainstorming name ideas with me (Amanda Wells, Angela Mathers, Becky King, Craig Richcreek, Erin Dost, Léon Lémieux, Opal Barclay, Red Ravenwood, Ruby McAleer Routledge, Stacy Affleck, and Uolevi L Lahti).

ABOUT THE AUTHOR

Emma Shelford loves magic and the ocean, and the Nautilus Legends is the result. She is also the author of the Musings of Merlin series and the Breenan series.